# FRIENDS AND LIARS

**Kaela Coble** is a member of the League of Vermont Writers, a voracious reader, and a hopeless addict of bad television and chocolate. She lives with her husband in Burlington, Vermont, and is a devoted mother to their rescued chuggle, Gus.
*Friends and Liars* is her first novel.

# FRIENDS
## AND
# LIARS

## KAELA COBLE

CORVUS

Published in trade paperback in Great Britain in 2017 by Corvus, an imprint of Atlantic Books Ltd.

Copyright © Kaela Coble, 2017

The moral right of Kaela Coble to be identified as the author of this work has been asserted by her in accordance with the Copyright, Designs and Patents Act of 1988.

10 9 8 7 6 5 4 3 2 1

A CIP catalogue record for this book is available from the British Library.

Trade paperback ISBN: 978 1 78649 205 0
E-book ISBN: 978 1 78649 206 7

Printed and bound by MBM Print SCS Ltd, Glasgow.

Corvus
An imprint of Atlantic Books Ltd
Ormond House
26–27 Boswell Street
London
WC1N 3JZ

www.corvus-books.co.uk

*To my crew, for the family kind of friendship that endures through all the drama, that feels the same no matter the time or distance between meetings, and that loves even when it doesn't like.*

# DANNY
## *Now*

Look at them. I'm dead and they're still pissing me off.
They're disgusting. Sitting in their pew, huddled together
like a pack of wolves. Each playing their part in mourning—the
bereaved, the wilted, the guilty. They clutch at each other, leaning
physically and emotionally for support. Shaking heads, balled
fists, crocodile tears. Asking why, how. Dabbing their swollen
eyes with crumpled tissues. Declaring their loyalty and love for
one another. For me.

Really they hate each other, and they hate themselves, and
they hate me for making them face their own mortality. And
they love me because it fuels their sick sense of pride in their
little clan. "The crew," they call themselves, even though they
haven't been whole for a decade. "Still supporting each other
after all these years," they declare, even though they wouldn't
know true support if it helped them climb out of a grave.

There's Ally, the great beauty of Chatwick, sitting tall and
stoic, practically cradling Steph in her arms. She shoots glances
at her husband, Aaron. High-school sweethearts; couldn't you
just puke? Her face is a marriage of self-righteousness and pride.
Steph is a girlfriend of the crew, not an original member. What
right does she have to this display? But no matter what, and

despite their resistance, *Ally* is their leader. *She* is the mother of the crew, the default person in whom to find solace.

Emmett and Aaron sit together instead of with their respective significant others, no doubt upon Emmett's insistence. He has always orchestrated the seating arrangements to split between genders. As the youngest of three brothers, he has always been uncomfortable with the noise, the gossip, and the full range of feminine feelings. The heightened emotional state caused by my death is no doubt more unbearable for him than my death itself. That he is allowing Ally to tend to his weeping girlfriend, offering no comfort of his own, comes as no surprise.

He and Aaron mimic the same posture—leaned forward, their elbows resting on the thighs of their cheap woolen pants. They face the front of the church, careful not to make eye contact with each other, so they won't have to utter one of the lame platitudes they've heard too many times over the past few days. "He's in a better place." "He's finally at peace." And my personal favorite, "Roger is watching over him now."

While they should be focusing on the tragedy that is (was) my life, instead my casket is a big fat polished-cedar reminder that one day this will be them. They ponder all the predictable questions that even people of the mildest intellect contemplate when faced with untimely death: *Where do we go when we die? What will they say about me when I'm gone? What does it all mean?* Tomorrow they will look into low-premium life insurance plans to take care of their burgeoning families should something happen to them. It will make them feel like men in control of their lives. But they're not. They're boys, and they're not in control of shit.

Speaking of boys, Murphy isn't here, the coward. He always picks the easiest option, and in this case (and many cases), that means hiding. I'm dead, lying here about to be carried off and buried, but all he cares about is winning the argument. Murphy showing up would mean I got the last word, or that he had forgiven me, and either of those would mean he's weak. He doesn't realize he's the weakest one of the bunch anyway.

That brings me to Ruby. She sits in the pew between the girls and the boys, the space between her and them so slight you would only notice if you were looking for it, like I am. She watches Ally comforting Steph, occasionally reaching out a hand to squeeze one of Ally's. I know Ruby feels genuine grief, but mostly discomfort. She doesn't know her place anymore, her role. I'm only now realizing that she never really knew it. She's been an official outsider ever since she dared leave Chatwick at eighteen, but even before that, she and I were always the ones straddling the curvature of the crew's closed circle. One foot in, one foot out. The dark ones.

I know it's terrible how much enjoyment I get from watching her squirm, but it's just too entertaining. Besides, with the fate of my soul no longer a question mark, I'm enjoying what I can. My death will be hardest on Ruby, for sure, but she'll never admit it, and our crew won't acknowledge it. She left. She abandoned us, so she can't possibly feel it as deeply as they do. It's amazing how grief turns so quickly from a group activity to a competitive sport.

It seems all of Chatwick turned up in their patent-leather shoes and cheap polyester blends. "To show their support," they say. For who? Me? I don't even know half these people. Four days ago they wouldn't have pissed on me if I was on fire. Most of them are only here to satisfy their morbid curiosity, whispering behind hands and rolling eyes, gathering tidbits to relay later to their neighbors who were unable to make it. But some are here for my mother, Charlene, whose deli (formerly my stepfather's) is where they happily depleted their food-stamps. Either way, I wish they wouldn't have come. It makes them feel too damn good about themselves, and they don't deserve it. And I don't deserve the show, either, even if it is fake.

Mom stares blankly ahead of her as the priest eulogizes yet another man who's let her down. I look—well, *looked*—just like her. If you shaved off her two curtains of waist-length blonde curls and straightened out her chest and hips, we would look like twins.

Nancy, Ruby's mother, sits next to Mom, holding her limp hand. Nancy is the one who made all these arrangements, and despite the overabundance of flowers, I still appreciate her efforts. She saved my mother from having to coordinate another funeral, and I think one is enough for a lifetime. Ruby's never forgiven her mother for the way she handled her illness back in the day, but as dicey as things got in the St. James household, they didn't hold a candle to my family. Besides, Nancy's one of the only assholes in this town who has any compassion, and I'm grateful she's decided to bestow it upon Mom when she needs it most.

That's all I ever needed. Compassion. If I'd ever gotten a shred of it from any of the people in this room, maybe I wouldn't be in this fucking box.

My "friends" all think once they've fulfilled this obligation they will finally be rid of me. They will go back to the "happy," normal, vanilla lives they lead, and their guilt will subside eventually.

Silly rabbits. They have no idea my mom found the letters this morning.

# CHAPTER ONE

# RUBY

## *Now*

I'm the first to arrive at Charlene's house, so I opt for street parking in case I need to make a hasty escape. I've never much cared for being caged in. Especially not in Chatwick.

Staring at the house, the last place my friend Danny was alive, I remember when he moved in here the summer after his stepfather died. Charlene used the moderate payout from Roger's life-insurance policy to buy it, and with what was left over she fixed up the apartment over the deli where the three of them lived so she could rent it out. She and her son needed a fresh start, she explained to neighbors who raised their eyebrows at the sudden move, so soon after Roger's death. Her first (and only) house project was to coat it with the hideous teal paint that remains today, enlisting the crew to do the bulk of the work. She paid us in subs that she brought over every day after the lunchtime rush. At the end of the day she served us iced tea she mixed in a large glass pitcher as we melted onto the front porch steps and teased each other about who smelled the worst after a hard day's labor. I can practically smell the iced tea, the paint fumes, and the sweat. It had been a happy time, mostly, but not as innocent as it should have been. At least for those of us who already knew that nothing was as it seemed.

The paint is now chipped and faded, but it still glows with the spark of Charlene's quiet defiance. She never said as much, but she had chosen it as a message: she no longer had to answer to anyone. She no longer had to rely on anyone else to keep her and her son alive. Her choices were hers and hers alone, and if she wanted a teal house, then by God she would have one.

My hands are wrapped so tightly around the steering wheel my palms begin to sweat. I consider driving away, straight out of Chatwick to Drummond, where the plane I am supposed to be blissfully seated on is currently being prepared for its flight back to JFK. In just over ninety minutes, I could be out of Vermont and back to my apartment in Manhattan, with the blinds shut. But I see Charlene's pleading eyes in my mind, asking me to please come to the private service Danny requested. There would be no public reception where my absence would hardly be noticed; it was just the crew. That's what Danny had wanted. I wondered briefly how she could possibly know what Danny had wanted, before it sank in. He had left a note. Up until that moment, none of us knew if the overdose was an accident or suicide, and no one knew which was worse. Now we know; this is worse, of course. Much worse. Charlene watched the realization dawn in my eyes before confirming it. "There's letters for all of you," she said.

Damnit. I wouldn't even be here if it weren't for Ally. I was the first person she called when she heard the news. My initial instinct was to not take the call, but when someone you haven't spoken to in ten years tracks you down at work at eleven o'clock in the morning, you take the call. If it had been anyone other than Ally, I would have had the receptionist take a message. Then I would have sent a nice card to Charlene (because Danny hated flowers), and I would have returned to pretending that nothing beyond the borders of Manhattan ever existed. It was

Ally's voice, the shock and the pain and the . . . *Allyness* of it. The way she hadn't asked but demanded my return. "I've never asked you why, Ruby, and I still won't. But you'll come for the funeral. You have to." What she meant, without saying it directly, was that I owe her. And I do. For leaving and never looking back. For leaving her behind and never telling her why.

If only I hadn't picked up the phone, I would be at my desk in New York, feeling guilty but safe. Not plagued by the ceaseless nerves bubbling under my skin. Not overcome by an urge to smoke that I haven't had in ten years. There are so many things in Chatwick that aren't good for me, and if I go in that house, I'll be sucked back into them all. I'll spin right back down the drain of this town.

Just as I make up my mind to get the hell out of here before anyone else arrives, Charlene swings open the screen door and stands on the porch with one hand on her hip, the other over her eyes, so she can see who's lingering outside her house like a private detective. She recognizes me and waves. Shit! You can't drive away from a grieving mother.

The door of the Sentra squeaks as I swing it open. I took a cab from the airport this morning because Nancy was busy helping Charlene get ready for the funeral, but since I had an hour between my arrival and the funeral, I went . . . home, I guess, is its rightful name. I no longer had a key to the house, but the code to the garage hasn't changed (my sister Coral's birthday, followed by my own). In addition to the spare key that hangs behind my old ice skates, I found, to my surprise, Blue, my high-school car, still a piece of junk with its four-gear standard transmission, power nothing, and heat that runs full blast all year long whether you want it to or not. My father purchased it second-hand for me the year he moved back in with us, a consolation prize for his absence. Despite my insistence I wouldn't need it after I left for college, Nancy has kept it here for me. The key was sitting in the ignition, and instead of going into the house I was not ready to face, I sat in the car and listened to a cassette tape—a cassette tape!—of songs I had recorded from the radio when I was sixteen years old.

I climb the rotting steps to Charlene, who stands on her tiptoes to hug me. I am not tall, five-foot-seven in my tallest pair of heels, which I left at home—my real home, that is, in New York—but Charlene is a teeny size two; the top of her head barely clears my shoulders. I feel like a beast descending on her.

"Oh, Ruby," she says, her hands on my face, her puffy eyes beseeching mine. "Thanks for comin'. It's so good to see you." She looks me all over and declares me as beautiful as ever. "Now, come have some iced tea with your long-lost mother-in-law." She includes this self-assigned title in the Christmas cards she sends every year, despite the fact that I haven't spoken to her son in ten years. She always hoped Danny and I would fall in love, as if I had the power to set his life on the right course. Now more than ever, perhaps unintentionally, it serves as a reminder that I could have saved her son.

As if reading my mind, she stops in her path to look at me warily. "I guess I should stop doing that," she says. "Pushin'. You know, now that there's nothin' to push."

I don't know what to say, so I just shake my head with a sad smile and follow her into the kitchen. Charlene deposits me on one of the red leather and chrome chairs she tells me she picked up at the Margie's Pub remodeling sale for five bucks a pop. I thought they looked familiar, although technically I shouldn't know what they look like. She pulls out the same pitcher from her fridge that she served us from fifteen summers ago and pours it into a glass I distinctly remember Danny serving us vodka-and-orange sodas in a few years later. She offers me vegetables from a platter that she next produces from the fridge, and I wonder how she's still standing, let alone serving me like I'm on a social call and her son will be home to join us any minute.

In keeping with this charade, Charlene insists I tell her about my "life in the big city." There isn't much to tell, so I talk about work. On the plane, I contemplated telling people who asked that I work at *The New York Times* and leaving it at that, letting them assume I've been away from Vermont for so long because I was busy achieving the ambition I listed in my high-school yearbook: to be a journalist. But now, at my first opportunity, I hasten to add that it's in the advertising department, because I don't want Charlene to think I'm putting on airs. Who was I kidding? For one, I'm sure she and my mother have talked about me and my career at least once since I've been gone. And even if by some miracle *Nancy* has let me fade into the sordid history of this town, it *is* Chatwick. Despite the fact that I don't have a Facebook page, I bet you could walk out on this street and ask anyone what Ruby St. James is up to, and they would reply: "Oh, the St. James girl? Reddish hair? Oh yes, she's living in New York, working at that big paper of theirs. I hear she's single, as always, and pays more in rent than this whole neighborhood spends on mortgage combined!"

My friends and I always called it "the Chat," this rapid-fire circulation of the unprinted news of Chatwick. The Chat is an intangible presence which cloaks the town in intrigue and fear. The houses are so close together here that every argument even one notch above normal speaking level is overheard by the little old ladies rocking the afternoon away on their screened-in porches. Their gossip filters down through whispered conversations at post-church-service receptions, then the parents repeat it at home it in earshot of their kids, who bring it to the playground. The other (and significantly more powerful) origin is Margie's Pub, which trickles news down to the Quik Stop clientele the next day, which brings it back to the "below the tracks" families, or the blockers. Subjects run the gamut from legal troubles to marital stress, right on down to who's dating who at Chatwick High. No one is immune. I remember Ally once having to defend herself against a neighbor who heard that Ally had broken up with her friend's grandson over the phone. We were in fifth grade.

Danny's family and mine were like gas pumps, fueling the Chat for years on end. From our home, the neighbors would occasionally hear Nancy crashing around the house trying to get from room to room, and shortly afterward a shouting match between my parents. At the Deusos' they heard much worse.

The doorbell rings, and Charlene escorts Ally and Aaron in. Ally carries a freshly baked pie, and the gap in time between now and the last time I saw her feels wide as a canyon. Her face—voted Prettiest in junior high and high school—is the face of the girl I stole my mother's car with before I even had a license, driving it all over town, smoking cigarettes. It's the face of the girl who told the crew what sex was, her giddy face lit by flashlight in the field behind her house, using the same hand motions she had seen her brother use when he explained it to his friend earlier that day. In that same field, years later, she would gather us together—me, Emmett, Danny, and Murphy, the original crew—to tell us her father had left. After a summer of her parents arguing over the rubbers her mom had found in her dad's pockets while doing the laundry, this came as a shock to no one but Ally, whose fierce belief in true love left her unprepared.

That was the night she made us promise to be friends always. To be loyal to one another above all else. Never to lie to each other. She needed something to cling to, and I could understand that, so I promised, like Ally promised and Emmett promised. Like Danny and Murphy promised, even though the three of us were already breaking it. Even though we've done nothing but break it since that night.

And now, Ally's a grown woman. From the clippings my mother periodically sends me from *The Chatwick Gazette*, I know she's recently been promoted to manager at The Cutting Edge, the salon where she's worked since she graduated from cosmetology school. I picture her ruling the roost from her position behind her chair, affectionately clucking directions to her junior hairdressers without taking her eyes off the clump of hair she's expertly snipping away at. Gathering bits of gossip from her clients like bits of feed. As we listened to the memorialization of our friend, I noticed Ally scanning my hair, and I know she was contemplating whether she would give me highlights or lowlights. She won't get the opportunity. I don't care how much practice she's had, I remember all too well the time in eighth grade when she convinced me to darken my hair to a chocolatey-brown. She dyed it out of a box we got at Brooks' Pharmacy. I cried for a week until the black streaks came out.

Since we've last seen each other, she's married the man beside her, the man we all knew she would marry since the moment he rescued her from a scum-of-the-earth date at Dunphy's field after homecoming. And I've become the girl who didn't even attend their wedding. Ally's become a person I don't know. Someone who knows that it's expected to bring food to a bereaved person. I imagine this knowledge was passed down to her in some kind of handbook that women receive on their wedding day, which tells you how to handle every uncomfortable situation that life presents.

Next in the door are Emmett and Steph, Emmett looking impossibly mature in a suit and tie that he moves in as comfortably as if he wears it every day. I get a flash of our eighth-grade formal dance, me straightening his tie for him every ten minutes. He was so obsessed with keeping it straight, but so uncomfortable in it that he couldn't stop tugging at it, ruining my efforts. He blamed me for tying it wrong, so I told him to screw off, which started the common splitting of alliances between the girls and the boys of the crew. Oh, the drama of those days, over a tie and a few harsh words. Over absolutely nothing at all. How I long for that now.

Nancy tells me Emmett works in finance now, in the loans department. Apparently he golfs with my father on Sundays. The WASPiness of it all turns my stomach. I half expected him to walk in with a cable-knit sweater tied around his shoulders. There is something different about the way Emmett moves now, and it takes me a minute to pinpoint it. He used to bound into a room, filling every molecule of air with nervous energy, constantly in motion. Now he moves slowly, cautiously, and only his eyes dart around the room anxiously. I attribute it to the situation; it must be difficult to attend the funeral of the boy you once treated like a fly to be swatted.

Steph, whom Ally had pointedly introduced to me at the funeral as Emmett's girlfriend *of three years,* (in case I didn't already understand how ludicrous it was that I hadn't even known she existed), is tiny in comparison to Emmett but just as smartly dressed. She has warm brown eyes, and when I hugged her at the service I felt an instant comfort with her. Perhaps this is because, comparatively, our embrace wasn't impregnated with ten years of absence, resentment, and disappointment. She carries a fruit basket, thus debunking my wedding day Uncomfortable Situation Handbook theory. I am feeling more and more inadequate with each guest.

Everyone takes turns hugging, even though we already went through this at the church and then again before leaving the cemetery. But it's something to do, I guess. When the ritual is over, there is nothing else to do but to shift uncomfortably until Charlene tells us the reason we've all been summoned here, and why we were the only ones invited.

"Must be weird for you to be back here," Emmett says, his talent for adding more tension to a room already humid with it still, unfortunately, intact. I feel my face instantly begin to burn as I search for an appropriate response. Am I to apologize for being gone so long? I know that's what they're all expecting. At the very least, it's what they deserve.

"At least she *is* here," Ally cuts in. "More than I can say for Murphy."

Even as it softens to Ally's defense of me, my heart jumps at the name. After all the anxiety at the thought of seeing him, Murphy wasn't at the funeral. When Charlene told us about the closed reception, she had asked me where Murphy was, as if no time had passed and I was still the keeper of his whereabouts. Ally had jumped in and offered to make sure he came. I had overheard her on her cell phone before I closed the door to my car: "Murphy Leblanc, if you don't put aside your stupid pride and get your ass over to Charlene's house—" In that moment, despite my leftover resentment, I felt sorry for him. He and I were in the same boat, helpless against Ally's authority, even if we were rowing in opposite directions.

We hear a vehicle pull up in the driveway, but when minutes pass without a knock on the door, Ally goes over to the window and peers through the curtains. "Speak of the devil," she says. My stomach drops. He's here. Like a ghost conjured by speaking its name, what I've been simultaneously dreading and looking forward to since I returned to Chatwick is now parked not fifty feet from where I stand, separated only by a rotting porch and a bright teal wall.

I can't help but join Ally at the window. There Murphy is, sitting in a truck I've never seen before. The side is emblazoned with the logo for Leblanc Johnson Construction, the contracting company Nancy tells me he has owned with Aaron for some time. His arms are stretched out straight, with the same death grip on his steering wheel as I had moments earlier. "What's he doing?" I ask.

Ally rolls her eyes and snaps her tongue. "Who knows? Aaron, can you go see if he's coming in for a landing anytime soon?"

"What am I supposed to say?" Aaron asks, a deer caught in headlights. Business partner or no, he wants as little as possible to do with the emotional turmoil that today is bringing up. He's a dude. A proper one.

Everyone is quiet. I lock eyes with Emmett, silently battling to relinquish this task to the other. I surrender more easily than I should. "I'll go." I head through the door before there can be any more discussion. The first time Murphy and I see each other should be just the two of us anyway, even if Ally has her nose pressed up against the windowpane the whole time.

I step out onto the porch, my breath catching in my throat as our eyes meet. I feel the pull. I'm circling the drain. Even though his window is rolled down, I can't hear the four-letter word his mouth forms as he breaks eye contact, but it puts an abrupt halt to the centrifugal force anyway. Thank God.

"That happy to see me, huh?" I ask as I approach the driver's side. Up close, I see that Murphy's jet-black hair is now peppered with grey that's too mature for his twenty-eight years, and his rolled-up shirtsleeve reveals a tattoo encircling his forearm, which is thicker, tanner, and more muscular than I remember. Otherwise, he looks exactly the same.

He exhales an unsmiling laugh but doesn't make eye contact again. "Didn't think I'd see you here." His voice makes it more real. The voice I talked to every night on the phone until one of us fell asleep.

"Ally didn't tell you I was coming home for the funeral?" Funny, Ally tells everyone everything, especially if she has a part in making it happen.

He ignores me. "Kinda forgot you even existed," he says, staring straight ahead.

Even though I know he can't possibly mean it, hearing the words and the icy tone of his voice feels like a bullet to the chest. A bullet I quite possibly deserve, although perhaps not fired by him.

"Why weren't you there?" My voice falters, and I realize I had wanted him to be there more than I had wanted him *not* to be there. In fact, I had *needed* him to be there. Suddenly I wish he would jerk his head in the direction of the passenger side, indicating that he wants me to get in. To ride around the back roads of Chatwick, head down to the bay. As dirty as *this* section of town is, the below-the-tracks section where Danny grew up, if you stick with the road for another mile, suddenly it breaks open to beautiful green rolling pastures of farmland. I can smell the cow manure from here; it's a sweeter smell than I remember. Past the farmland is Chatwick Bay, where we used to escape on the boiling hot summer nights—skipping rocks, talking about life, skinny-dipping. I suddenly ache to be sitting in Murphy's passenger seat, my legs stretched out, my toes cold in the wind, headed away from the center of town and into our own little world.

Murphy still stares straight ahead, so I risk putting my hand on his arm. "Hey. Look at me."

When he finally does, I see the anger and hurt burning in his eyes. I wonder if he can see the same in mine. "You're not the only one I haven't seen in a while," he says, breaking our gaze almost immediately.

"You fought?" I ask, knowing the answer is yes before he nods, but not wanting him to *know* I know. It works in my favor that they stopped being friends just two weeks before Danny and I did. If they had continued to be as close as brothers, Murphy and I would be having a very different conversation right now. "What was it about?" And this I have truly never known, have tried not to want to know.

His face finally twists into a smile, although not the warm, easy one I remember. "It wasn't about *you*, if that's what you're thinking."

My mouth drops open in feigned shock, because that's exactly what I was thinking. "That's not what I was thinking!"

He snorts out an infuriating laugh.

"Excuse me for trying to figure out what could make the best of friends completely cut off communication for ten—" I stop, realizing what I'm saying. I am a huge pile of hypocritical crap.

Murphy doesn't say anything, he simply continues to smile that scary, un-Murphy-like smile.

I raise my hands against the gun I imagine he's about to reload. "Okay. You're right, I'm no master communicator myself. It's just . . . I *know* what happened between the two of us," and I wave my finger between him and myself. "And I know what happened between me and Danny. What I *don't* know is what happened between the two of you."

"Ruby, not everything is some dramatic thing. I told you it wasn't about you. So mind your own damn business!" he says.

I spin to go back inside, anger and hurt stinging my eyes. I hear him curse and then the door of his truck opening and closing. He grabs at my elbow and I shrug him off, turning back to face him with my arms crossed.

"Tuesday!"

The nickname stops me in my tracks. Only he and Danny call me that. Now, I guess, it's only Murphy. It used to drive me crazy, the way they would walk behind me in the halls in elementary school, singing that song over and over again until I shouted at them to stop. Now, I would give anything to hear Danny sing just one horribly out-of-tune chorus of "Goodbye, Ruby Tuesday."

"Listen, I'm sorry," Murphy says. "I'm a little shook up. It was a long time ago and neither of us got over it . . . in time. I don't want to talk about it, because it seems stupid now. Everything seems kinda stupid."

I know this is as much as I'm going to get from him. "Well, I tell you what's stupid: us standing out here fighting while everyone else is inside, ready to hear what Danny has to say for himself. No one is looking *forward* to it, Murphy, but maybe . . . it will . . . help." When the tears come to my eyes, I see, finally, graciously, his face soften. He takes a step forward, opening his arms to hug me, and I get a whiff of his cologne, the same stuff he's always worn. I step backward, away from him, shaking my head. I can't be hugged by Murphy. It will kill me; I'm sure of it. When I turn to climb the steps, I feel him hesitating behind me, but eventually he follows.

Charlene makes even more of a fuss over Murphy than she did over me. He looks sheepish, undoubtedly feeling the full weight of the rift between him and Danny, now that he's in Charlene's house with Danny's school pictures lining the walls. Neither Murphy nor I will resolve our final fight with Danny, and both of us should have been fighting to keep him with us.

Charlene leads us into the basement, which is different from the last time I saw it. There's a futon, a bed, and a mini-fridge. Danny must have adapted this room into an apartment of sorts, giving him the illusion of independence and the privacy to numb himself against the world. The hairs on the back of my neck stand up, and suddenly I know: Danny *died* in this room. I picture Charlene coming down with a basket of laundry, calling out in forced cheeriness, "Get up, lazybones!" only to find . . . I shudder. I can't even go there. God help me from ever going there.

Aaron hands out the folding chairs we used to use for poker nights. He offers Charlene a chair, but she shakes her head. She stands in front of the old television we once screened porn on; the girls curious to see what all the fuss was about, the boys simply horny teenage boys. We arrange ourselves in a semicircle to face her, reluctant pupils in a class we never elected to take. The couples sit together, holding hands, while Murphy and I are lumped together off to the side. As always, the single ones.

I close my eyes, just for a second, and picture the crew as it used to be. Aaron and Ally remain unchanged, save for the wedding bands on their fingers, but suddenly it's Emmett's high-school girlfriend, Tara, by his side instead of Steph. Danny is in the corner, making out with whatever blocker he's found to entertain him this month. And I—without anyone thinking anything of it—am able to lean into Murphy for support. In this world, at the end of the night it's quite possible I'll return home to find Nancy either high or low, or one of those plus drunk, but it still feels lighter and simpler than the reality I return to when I open my eyes.

Charlene holds a stack of envelopes and two sheets of loose-leaf paper. I can see Danny's scribble through the white-lined sheet, and I remember the first time I looked over Danny's shoulder at this same handwriting. He was showing me a poem he had written, which was better than I expected, much better than my own drippy attempts anyway. Charlene reads:

*"Dear Mom,*

*I'm sorry I have to leave you this way. With all we have been through together, I always hoped I could someday make you proud. But life is hard, and sad. It has been for a very long time. At first, pot made it better, and then it didn't, so I moved on to other things. They all helped at first, but then they didn't anymore. And now I'm nothing but a junkie."*

Charlene's voice falters here, and it takes her several minutes to get through the rest of the letter:

*"I'm a disappointment as a son and as a human being. Nothing I do now can change that. I hate myself for what I've done. For what I am. I don't even deserve the grief I know you must be feeling. Please don't hate me. Try to be happy I'm finally at peace. I want you to know there is nothing you could have done to prevent this. You tried to help me as best you could."*

I can tell when she breaks down at this part that, no matter what Danny says, Charlene will *always* wonder what she should have done differently. As will we all.

> *"The trouble is, if a person has no hope things can get better, there's not a whole lot anyone else can say to change that.*
> *I love you very much,*
> *Danny*

> *P.S. There's another letter I'd like you to read to Ruby, Murphy, Emmett, and Ally, if you can get them all together. Please read it before you give them their envelopes, or else they won't understand."*

I barely hear the last part, I'm so furious with Danny. *I'm sorry I have to leave you this way.* As if he had no say in the matter. I could kill him, if he hadn't already done such a thorough job of it.

"Got the autopsy results back yesterday," Charlene whispers. "It was heroin. But I wasn't sure if it was on purpose or not, until . . ." She flaps the piece of paper. "I found it when I finally made myself strip his bed this morning." My eyes dart over to the bed, which I had been avoiding until this moment. The little twin mattress is made up with sheets so crisp and tightly tucked in, even Nancy at her most manic would approve. Then I remember Nancy telling me she was helping Charlene out with the arrangements, and realize this was probably her handiwork.

Heroin. Suicide. The weight of the words hangs in the air, already dense with emotion. Ally's hand springs to her mouth, and Aaron wraps his arm around her. Murphy leans forward and hides his face in his hands. My hand shoots out instinctively to rub his back, freezing about an inch above his shirt when I realize the intimacy of what I'm about to do. I pat him awkwardly a few times and then return the disobedient hand to my lap. I look over at Emmett. Steph is looking at him too, but he stares straight ahead, white as a sheet. No one knows what to say. I mean, what do you *say*?

Finally Emmett seems to return to himself. He clears his throat. "The note says there's letters for us?" I shoot him a sharp look. He's trying to get this over with, and I understand the urge but don't think rushing Charlene is very kind. He doesn't notice my glare.

"Yeah," she says. She puts the first sheet behind the second. "I haven't read this one yet, since it ain't addressed to me." Even with her bastard ex-husband and her troubled son in the ground, Charlene is still waiting for someone's temper to explode. She sniffs deeply and reads:

*"To my old friends,*
*So here you all are. Nice to see you can show up for a person once he's dead."*

Charlene stops, her mouth open, her eyes horrified at the abrupt change in tone. Her expression almost exactly matches those of Ally, Aaron, Emmett, and Steph. My face and Murphy's have not changed; he and I were expecting this. Probably because we know we deserve it. Charlene's eyes scan the rest of the page, and then she looks at me, as if she's asking permission to continue. I nod my head to grant it.

She looks down at the page again, her hands shaking visibly. She looks back up at me and shakes her head. The first note was bad enough. She doesn't want the last memory of her son to be *this*. I stand up, grab the box of tissues from the top of the TV, and guide her back to my seat with them. Murphy takes one of her hands. With the other, she dabs at her eyes with a tissue. I take Charlene's place at the head of the class and continue reading:

*"I haven't heard from any of you in a while. Some of you I see down at Margie's Pub every weekend, so I don't know what makes you think you're so much better than me. I doubt Ruby and Murphy are even here. They're both really good at ignoring problems."*

I look at Murphy, who glances at me and then returns to staring straight ahead.

*"If any of you actually showed up at my funeral, don't feel like you deserve some medal. None of you bothered to try to help me when I was alive, when it counted."*

Ally is crying audibly now, her head in her hands, slumped into Aaron's chest. Charlene's eyes dart between each of our faces guiltily, as if she were the one who wrote the hateful words. "I'm sorry," she says to us. "I didn't know. I thought it would be like mine, not . . ." She waves her hand at the letter in mine. "Maybe we shouldn't—"

But something in me tells me that Danny's last words deserve to be read. Maybe the part of me that feels I contributed to his demise by abandoning him all those years ago. I turn my eyes back to the page and continue:

*"You always talked about 'the crew, the crew, the crew,' like we were some untouchable entity. But when it comes to things that really matter, you guys barely even know each other.*

*I think it's about time you did, if you're going to continue to pride yourselves on being friends since the womb. I know things about most of you that you didn't trust the rest of 'the crew' to know."*

Here I pause, a hot spring of acid appearing in my throat. But I know if I choose not to continue reading, someone else will snatch this piece of paper away from me. If I read it, I can control the information if it reveals too much.

*"There is one envelope for each of my dear friends who once pledged always to be honest with each other, and each envelope contains evidence of your betrayal of that pact. I'll leave it up to you. You can either share the envelopes with each other, or keep them to yourselves. Just remember that all things done in the dark have a way of coming to light. If you don't tell each other your secrets, you never know how, or when, I might have arranged for them to come out."*

He didn't sign the letter "Love, Danny," which is no surprise after the content. He simply dashed off a large, loopy "D." I'm not sure what to do with the piece of paper. I don't want to give it back to Charlene, so I place it on top of the television, next to the pile of envelopes, which I pick up. Each has a name on it. There is one for me, one for Ally, one for Emmett, one for Murphy, and one, oddly enough, for Danny himself. I hold them in my hands, little grenades of paper. If I tear them up now, will it stop them from detonating? Judging by the ferocity of Danny's letter, I'm guessing not.

I hand out the envelopes, and as I do so each person looks at me, searching for answers to the questions on all of our minds.

I drop the envelope with my name on it back on the TV set, left now only with Danny's envelope in my hands, which says, "I'll go first." I know what it will say, and I wish I could somehow shrink down and disappear inside the envelope so I don't have to deal with any of what's about to happen. But I don't debate with myself if I should open it or not, or if I should give it to Charlene for her to sort out instead. I just rip open the seal and pull out a small piece of paper. It says what I thought it might say.

I read aloud the truth that changed everything for Danny:

*"I killed my stepfather."*

# CHAPTER TWO

# RUBY
## *Back then*

I'm used to waking up in the middle of the night. Danny throws rocks at my window every couple of weeks. So tonight, when I bolt upright in bed, I wait to hear the next pebble before I bother getting up. I hold my breath, waiting for the ping! against the glass to slice through the thick summer air, but I don't hear it. I draw the curtain to look out to the street, but no one's there.

I lie down and try to fall back to sleep. Sometimes my ceiling fan, tired from the effort of keeping my room cool in the humidity of the Vermont summer, starts to creak in the middle of the night, and in the past I've mistaken the noise for Danny's SOS. But my fan hasn't been on since the storm knocked out the power hours ago. My phone call with Ally cut off mid-sentence after a flash of light, which I'm sure made her more worried. The first night I had a sleepover at her house— we were maybe five or six—there was a thunderstorm so big I couldn't help but tell her I was scared, and she stayed up with me all night playing Go Fish, giving my hand a squeeze with every boom of thunder. Ever since then, she calls me to make sure I'm okay when it storms. Even though I'm over the fear, I love that she still checks on me.

After we lost power I tossed and turned, replaying a much more powerful storm that swept through earlier: Hurricane

Nancy. She's off her meds again. "You don't understand how they make me feel sweetheart," she raced to say as she paced my room, gathering discarded clothes from the floor and hanging them in my closet, picking up items from every surface to wipe imaginary dust away with her hands. "I just can't live underwater anymore. You know what they say: water is for fish and seaweed and coral and speaking of Coral that sister of yours keeps antagonizing me she's so ready to get out of this house well she's in for a surprise when she gets out into the real world and realizes there are people in this world a whole lot crazier than me and . . ." On and on she went, climbing farther up the ladder of hypomania without taking a breath.

The power must have come back on just before I fell asleep, because I could hear her banging pans and cabinet doors in the kitchen, preparing to bake. When I was little, I used to sneak into the pantry and watch her as she kneaded and rolled out the dough in perfect, flat circles. Her baking was magic to me. Now that I'm almost a teenager and have been through this enough times, I know I will wake up in the morning to fresh scones and a mother who has crashed so hard she can't get out of bed.

I am so sure I feel trouble that I keep sitting back up to check the window. Finally, I get out of bed and tiptoe downstairs. Sure enough, a tray of baked goods cools on the counter, although the kitchen is dark except for the blinking digital clock on the stove and microwave. I open the back door—slowly, so the creaks in the old hinges will be quieter. I don't turn the back porch light on. I never turn it on, even though the dark scares me, because I can't risk waking anyone up. The earth smells damp and clean, but the humidity hasn't broken. Steam rises from the driveway. Wind chimes collide on the Bronsons' porch, but there is no breeze. A chill runs down me in spite of this.

Danny is not on the rocker where he usually waits for me. I suppose it's possible I woke out of habit, or heard the clinking of Nancy washing her dishes before turning in for the night. Still, I can't shake the feeling that something's out of place. I'm about to chock it up to paranoia and go back to bed when I hear a rustling coming from the lilac bush in the farthest corner of the backyard. I stand on the rough wood of the deck, staring at the bush and telling myself I'll be thirteen next week—too old to believe in monsters in the bushes. But I hug my arms to my body anyway, goose bumps popping up on my arms despite the heat, too scared to move. Feeling stupid, I whisper, "Hello?" into the darkness.

I hear the noise again, and right when I'm about to wet my nightgown, I hear, "Don't be scared, it's me." A few seconds later, I make out Danny's figure coming out from behind the bush.

"Jesus, Danny, what are you doing?" I whisper-yell at him. I want to punch him, but by the look of the bruises on his cheek, he's gotten it bad enough tonight.

"I just needed a place to hide out for a while," Danny says. "I didn't want to drag you into this."

This is weird of him to say, considering he's been "dragging me into" every beating his stepfather has handed him since we were in second grade. When Charlene started dating Roger Deuso, our parents told us how lucky Danny was to finally be getting a father. His real dad left when Danny was only a baby. And Roger, who owns the below-the-tracks landmark Deuso's Deli, is practically famous for his charity. He's always giving free subs to "neighbors in need," and considering where the deli is, I'm surprised he makes any money at all. He became even more of a hero when he married Charlene—"A single mother and her 'troubled' child?" the Chat said. "That Roger Deuso sure is a saint."

So when, a couple of months after they got married, the neighbors started hearing Danny screaming bloody murder, they decided he is just "a little hell-raiser," and "God bless Roger for putting up with it." Danny's bruises and cuts are waved away. "Must have gotten into a scuffle at school," they say. He's called a "sour one" and a "bad egg," and even though he'd never exactly been an angel, it wasn't long until Danny really started living up to his reputation. Murphy, who's been his best friend since First Communion, has to pull him off boys at recess more days than not. Danny is not even allowed at Emmett's, and while Ally never comes out and says it, when Danny is with us we always play in her back field instead of going into the house. It makes me so angry he gets all the blame, but Danny made me promise not to tell anyone. I think he's afraid his mom will pick Roger over him. Can you blame him? She's not deaf, dumb, or blind. In a way, it's like she already has.

That's why Danny comes to me. He knew I understood discretion, back before that was one of our vocabulary words in fifth grade. I know how to hide stuff, because my family's almost as screwed up as his. Almost. I'll take my mother, and her tendency to medicate her bipolar disorder with alcohol, over Roger any day.

We sit on the rocker, and he winces when I reach out to examine his face. Because I wasn't sure Danny was here, I am not prepared with the first-aid items I usually meet him with—a towel of ice, Neosporin, and some Band-Aids. His eye is swollen shut. If I hadn't seen him from the other side, I would barely be able to tell it's Danny. I get up to go inside and retrieve my supplies, but he grabs my hand.

"Don't go." He whispers it so quietly I'm not sure he really said it. He starts to shake, so I sit down and wrap my arms around him sideways, to warm him up, to steady him, whatever he needs. But he jumps away from me. He usually flinches when people get too close to him—in fact, that's what most of his recess fights are about—but he's not usually like that with me.

"What set the asshole off this time?" I whisper, savoring the feeling of the swear word on my tongue.

"Don't call him that," he snaps.

This is also new. Usually Danny doesn't start defending Roger until he's already called him every name in the book and is trying to prepare himself to return home. He'll say stuff like "I shouldn't have left my skateboard in front of the shop, he says it looks trashy," or, "I shouldn't have left the laundry basket open, he's told me a million times to keep it shut." I mean, my house has a lot of dumb rules like that, too, but if I break one of them, I get yelled at. I don't get *hit*.

"What happened?" I demand. I don't usually push like this, I wait until Danny's ready to talk, but tonight something is off. 1) He didn't wake me up. 2) He was hiding in my backyard, not sitting on the rocker like usual. 3) He said he "didn't want to bring me into it," but he's been bringing me into it for years, so why is tonight any different?

The eye that can still open looks around wildly before settling on my face. "I think you should call Murphy."

It's only when Roger is so fired up that he screams at Danny to "never show his rotten face here again" as he (literally) kicks him out on the street, that we call Murphy. Danny always comes to my house first, because he knows I'll tend to his wounds and let him cry if he wants to. After that, we assess whether it's worth waiting it out, giving Roger some time to cool off before he sneaks back in, or if we need to give Murphy the warning call that Danny's on his way and he'll need to be snuck into the basement again.

The first time we called him for help, his terrifying mother screamed at us in French and hung up before even asking who was calling. Since then, Murphy's learned to keep the portable phone next to his bed. So I'm not surprised when he answers on the first ring.

"Yeah, I'll wait for him on the side porch," Murphy says groggily, before I even speak.

"No, Murph," I say. "He wants you to come here this time."

"What? Why?"

"I don't know. He's acting really weird. Just get the hell over here!" I whisper-yell into the phone.

While we wait for Murphy to arrive, I hold Danny's hand and use my feet to keep the rocker moving back and forth. I hope the motion will soothe him, but I get no sign either way. He is silent, staring down at the pool like he's thinking of jumping in and never resurfacing. It seems like hours that we wait for Murphy, but it can't be that long because he only lives three blocks away. None of us live more than three blocks away from at least one other member of our crew, except for Danny, who is ten blocks. The deli is below the tracks.

Finally Murphy climbs the back steps and joins us on the deck, wearing the same shorts and T-shirt he wears to my house to swim in to cover up the baby fat he hasn't shed yet. He looks at our clasped hands, confused. I realize he probably thinks he's been called here so Danny and I can announce we've become a couple. Or maybe ask permission, since Murphy and I were boyfriend and girlfriend for like a week last year before we realized we can't stand each other when no one else is around.

He *would* think that's what this is about, despite all the times Danny has been our mutual crisis. What an idiot!

Then, without looking at Murphy or me, Danny starts talking. "It was just like always," he says. "I was sleeping, and then suddenly Roger busted open my door and yanked me out of bed. He lifted me by my shirt," and he grabs the top of his shirt at this, twisting it into a knot, "so I was looking right into his eyes, and he had that look, and I knew I was in for it. He asked me what the hell was wrong with me, and when I didn't say anything, he dragged me into the living room and pointed at the Sega. I forgot to put the controller away. I said I was sorry and went to wrap the cord up and put it in the drawer under the TV, but he smacked it out of my hand and picked it up and started hitting me over the head with it. Hard.

"My mom woke up from the noise. I always try to be quiet, to keep her out of it, but when he hit me this time, it felt like my skull was cracked open. When she yelled at him to stop, he turned on her and started shaking her. 'This little bastard has no discipline! I take you into my home, and this is the thanks I get?' Same as usual. When she begged Roger to leave me alone, he slammed her head into the wall. He went to do it again and then, suddenly, he stopped. Roger *never* stops hitting until someone's on the floor crying, so right away I knew something was wrong. I couldn't see his face, but his back kinda stiffened up, and then he bent over, grabbing his arm. When he dropped to the floor I could finally see his face, and it was redder than I've ever seen it. Including the time I called him a 'dickhead' and he broke two of my fingers.

"My mom called out his name and kneeled next to him, crying. She told me to call nine-one-one, say that Roger was having a heart attack, but I didn't move. She asked me again, but I just stood there and waited for her to look at me. Roger was rolling around on the ground, begging us to help him, but I simply looked at my mother and told her to go back to bed. She shook her head at first, saying we had to do something, and I yelled at her to get back in her room and not to come out until I told her to. I sounded just like Roger did when he yelled at her for not loading the dishwasher right. But she listened. She got up, went back to her room, and closed the door."

My hand is over my mouth now. I know how the story is going to end, but Murphy either doesn't know or he needs to hear Danny say the words, because he asks, "Dan, what happened to Roger?"

Danny looks at Murphy like it's the first time he's really seeing him, then he answers. "After a few minutes, Roger stopped rolling around. He just looked at me, mad as hell, but scared, too. And I sat down on the couch and looked right back at him. Until he stopped moving."

I wait a beat before I ask, "And then you left?"

Danny nods. "I knocked on my mom's bedroom door and told her she should call nine-one-one. I knew it would . . . look funny if she didn't."

Murphy and I look at each other. We both know this is way over our heads. My hand is still on top of Danny's, and the squeeze I give him is like the flip of a switch. His face crumbles and he starts crying. He cries so hard I'm worried he's going to choke.

"Breathe, Danny, breathe," I say, rubbing his back.

"I just wanted it to stop," he says between moans. He repeats it over and over, and I pull him to me. Finally, he lets me. He feels so small. He sounds like he did in kindergarten, when Emmett used to steal his lunch, and I realize the part of Danny that was still in any way a child an hour ago is making its final appearance tonight. And the parts of Murphy and I that are supposed to be children—supposed to be worrying about whether we're going to make the baseball team, or who we're going to take to the end-of-year dance—they're gone now, too. We can't ever un-know what we know.

We're not paying attention to how loud Danny is being, so we're all shocked when the back porch light flicks on. My mom is standing in the doorway. "What on earth is going on out here?" she screeches. Murphy and I look at each other again. He shrugs. It's up to me to decide how this all moves forward.

"Roger had a heart attack," I say, looking not at my mom but at Murphy. "Danny's mom found him, and Danny was upset, so he came here." I look at Murphy again. I've learned from watching Danny make excuses for his cuts and bruises that the trick is to stay as close to the truth as possible, and that's as much as I can say without cracking.

Murphy nods and takes over. "Danny's really worried," he says. "Can you call Mrs. Deuso and see if he's okay? They should be at the hospital by now."

# CHAPTER THREE

# STEPH

*Now*

Well, this is awkward. First time I meet Charlene, I'm sitting here listening to her son's murder confession. First day meeting Ruby, and she's reading it. Her words—well, Danny's—hang in the air like when church bells stop ringing but you swear you can still hear them. The echo survives Ally's gasp, and Charlene's, too. I suppress mine, so I won't get another lecture from Ally about how I can't possibly understand the pain of losing Danny, like she and the rest of the crew who've "been there since the beginning." Honestly, if she even knew the real reason I lost it at the funeral, I bet she wouldn't have given me such crap. I won't have time to bet, though; they're all about to find out. They have to. It's the only thing I can say to distract them from what's really inside Emmett's envelope.

Charlene shakes her head, saying, "No" over and over again. Of course she doesn't want to believe it. That her son killed her husband? That's like something straight out of a Greek play. And hasn't Charlene been through enough? She shouldn't beat herself up. The more I learn about Danny—and I hate to think this about anybody—the more I think maybe he really was beyond help.

Charlene stands up, and Ruby puts her hands on Charlene's shoulders, tells her it's okay, that it's going to be okay. I've only met Ruby today, but already I like her way more than I thought I would. Emmett puts her on such a pedestal, and from what Ally tells me about her, I was expecting Ruby to be a little stuck-up. I mean, she's lived in New York and London, and God knows where else, and she hasn't talked to any of them since high school. Imagine my surprise when, at the funeral, Ally introduced me to a pretty, but not overgroomed or overperfumed, average-sized girl in non-labeled clothing, who smiled and hugged me as if I were one of her long-lost friends. She seems     down to earth. Sweet even. Ruby's the one from the stories—All. The. Stories.— who is decidedly fearless: the first girl to leap from the fifty-foot jump at the quarry; the girl who stole her parents' car when she was thirteen; the one who's traveled and moved to big cities on her own. And yet, when she entered the church, she looked like every step was a calculated decision to move herself toward us. When she got closer, I could see the quiver in her smile, and something told me it wasn't just the circumstances. She was nervous to be among people she's known since preschool. And yet now, in the tensest of moments, she is in complete control. Maybe Ally was wrong when she said Ruby thinks she's better than all of us, but she *might* have been right in her description of her as an "odd cluck," if what she really meant was an "odd duck" (Ally has a tendency to mess up all those old sayings; I don't have the heart to tell her).

"It ain't what you think," Charlene pleads, as if we were walking out the door in disgust. But none of us have moved. We're frozen to our seats. I look over at Ally. Her face has been white as a sheet ever since the envelopes were handed out, which, of course, makes me wonder what hers says. I know what Emmett's says. Or, at least, nothing in that envelope could be *worse* than what I already know.

Charlene tells the story of the night Danny's stepfather died. Apparently Roger was abusive, and one night when he was hitting both of them he had a heart attack. Instead of calling an ambulance right away, they waited until . . . well, you know. So Danny didn't exactly *kill* Roger, but he didn't exactly *not* kill him, either.

"It sounds like maybe Danny was just scared," Ally says quietly. "Like he was in shock and didn't know what to do."

Aaron shoots her a look, which makes Ally cry out, "What?" Aaron simply shakes his head, shrugs.

"Ally, don't be so simple," Emmett says. "Danny meant for Roger to die, it's pretty obvious." Geez, Em, don't hold back or anything.

"Watch how you're talking to my wife, Emmett," Aaron says.

"Well, come on," Emmett says. "Why *confess* in a suicide note, if it isn't true?"

"Maybe Danny just feels guilty because he couldn't save him," Ally says. I notice everyone is still talking about him in the present tense.

"Stop being such a Pollyanna, Ally. You know that's not what he means." Emmett's ears are getting red now, which always happens when he's about to blow his top and storm out. This isn't the place for that, and it's really important Emmett doesn't get too stressed, especially now. So I hook my arm through his, our little sign that he needs to calm down. I feel his muscles relax a bit. He nods at Charlene. "Not that I'm saying what happened was right or wrong," he says to her.

Charlene dissolves into tears and flees up the stairs. Moments later, we hear the door to her bedroom close.

"Jesus, Emmett," Ruby says. "Why don't you just punch her in the face?"

Emmett shoots her a look.

Ally says, "Well, I don't care what happened that night. If Danny let Roger die, then Roger deserved it. As far as I'm concerned, Danny acted in self-defense. I didn't want to say it when Charlene was here," she lowers her voice to a hiss, "but if Roger was hitting them, *someone* had to stop him, and it obviously wasn't going to be her."

Aaron chimes in, "Now that I think about it, as long as I've known him, Danny's always been pretty protective of the people he cares about. Remember when he got in a fight with that carnival guy at the Maple Festival for grabbing Ally's ass? I bet the whole thing was more about protecting his mom than himself." Aaron has hereby redeemed himself to his wife for the skeptical look he gave her earlier, no doubt avoiding a blow-out at home later.

Meanwhile I'm silent. It's not my place to speak. Maybe it's the Catholic in me, but I can't help but think being responsible for someone's death, in whatever way and for whatever reason, is still called murder. I didn't know Roger, and it sounds like he was an awful man, but it wasn't up to Danny to decide whether he lived or died. Besides, only half of me is keeping up with the conversation. The other half is trying to find my opening.

I think Emmett is speaking to me when he says, "You've been awfully quiet," but when I look at him, he's glaring between Ruby and Murphy. "What do you think about all of this?"

They look at each other, like they're trying to decide something. Murphy nods, then Ruby says, "We knew."

Another round of gasps ensues. "Since when?" Ally says.

Ruby is quiet; more decisions about how much truth to tell. Her shoulders fall and she says, "Since the night it happened."

"You've known since we were twelve years old that Roger was beating Danny and his mom, and you didn't *tell* anyone?" Ally cries.

The first crack in Ruby's poise shows in her voice when she says, "Actually, I've known about the *abuse* pretty much from when it started, and that wasn't long after Roger and Charlene got married."

All eyes grow wide.

"We were in *second grade* when they got married!" Ally is all but screeching now. "That's *four years* before Roger died!" Aaron folds his hand over hers. Their little sign.

Ruby looks at each of us; her eyes seem to have gotten bluer. They have the same deep sadness as Charlene's when she looked at us, pleading for understanding. For forgiveness.

"Unbelievable," Emmett says, and I know he's about to put words to the accusation formulating in all our minds. I squeeze his arm hard now, hoping he will back off. "Ruby, do you realize if someone had stopped Roger, maybe Danny wouldn't have been put in that situation in the first place? That maybe he wouldn't have tried to drown his guilt in drugs? That maybe—"

"Okay, that's ENOUGH!" Murphy roars as he jumps out of his seat. "I get it, we're all upset. Keep in mind, when all this started we were EIGHT YEARS OLD. In case you don't remember, Emmett, when you were eight, you were playing with Hot Wheels and collecting Pogs. Not exactly old enough to know what to do when your friend is getting beaten up by an adult. You do *not* get to pin this all on Ruby. No. Way."

Ruby looks at Murphy with gratitude, and a little hint of something else that piques my interest.

"Who should I pin it on, then? You? What did you have to do with this?" Emmett and Murphy are now practically toe-to-toe.

"Sometimes it was bad enough that it wasn't safe for Danny to go back home right away, so Ruby would call me and tell me Danny was on his way over, because he needed a place to hide out until Roger cooled off. He never wanted to talk about it, but I knew anyway. It doesn't take a fucking rocket scientist," he says and looks pointedly at Emmett, then at Ally. "The night Roger died, Ruby told me to come over instead, and Danny told us what happened."

"And you didn't think to tell the rest of us? So we didn't look so stupid when we were all telling Danny how *sorry* we were that Roger died?"

I want to smack my forehead. We're talking about some of the heaviest stuff you *can* talk about—child abuse, murder, suicide—and Ally is concerned that she reacted inappropriately to a situation that happened over sixteen years ago.

Ruby gracefully ignores Ally's point of focus. "We talked about it afterward and decided the fewer people who knew the truth, the better. We didn't want Danny getting in trouble, when all he was doing was protecting himself."

"You should have gone to the police," Emmett says. Ally whips her head around, her mouth hanging open.

"Emmett. Come on," Ruby says.

"What? He was a minor! A little *boy*, for Christ's sake! They wouldn't have thrown him in jail. But at least the truth would have been out, and Danny wouldn't have to live with this giant secret his whole life! He could have gotten help. *We* could have helped him through it."

There it is. My boyfriend's hypocrisy gives me the *perfect* opening. "Emmett, calm down," I say. "You're not exactly the poster boy for being honest." Emmett spins around and looks at me, a look of betrayal on his face. I widen my eyes, trying to beam a telepathic message that it's okay, that I have a plan.

"Steph, you keep your mouth shut," he says.

Clearly he didn't get the message, but since he said it so nicely, it makes my part all the easier. "Fuck you, Emmett," I say. "I've kept this goddamn secret for you because I love you, and it's what you wanted. But they should know." This part is true, at least for what I'm about to tell them. Talk about secrets turning you into something dark; Emmett's temper has been out of control these last few months, and I've had about enough. I snatch the envelope from his hand and stand up, holding it over my head. This next move is risky, but I need to do it in order for them to believe me. I pull out the piece of paper, nod like it's only confirming what I'm about to say, and slip it back in the envelope before I speak. "Emmett's got a bum heart."

"Steph—" Emmett starts, and then stops, realizing that's all I said. He's not happy this is getting out, but this is not what he was expecting me to say.

"What does *that* mean?" Ally asks. She stares at me accusingly. I know what the look means. *How dare you keep me out of the loop? You're just the girlfriend, but I've been here since the beginning.*

"He's got a condition called Hypertropic Cardiomyopathy."

"Hyper-*what?*" Ally asks.

"It's HCM, for short. It means the walls of his heart are thicker than they should be, which causes problems in the heart's electrical functions."

"That sounds pretty serious, man," Murphy says.

"It's not that big—" Emmett starts.

"It is serious," I interrupt. "In most cases, people don't know they have HCM until their heart stops. Especially in younger people."

"So how did you find out?" Ruby asks. Everyone is still directing their questions at Emmett, hoping he will look up from the spot on the floor he's currently drilling a hole into with his eyes. He is red to the tips of his hair follicles.

"He was lucky," I continue. "For him, it started with what's called A-fib, which is like a rapid fluttering in your chest. About nine months ago he was playing basketball with his work buddies at lunch and had to stop because he couldn't catch his breath. He started to say something about his heart, before he passed out for a minute. They thought he had a heart attack, but at the hospital they ran all kinds of tests and diagnosed him with HCM." A chill runs through the group. There's a lot of heart problems in the air.

"How do they treat it?" Ruby asks.

"Well, the danger of HCM is that your heart will stop, so if no one is around to start it again . . . well, you can imagine." I can't say the words. "So they . . . *installed* . . . a defibrillator. You've seen doctors on TV rubbing those big paddles together and yelling, 'Clear!' until all the nurses get out of the way? It's a miniature version of that. It will start Emmett's heart again if it ever stops beating."

"So then, you're fine!" Ally says, brightening. "As long as you have that, you're fine, right?"

Emmett nods slowly, not removing his eyes from the spot on the ground.

"Not really," I interject. Might as well give them the whole ball of facts, as Ally would say. At least about this part of it. "He has to be on medication that makes him dizzy and sometimes nauseous and drowsy, and he has to be a lot more careful about his heart rate. Which means no strenuous exercise."

The crew is silent at this, and I know what they're thinking. Emmett is as active as they come; even when he's not playing basketball or hockey, he's running or swimming, always in motion. Or at least he *was*. It's not that he can't do any of those things anymore, it's just that he has physical limits that he can no longer push, which is what Emmett has always prided himself on. Getting the defibrillator put in and all that, we thought that would be the worst part, but it wasn't. The hard part has been the aftermath. The changes in his lifestyle. The struggle to regain a sense of normalcy, the loss of the confidence that made me fall in love with him in the first place.

"Steph," Murphy pipes up, "when you say *installed*, do you mean . . .?"

I nod. "Surgically."

He rounds on Emmett now. "You had your *chest cracked open,* and you didn't tell anyone about it?" Murphy asks. I breathe a silent sigh of relief. Just like I had hoped, this part of Emmett's secret is big enough for them to believe. "How is it even possible to pull something like that off?"

"I don't know, Murphy, how is it possible to cover up a murder?" Emmett shoots back. They glare at each other.

I interject, "He didn't want anyone to know. Emmett didn't even let me call his parents until after he was out of the hospital. I was so concentrated on him staying alive I would have done anything he asked me to."

"But *why*?" Ally asks, her voice more full of hurt now than anger. And I understand it. Why wouldn't he want his friends to be there for him?

"I didn't want people treating me differently. Ally, you would make a big fuss and start bossing me around. Don't—" he holds up one hand as Ally starts to open her mouth to protest, "act like you wouldn't. We all know you can't help yourself." The crew laughs at this, one sweet moment of relief after all this awful news. "And you guys," he looks at Aaron and Murphy, "you'd start taking it easy on me on the court, looking at me funny. I just couldn't take it. I still can't. That's why I'm always 'too busy' to play."

Everyone nods in agreement. They are promising to themselves, to each other, that they won't treat him any differently. That they won't pity him. But they will. I know, because I made those promises, too.

"We thought you were just whipped," Aaron says, lightening the mood.

After a moment, Ruby asks, "The thing I don't understand, if you kept this under such tight wraps, is how did Danny know?"

Emmett turns to me, trying to hide the panic from his eyes.

"He didn't exactly choose Danny," I pipe up, looking straight at Emmett. "After the diagnosis, Em didn't have much of an appetite, and I had trouble sleeping. We needed something to . . . ease the anxiety."

I watch as they struggle to connect the dots. Then Ruby claps her hand to her mouth, stifling a bark of a laugh. "You went to Dan to get *pot*?"

Emmett's face flushes and he shoots me a glare that says I'm in for it when we get home. But who cares? His reaction still perfectly confirms Ruby's theory. It's close enough to the truth that no one will question it, and far enough away to keep us safe.

The crew howls with laughter.

"What is so fucking funny about that?" Emmett demands, losing his already minuscule amount of patience.

"I'm sorry," Ruby chokes out between giggles. "It's just . . . the guy who gave us a Nancy Reagan lecture every time we lit up a joint, a pothead at twenty-eight years old!" Fresh waves of laughter ripple through us.

"'Just say no,'" Murphy says, imitating Emmett's serious voice, wagging his finger. More laughter.

"'Ruby, you're acting like a blocker,'" Ruby says, doing the same.

"Well, you were," Emmett says.

Even I have to giggle at the way he stands with his arms crossed, in perfect Stern Dad posture.

"And now you are!" she roars. It's not really all that funny, but the laughter is needed after the day we've had. After the *year* Emmett and I have had.

"*Any*way," Emmett says over the din, "Dan, of course, had to give me the same hard time you're giving me—"

"—Or he was concerned about you, because twenty-eight is a little old to start experimenting with drugs—" Ruby interrupts.

"—And I lost my temper—"

"—Shocker."

"—And I ended up telling him. Honestly, I didn't think he would remember. Towards the end he was, you know, pretty out of it."

That sucks the laughter right out of the room.

"All right. Your turn," Emmett says, his arms still crossed. He looks straight at Murphy.

"My turn for what?"

"Your secret. I went. Your turn."

Murphy breathes a laugh out of his nose. "You didn't exactly *go*; your girlfriend went for you." Again, three years with these people and I'm still only the girlfriend.

"Whatever. I don't care. Out with it."

"We just talked about it, dude. Ruby and I knew about Danny and . . . the thing . . . with Roger."

I wonder if anyone else notices Ruby snap her head to Murphy.

Emmett narrows his eyes at them, but he must decide it's better not to press, considering that he's lying, too. He turns on Ally. "And you?"

Ally hesitates, looking at Murphy and Ruby as if she's hoping they will take their turn again. "Mine is . . ." She looks at Aaron, who shrugs his shoulders. She's on her own. Her face suddenly brightens, her posture straightening. "It's nothing bad, and I'll tell you guys, I just don't want to say it today. Not after the day we've had. Okay?"

She looks at each of us, waiting for us all to nod, which we do.

Ally's, Murphy's, and Ruby's envelopes all lie unopened, their hands clutched around them.

*When it comes to things that really matter, you guys barely even know each other.*

And how.

# CHAPTER FOUR

# RUBY

*Now*

"Remember when Emmett mixed up mayo and ketchup and hot sauce and Kool-Aid and dirt and all that shit, and then paid Danny a dollar to eat it, and when he didn't pay up, Dan threw up on his shoes?"

"Remember when Ruby drove us home from the homecoming party during that freak snowstorm, and when she started to skid, Murphy panicked and pulled the hand brake and we ended up in that ditch, facing the other way? And the cops brought us home?"

"Remember when Ally's bikini top popped off when she jumped into the quarry, and she was so shocked by the cold water she didn't realize it for, like, five minutes?"

The stories from fifteen years of friendship flow like a faucet that won't turn off. Despite Aaron's signature method of peer pressure (one hand clasped on my shoulder in what the crew lovingly calls "the claw," the other holding a shot of bottom-shelf liquor), I have stood strong, shaking my head at each one-ounce parcel of liquid courage. The crew, who do not have my self-imposed three-drink limit, have partaken enough to get us to this point: the proverbial walk down Memory Lane.

Adhering to our old customs, already I have gotten complete histories on two high-school classmates I only vaguely remember; I've debated the upcoming election with Emmett while the crew rolled their eyes in the background; and when he realized he was losing, he resorted to picking apart my outfit (Ally's black top and dark-wash jeans passed inspection, but as I couldn't squeeze my big feet into Ally's dainty shoes, we fished out my cowboy boots from my high-school closet, which Ally had declared "classic").

But not everything is the same. A welcome addition to the night's proceedings has been getting to know Steph. As well as siding with me while Emmett and I debated equal pay (Emmett refuses to acknowledge it's a problem), Steph works at the Chatwick Community Library, which explains the instantaneous case I felt with her earlier. She carries the scent of the musty stacks of my childhood—perhaps the only place in Chatwick I have ever felt truly comfortable.

An unwelcome change is the way Murphy and I sit on opposite ends of the row of stools the crew occupies, although the scent he carries isn't having any trouble infiltrating my nose from there.

I try to remain present, but every few minutes I find my eyes wandering to the Exit sign. I don't want to be here. Not in Chatwick, and definitely not in Margie's Pub, otherwise known as the congregation of Chatwick's finest. Chatwick Town is made up of rednecks, who farm on the outskirts of Chatwick City (which is really a bunch of neighborhoods, a few blocks of shops, and the high school); white trash, who live below the tracks and off the government; and "richies," a relative term that the other two camps invented to make people like me and my friends feel like snobs for living in the hill section of the city and having parents who own local businesses or commute to more affluent communities, like Drummond, to work. All three groups are fairly represented tonight, and they've all spent the evening staring at me, trying to decide exactly how to enter my description into the Chat tomorrow.

But the biggest reason I am so uncomfortable at Margie's is the memories. Memories I shouldn't have, considering I left Chatwick when I was eighteen years old, well before I was legally allowed to be in a bar. The last time I was here was my sixteenth birthday, but I wasn't here to celebrate. I was here responding to a courtesy call from Monty, the 400-pound bouncer, to warn me Nancy was approaching her cut-off point and I had best get down here before she pitched a fit and then hopped in her car. This was not an unusual occurrence, but on this special day Nancy told me she wished I'd never been born, so she could actually have a little fun. Happy Sweet Sixteen, right? That was the last time I tried to save her, and the day I stopped calling her Mom.

I was surprised when Monty slapped my hand away as I tried to show him my driver's license and pulled me into a hug instead, although we did have quite the special relationship back then. Besides the warning calls, there was the time a beer-bellied redneck got handsy with me as I pulled him off my mother. Monty dragged him into the alley and beat the shit out of him. So I guess Margie's has produced one happy memory for me. Of course, that was followed up by two months of harassment at Chatwick High from the redneck's kids, who were forced to pick up the slack around the farm for a week because their father was out of commission. So, bittersweet memory, I guess.

Before I could even ask Monty how he was, he assured me Nancy wasn't here tonight, that she hadn't been in over ten years. Ally, who had her hand clamped on my elbow (I imagine more in an effort to prevent my escape than to stay linked as we navigated the crowd of smokers outside the bar), had to explain to Monty that I am here to be with friends tonight, not to drag my mother out by her hair so that she won't drive home and wrap her car around a tree.

By the time the crew was exhausted from the day's drama, it had grown dark outside the basement windows. Ally and I were unsuccessful in our attempt to coax Charlene out of her bedroom, so we joined the crew in the driveway, where they were making plans to meet up here. I had nodded with my fingers crossed behind my back—*my* plan was to shut myself into my childhood bedroom, pretending to answer client emails but really refreshing my computer screen every thirty seconds to see if a flight back to New York became available. Because Vermont's main airport in Drummond is so small, the seat I vacated today to attend Danny's "private reception" was the last seat back to New York until Sunday night—three days away.

But Ally was one step ahead of me. I had barely settled in and booted up my laptop, suddenly unsure if I could even connect to the Internet in this house, when she showed up. She waved Aaron off in his LJ Construction truck as soon as her foot was in the door. "He has to go save our seats," she said. "It gets rough down there." As if I didn't know that. "Plus, I thought it would be fun to ride down, just us girls. I know Nancy hasn't gotten rid of Blue. I see her tooling around town in it sometimes." She even brought an assortment of clothes with her, assuming—since I hadn't planned on staying past the funeral—that I hadn't packed an appropriate bar outfit.

We really didn't need to drive; Margie's is only about six blocks from my parents' house—an absurdly lucky walking distance in New York, but unheard of to walk here. Everyone drives everywhere in Chatwick. If you're walking, you're a blocker who can't afford a car. The neighborhood had a conniption when Nancy quit drinking and started taking daily walks "to keep her centered."

The short ride down to the bar was quiet, and not in the comfortable, peaceful way our rides around the back roads of Chatwick used to be. The air was thick with questions we were both too afraid to ask, for fear of them being turned around back to ourselves. Now that doesn't seem to be a problem. It only took a dead friend, a threatening letter, and three hours at Margie's to catapult us from awkward estrangement to our new sense of normalcy. The one where we are all together without Danny.

In an effort to fit in, I pipe up with my favorite story from our high-school years. "Remember when Emmett ate the mushroom pizza?" I ask, eyeing him.

"Oh. My. God. The mushroom pizza!" Ally cries. Murphy and Aaron throw their heads back in laughter.

"What pizza?" Steph asks.

I cock my head, not taking my eyes off Emmett while I ask, "Oh, you mean he *never told you that story*?"

"Ruby—" he warns.

"So we're all at Danny's, about to try mushrooms for the first time," I start, ignoring Emmett to the rest of the crew's utter delight. "Emmett, of course, is all bent out of shape about it, because he was all 'Just Say No' about everything but booze. Back then, anyway." We giggle, thinking about his recent dalliance with marijuana a good half-life after the rest of us. "So when Danny goes to dole them out, Emmett *slaps* the bottom of Danny's hand and the mushrooms go flying everywhere. Now, we're out in the woods behind Danny's house, and it's dark out, so we can't see where they land. So Danny goes to get the flashlight Charlene always kept in the kitchen junk drawer, but it's not there, so we have no choice but to give up the search until the next morning."

The others are hanging on my every word, Ally and Murphy and Aaron clutching at each other, knowing where the story is going but in suspense for the punchline nonetheless. Emmett crosses his arms and purses his lips, shaking his head, his face the color of Pepto-Bismol.

"So we're all pissed at Emmett, even though he *swears* up and down he didn't mean to lose the 'shrooms; that he was even thinking about trying some—like we believed that! So we spend the night drinking instead, but what Emmett doesn't know is that before we went into the woods, Danny had cut up a couple of the 'shroom stems and spread them over the leftover pizza in his fridge—Charlene *always* had leftover pizza, and Emmett *always* ate it late night when things started winding down. You could almost set your watch by it: when Emmett started eating pizza, it was twenty minutes before everyone went to bed."

"He still does that," Steph says, glancing lovingly at her boyfriend before seeing his now fuchsia face and darting her eyes back to me, tucking her lips in to stifle a laugh.

"So we all go to bed: Danny in his room with Jenny or Heather, or whoever he was dating at the time; Aaron and Ally in the spare; Emmett in the basement, *or so we thought*"—I leave Tara out of the sleeping-arrangement discussion, because Emmett's pissed enough at me already—"and Murphy and I on the trampoline in the backyard, where we always slept in the summer because the couples always claimed all the beds. Well, the next thing I know, I feel like someone's staring at me and when I roll over there's Emmett, standing by the trampoline, his eyes so alert and wide open they practically glow in the dark, and he just says, 'Hi,' with this big dopey grin on his face." I pause, giggling at the image of how cheerful he was, blissfully unaware of what was happening to him.

"Then he starts babbling at the speed of light about how drugs are bad and we don't need them and didn't we have a great time just drinking and hanging out"—Ally points out here how ironic this is—"and then he gets distracted by something and starts running around the yard mumbling something about 'the goddamn fairies.'" This gets big laughs, although I remember being completely freaked out about it at the time. "I wake up Murphy, to help me get him under control, but he of course makes it worse, pointing out things in the woods that aren't really there and then pretending like he never said it." I give Murphy, who's moved closer to me now, a playful punch on the arm, and Emmett does the same.

"Dude, I was sixteen!" Murphy says, laughing. "I was an asshole." At least he admits it.

"So Emmett takes off into the woods, and Murphy the hero passes right back out and I can't wake him up again, so I have to go inside and wake Danny and Aaron to go out and find Emmett—with no flashlights, mind you—while Ally and I argue over how long to wait before we wake up Charlene or call the police."

"I still feel like we should have woken her up right away," Ally says. She also doesn't mention Tara's role in the story, which was to cry and wail, convinced her boyfriend had been abducted.

"I didn't want to get Danny in trouble!" I say. I'm momentarily knocked off-course when I hear myself say the words I've said too many times before.

"So what happened?" Steph asks, prompting me back on track after a minute of staring into space.

"Right. So just as we're about to go wake up Charlene, Danny and Aaron drag Emmett in, dirt *all over* his face, and he's holding . . ." I pause here for dramatic effect, and Steph leans in, her eyes wide, ". . . the missing flashlight!"

We all laugh at this, including Steph, but not Emmett. When

I come up for air I add, "He purposely hid it under the porch before we went out in the woods. He planned to ruin our night all along. Serves him right!"

As the laughter dies down, Emmett starts nodding his head, slowly, and with a sadistic smile on his face. I know I'm in for it.

"I could tell some stories about Ruby, too," he says, not taking his eyes off me.

I ignore the tingling in my gut and put a challenging look into my eye. "Oh yeah? Try me." I take a sip of my last allotted beer for the evening and wait. Emmett and I go way back, but we've never been the type of friends to confide in each other. I'm reasonably confident my secret is safe.

"Remember the time when Ruby *finally* got drunk, and she gave up her vir—"

"Hey, let's dance!" Murphy cuts in, his voice louder than Emmett's and the hubbub of the crowd and the band combined. At the same time, he practically shoves me out to the dance floor, leaving no time for Emmett to finish his sentence or for me to respond. The band plays "Folsom Prison Blues," to which everyone roars approval and starts stomping around, clapping their hands. I stand stock still, too stunned at what Emmett was about to say to move my body in any kind of rhythmic fashion. I open my mouth to protest at what just happened, but Murphy holds his finger to his lips and takes my hand, spinning me under his raised arm. Soon Ally and Aaron join us, and I feel the sensations return to my feet. I look over to the bar, where it seems like Emmett is getting a dressing down from Steph before she leaves him there to join us on the dance floor.

I like her. I really like her.

After a few minutes, Emmett makes his way over to us. He clasps onto my arm—to prevent me from leaving or socking him one, I'm not sure—and mouths, "I'm sorry." It's so surprising that he's apologizing, I instantly forgive him. I remember now. This is what it's like, what it was always like, the constant ebbs and flows of being with the crew.

The song changes to "I Love This Bar," which my friends seem to know every word to. They couple off and, as always, leave Murphy and I standing alone. He pulls me to him, and when I instinctively stiffen and try to pull back, he clutches me so tightly I can't help but laugh. "No running away," he says into my ear. "No more running away." I keep the smile plastered on my face, but my eyes water, and I'm grateful we're dancing the grade school way—my arms around his neck, his encircling my waist, my head safely looking over his shoulder. If we were dancing the traditional way, he would be able to see my tears and feel my sweaty palms.

We turn slowly around the dance floor, every muscle in my body on high alert. His smell overwhelms me. Since I can't seem to get away physically, I try to detach myself from this moment mentally by scanning the room as we spin. I notice at least four beams of hatred trained on me, and wonder if the last dance with Murphy Leblanc is a coveted privilege. I think about asking him but find myself breathless, and not just because he's holding me so tight. We've danced together like this a million times, always the ones left out together. The last time was senior prom. I can't think about senior prom.

"You're welcome," he says into my hair.

"Oh," I say, "thanks for the save, Emmett's such an assh—"

"I'm not talking about Emmett."

I look at him now. Murphy's eyes shine with the familiar spark of something only we know, a spark we've shared ever since the night Roger died. But this has nothing to do with Roger, just like our secrets don't. I wasn't sure before whether he was covering for us or not, but now I know.

When finally, blessedly, the song ends, the bright overhead lights turn on and bathe the bar with a shocking reminder that there is life outside Margie's. I hug everyone goodbye, thinking as I do that I've actually made it through this rollercoaster of a day. More importantly, I've made it through without my secret being outed. Now all I have to do is hide in my room for the rest of the weekend.

But as the girls and I collect our purses from behind the bar, where Murphy had "his buddy" the bartender keep an eye on them, someone from the other side of the bar catches my eye. It takes me a second to place her, and by the time I do she's already made a beeline for me.

"Ruby St. James," she says, sneering her emphasis on the "Saint." She is thinner than I remember her, almost sickly thin, and her hair frames her face in two greasy curtains. Her eyes are bloodshot; her nostrils pink-rimmed. The years have not been kind to her. I try to appear as if this girl's presence is a happy surprise, but my breath is caught in my throat.

"Brandy . . ."

"McCallister," she scoffs, mistaking my panic for forgetfulness. If only she knew I have never forgotten her full name. That sometimes I wake up in the middle of the night with it on the tip of my tongue.

"McCallister, right. How are you?" I smile weakly. The fluorescent lights grow brighter, doing nothing to hide the harsh reality of Brandy's appearance.

"It's actually not McCallister anymore," she says, flashing a diamond the size of a flea.

"Oh?"

"It's Crane. Mrs. Hardy Crane." The name causes an instant-aneous flutter of anxiety in my stomach, but she says it with a flourish, like she's been rehearsing this moment for a decade.

Suddenly it feels like I'm trying to swallow sand. "Oh!" I say. "How wonderful." I risk a glance around to see if Hardy himself is here to haunt me.

"He's not here," she says, following my gaze smugly, mistaking my fear for interest. "He's at home with *the kids*. Girls' night out." She points to a posse of girls who are watching us carefully. Like Brandy, they are dressed in age-inappropriate clothing fished out of the clearance bin at the Fashion Bug off I-89. If their outfits weren't so tight, I would have been worried about concealed weapons, the way they're looking at me.

"Well, best of luck to you," I say, and turn to leave.

She grabs my elbow, clamping down with all her might. She leans in and snarls into my ear, "If you think you can just saunter back into town and—"

"Back off, Brandy." Ally steps in between us.

Brandy instantly drops her grip but doesn't step back. "I'm just telling her—"

"I know what you're telling her. You're the only person in this town who thinks Hardy Crane is some prize to compete over, but you're embarrassing yourself. I think it's time for you to head on home."

Brandy looks at Ally through narrowed eyes, drunkenly trying to decide whether to press the issue. She opens her mouth again, but then Murphy steps in.

"You heard her, Brandy, go on home to your family." It's so strange to hear those words coming out of his mouth. Here we are, rehashing a drama straight out of Chatwick High as if I'd never left, but he's talking like a grown man, to a grown woman who has a *husband* and *children* at home. The surrealism makes me queasy.

Shaken, I thank Ally, giving her and the rest of my friends a farewell hug. How sad it is for the evening to end this way, after the already tragic day we've had. Who knows when I will see my old friends again, and the last thing they will remember of me is the old business with Hardy Crane.

Murphy hovers nearby as I shrug off Ally's attempt to further engage about what just happened. He puts his hand in the small of my back and starts to guide me through the crowd. When I look at him questioningly, he smiles sadly and says, "I'll walk you to your car." In that look, I know he knows I'm not planning on attending any more reunion events. And he's not letting me leave without a private goodbye.

Once we're outside, I point to the farthest corner of the lot, where I'm parked. The lot is not large, but the walk seems endless. I haven't been alone with Murphy since the summer before I left for college. I cringe, thinking about that summer. "So, Ally tells me your business is doing well," I say. I'm trying to rebalance from the drama that just occurred, but my voice shakes. My mind is still trapped in a time I have fought so hard to put behind me.

When he doesn't answer me, I risk a glance at him. His hands are in the pockets of his jeans, making him look like he's mid-shrug. I try not to notice the muscles showing through his long-sleeved, form-fitting T-shirt. I prepare myself to tell him I don't want to talk about my run-in with Brandy, but he only nods with a bemused smile and stares off. When he finally speaks, it's not to talk about that.

"Where you been, Tuesday?" It's the question I didn't think he'd ask. We walk in silence the last few feet to my car.

I sigh. "You know where I've been, Murphy. New York. London."

"No phones in New York or London? I mean, I can understand why you didn't call *me*, but Ally? Emmett? Danny?"

"I . . . got busy." The excuse is pathetic, and untrue. I look down, my hands trembling as I search for the right key through the tears that fill my eyes again. He takes both of my hands in his and pulls me to face him. His eyes are like magnets, and I don't know how long we look at each other before he reaches into my clasped hands, fishes out my keys, and swiftly inserts the one with the Nissan emblem on it into the keyhole. Our gaze breaks along with the tension.

"Still drivin' this thing around, huh? Old Blue?" he teases, his tone suddenly jovial again.

"It's been in my parents' garage all these years. You know Nancy," I say as I open the door and climb into the driver's seat. It's the middle of September and just cold enough for an open window to be unnecessary. I crank it down anyway, to get another few minutes with him.

"It's a perfectly good car!" Murphy says, in a spot-on imitation of Nancy. "No use getting rid of something that works just fine!"

I laugh, and he crouches down and rests his arms on the windowsill. "Nice to hear that sound again," he says. I'm starting up the car, so I don't know if he's talking about my sad little engine or my laugh. Again our eyes lock. Suddenly the smile is gone, and his face is moving toward me. *No*, I think, but my head moves toward him despite it.

"Hey, Murphy! Wanna get a move on? The bar's closed and I need to take a piss!" Emmett. Sweet, eloquent Emmett.

"Yeah, I'm comin'," Murphy says.

He looks at me one last time, smiling, and gives his shaggy head a shake.

"Drive safe," he says. He stands up, but seems to change his mind and leans in again. "You know, you've come a long way since Hardy Crane, Tuesday."

I watch as he walks away with a sad smile on his face. As soon as I pull around the corner and am out of sight, I cry the whole way home.

# CHAPTER FIVE

# ALLY

## *Back then*

I don't like what I'm seeing with Ruby and Hardy Crane. Hardy has that look in his eye, the same look my dad used to get before he went out hunting with Uncle Charlie. And he's refilling Ruby's shot glass like he's looking for a tip, and I don't mean a dollar bill. His antenna is up, for sure—the one that tells him when there's a vulnerable girl around. Meanwhile Danny and Emmett just sit there, laughing as Ruby gets wasted, both trying to be Mr. Cool because we're sophomores and Hardy is a senior. Who cares? It's his second time being one, that doesn't exactly make him Top Shit.

I figured Hardy would leave after Danny sold him whatever it was he wanted, but he's still here and for no good reason. I mean, he's on the hockey team with Aaron, but they are *not* friends. Aaron *knows* what happened when Hardy and I dated. It's actually how Aaron and I met. When I was a freshman, Hardy took me to the homecoming after-party at Dunphy's field, got so drunk he pissed his pants, and slapped me across the face when I tried to point it out quietly. Hardy's friends hauled him away, and I was too shocked to move. Then Aaron came out of nowhere, this handsome guy I'd seen around the halls at Chatwick High who came from the Town School. He offered me a ride home in his brother's car, and we've been together ever since.

I don't know why Ruby is even *talking* to Hardy, let alone going shot-for-shot with a guy who uses his liver like a toilet. She's never really been a big drinker, at least not compared to the rest of us. I'm guessing because she doesn't want to end up like her mother. I mean, she'll have a beer or two and takes a poke of whatever's being passed around, but I've never seen her *drunk*. That would mean she'd have to lose some control, and we all know Ruby can't do that.

I think I've been pretty good about giving her space since she's been staying at my house (as much space as you can give when you're sharing a bed), but *clearly* she isn't dealing with her family drama as well as she'd like us all to believe. Wouldn't you think if your mother landed in rehab and your father told you he's not coming back until she's sober for a year, you would want to talk about it? Especially with someone who knows what it's like for your dad to quit on you? Not Ruby, though. When she's going through stuff, she wants to be left alone. And if you push her, she'll just clam up more. So I let her be, and try not to be too mad when she sneaks out of bed and brings the cordless into the bathroom to call Murphy. Ruby is usually pretty serious, especially these days, but you'd think she was at a comedy show from the sounds I hear coming from that bathroom. He's not even that funny.

Her dad made arrangements for her to stay with us and left her plenty of money, but Ruby still insists on working at that second-hand store. I used to think she just liked having clothes different from the rest of the kids at school—although I *personally* don't see what's wrong with shopping at the Gap or American Eagle at the Drummond Mall for brand-new clothes that haven't been sweated in and who-knows-what-else by some stranger. But now I think it has something to do with the old ladies she works for. They're like forty and fifty, I don't know what they could *possibly* have to talk about, but every time I walk in there to visit Ruby, they're chattering away. Maybe it's because she's like an old lady herself. No one knows that about her, because she's been through so much and talks tough and smokes cigarettes like a chimney. But underneath that, all she cares about is getting good grades. I swear when we used to ride the bus together, she would pull out a *book* and just sit there and *read.* What a nerd! I mean, I'm sitting *right there* for her to talk to and she's got her nose stuck in a book. How rude!

And *speaking* of rude, the boys are offering no help in this situation. Danny's already passed out in his room, Emmett and Tara left twenty minutes ago to take advantage of Tara's empty house, and Aaron and *Murphy*, Ruby's so-called best friend, haven't gotten back from their munchie run to the Quik Stop, leaving me all alone as Hardy moves in on Ruby. I have to do everything around here. When Hardy goes to refill Ruby's glass again, I finally say, "Ruby, I think you've had enough."

Ruby just glares at me—like I'm the bad guy here!—and Hardy says, "Oooh-hooo, looks like someone's jealous she's not getting all the attention anymore."

"Oh, fuck off, Hardy, that has nothing to do with it. Look at her! She can't hardly stand up!"

"Ally, I take care of m'self," Ruby slurs.

"Clearly," I say. She nods her head self-righteously, not picking up on my sarcasm.

Hardy mutters something about being "over this business," and makes like he's going to leave. Good riddance to white trash. This town is crawling with it, and Hardy is just one example of white trash who happens to be good at something (okay, two things: hockey and funneling beer), so he's actually popular in spite of it. When I'm about to breathe a sigh of relief, he turns to Ruby. "Wanna get out of here?" he asks, like he couldn't give a shit whether she said yes or no.

Ruby just nods. I stand in front of her as she goes to follow him. "Ruby St. James, you are not getting in a car with someone who's been taking shots all night."

She pushes past me, says again that she can take care of herself. "You're not my mother!" she yells as she struggles to slip on her shoes.

"Yeah, I know. Because if I were, I would be in REHAB!" I yell back. Maybe that's mean, but for one, it's the truth; for two, she's treating me like shit just because I'm trying to protect her from being killed; and for three, I'm hoping it will make her mad enough that she'll stay here and fight with me.

It doesn't work. She slams the door behind her, and I hear the tires screech out of the driveway a minute later.

It isn't till *4 a.m. in the morning* that Ruby comes back to Danny's house. I know because I'm sitting up in the living room, waiting for her like her goddamn mother should be doing.

The thing you should know about Nancy, in case all this comes back around to me, is that she's not *always* a useless crazy drunk. Most of the time she's like June frickin' Cleaver. Like bake-sale director, food-drive organizer, Halloween-costume seamstress for Ruby *and* me (because my mother has a job, and zero sewing skills), cheerleader at Ruby's debate club *and* my tennis matches *and* Murphy's baseball games *and* Emmett's basketball games *and* Danny's . . . well, Danny isn't heavy into extracurriculars that don't involve getting high, but you get the point. And the

St. James' house is so neat, with every last thing always in its proper place. Sometimes we rearrange her trinkets just to see if she'll notice. She *always* notices.

Then every once in a while, Nancy will get in this mood. Ruby calls them black periods, and it has something to do with being manic-depressive. She stops coming to our games and she stays in her room when we come over, and she stops doing all the stuff that makes her Top Shit Mom. After a week or so of that, she starts drinking. I don't know if she's trying to cheer herself up or what, but she drinks at home for a few days before she runs out of booze at the time of night when it's too late to restock at the gas station. When that happens, she heads down to Margie's and doesn't leave until she's forced to. It used to be Mr. St. James who would fish her out, but if the rumors are true, he said he was done rescuing her the night he found Nancy making out with some 'necker. So since before either of us even had permits, Ruby's been taking her dad's Beamer to drive the four blocks down to Margie's and back. The whole town knows she does it, but they don't say anything, because she can't be expected to drag Nancy up that hill all by herself, and it's better than Nancy's drunk ass driving home.

Aaron and Murphy get back and have already devoured the entire food supply on the way back. Aaron is so stuffed he's too tired to stay up with me, so he goes to bed in the basement. I love him, but sometimes I could pop him one. Murphy asks where Ruby is, and I tell him *exactly*. He looks all worried for a second, but then he just goes to the spare room to sleep. Now I'm sitting here in Charlene's La-Z-Boy, flipping between the "Are you my daddy?" talk show and an infomercial for this vibrating belt that you strap to your stomach to lose weight. As I'm about to give up and go to bed, Ruby waltzes in.

She's not drunk anymore. At least, she's not stumbling all over the place. But she does look like hell. Her hair's all messed up, her eyes are puffy, and her shorts and tank top are wrinkled to shit. It doesn't take a genius, but I still can't believe it. Ruby St. James, Miss Top Shit Honor Roll, losing her virginity to some dumbass second-year senior?

"Have fun?" I ask, in a way that should tell her I'm pissed. I worried all night, and here she just strolls in without a word.

She pretends she's real into the talk show, even though she always teases me for watching this shit. "Yeah," she says, casual as anything. "Hardy is actually pretty cool. We talked about our parents. His are even more fucked up than mine, if you can believe it." She says it like she rehearsed it. "Hey, are there any smokes left?"

Oh, and now she's going to *lie* to me and act like nothing happened? I've been walking on horseshoes for two weeks while she pretends everything is fine, and now she's going to treat me like I'm *stupid*? "Really?" I say. "In all this time you spent 'talking,' did Hardy tell you all about his girlfriend?"

That gets her attention. She narrows her eyes at me and shakes her head. "He said he wasn't seeing anyone. That he just broke up with—"

"Brandy McCallister?" I say. Ruby nods. "Well, that's funny, because Brandy McCallister called here about two hours ago. She said she was waiting for her boyfriend to get back with the weed. Wanted to make sure he was okay."

Ruby's face gets even whiter than usual. She swallows. "What did you tell her?"

"I told her he got you drunk and fucked you, Ruby," I say sarcastically. "What do you think? I lied! I told her he left hours ago and I didn't know where he went. She was probably worried out of her mind he was in a ditch somewhere. Too bad she was right."

"Ally, cut it out," I hear from the doorway behind me. Oh, perfect. This is when Murphy decides to make an entrance, swooping in just as Ruby starts crying, so I look like the bad guy and he gets to be the big hero.

Ruby crosses the room to Murphy and he hugs her. Without a word, he leads her into the spare room where he's been sleeping while I've been up worrying. I'm about to sneak over to the door to see if I can hear them talking when Murphy comes back.

"Ally, what the hell is wrong with you?" he whisper-yells at me.

"With *me*?" I whisper-yell back. "What's wrong with *me*? I'm the one who's actually looking out for her, Murphy. What the hell did you do to help?"

"I wasn't even *here*!" he says.

"Exactly. You're supposed to be Ruby's 'best friend,' and you didn't think it was important to stay close and protect her, when she's obviously going through a rough time?"

"Protect her from what? As far as I knew, *our friends* were supposed to be here shootin' the shit in Danny's basement, like always. Was I somehow supposed to know some predator would be here, just waiting to get Ruby drunk so he could—" He swallows. He doesn't want to say it. He doesn't want to think of Ruby acting so . . . well, I don't need to say it out loud. You know what I'm thinking.

"Whatever, Murphy. All I'm saying is: don't yell at me for not being able to stop Ruby from leaving with him. I *tried*. But you know Ruby, once she gets something in her head, she's going to do it no matter what anyone says. If you had been here, maybe you could have stopped her. God knows, you're the only one she listens to."

Murphy just looks at me. We're both pissed; at each other, at ourselves, at Hardy, but really at Ruby. And I think we both realize it, because we stop yelling. "I'm gonna go check on her," he says. I follow him, thinking I could probably comfort her better than "let's have a farting contest" Leblanc, but he closes the door on me before I can set foot in the room. As the door is shutting, I see Ruby sitting on the bed with her head in her hands, and something is strange. I realize, after the door shuts, what's bugging me—the bed was made and the curtains were wide open on the window that faces the street. I don't know what Murphy was doing in there all night, but he wasn't sleeping.

I rest my ear against the door. I mean, it's only right to listen and make sure she's okay. I guess I *was* kinda harsh, but that's tough love. What was I supposed to do? Congratulate her on her first time being with a lowlife like Hardy? Pat her on the back for throwing out her virginity with the bathwater? She didn't confirm it, but I know what happened, because I know Hardy. And I *thought* I knew Ruby, but I guess not. She's supposed to be the smart one. Even if she didn't already know what Hardy did at Dunphy's field, she's still lived in this town all her life. She's pulled older versions of Hardy off her mother long enough, she can smell a bullshitter coming from a mile away.

All I hear for a few minutes is muffled sobs, and every once in a while Murphy shushing her and saying it's okay. I *do not* understand their relationship. They used to bicker like cats and frogs, and suddenly in eighth grade they were, like, inseparable. I heard Nancy complain once that the phone bill was out of control from Ruby and Murphy talking on the phone all night. I thought she was simply exaggerating at the time, but now I believe it.

The sobbing seems to be slowing down now, a good sign. I hear a sniffle and then "Oh God, I didn't know, Murph."

"I know," I hear him say.

"How could I be so stupid?"

"You're not stupid, Tuesday, you just made a mistake."

"Yeah, a really fucking stupid mistake." *Amen, sister*, I think. "I already catch shit for Nancy being a slut. I can only imagine what's going to happen when people find out *I*—"

"Ruby, stop it. You are not a slut."

"I am! What else do you call losing it to someone else's *boyfriend* in the back of a *truck* on the side of the *road*? I'm a slut and a terrible person. Oh my God, I think I'm going to throw up, I'm so disgusted with myself."

"You are not a terrible person. You're one of the best people I know. And I bet the puking thing has more to do with the vodka."

I hear a small laugh, a sniffle, and then silence. Then Ruby says, so quietly I have to really press my ear against the door to hear, "School starts next week. Everyone's going to be talking about it. Nice way to kick off junior year."

"No one's going to find out."

"Murph, she knows. There's no *way* it's going to keep quiet."

"I'll talk to her, she won't say anything."

Who the hell are they talking about? Brandy? How would Brandy know? *Hardy* certainly isn't going to tell her. And if she does figure it out, how is Murphy going to stop her from spreading it all over school? Hell is not as furious as a woman . . . who's furious, or whatever.

"Yeah, but she's definitely going to tell Aaron. And Tara. And Tara will tell Emmett, and then all of a sudden the whole hockey team knows—"

Bitch! She's talking about *me*? After all I've done for Ruby, here she is acting like I'm some enemy? I would never ever tell anyone this. I mean, Aaron was *there*, he already knows. And of course I would talk to Tara about it, but only because we need to figure out how to help Ruby through this situation. It's not some big betrayal. We're *friends*. Am I the only one who remembers the night before we started ninth grade? Everything was changing so fast—my dad leaving; my brother already away at college; starting high school, with kids from all over the county upsetting our place on the social ladder. I just wanted to pump the brakes before everything was gone. What did we say to each other? "I promise to be loyal to the crew above all else, always to be honest and true, through good times and bad." And it worked, I thought! If it weren't for those promises we made—the promise to stay close, to trust each other—would we even still be friends? How are we supposed to take care of each other if we have secrets from each other?

And now Ruby is talking like I'm some monster who just wants to ruin her reputation. Well, I'm washing my hands of this whole mess. If Ruby thinks staying out of each other's business is what friendship is, then I will. And I will keep her out of mine. From now on, we're merely roommates. She can have all the time she wants to talk on the phone with *Murphy*. She's his problem now.

# CHAPTER SIX

## RUBY

*Now*

The smell of the linens tells me I'm home before I even open my eyes. They smell like the cedar chest at the end of my bed, where they're stored between uses. I slept on these pale blue sheets (alternating with their fraternal twin set of pale green) for over fifteen years, ever since I graduated from a crib to a big-girl bed. Coral used to tease our mother—back when she still spoke to her, that is—about never updating or replacing any of the furniture or decor, but Nancy would always reply, "They're perfectly good sheets! There's no use spending the money on something we don't need!", which is where Murphy's impression of her comes from. Swap out the word "sheets" with "dresser," "couch," "throw pillows," "shoes," "car," or anything with the potential, but not the necessity, for updating, and you could pretty much script any conversation from my childhood that included a request for material goods.

Nancy was raised by a poor single mother in North Carolina, back when they were called "unwed mothers" (a.k.a. "whores"), and therefore balks at the idea of buying something just because you want it. They moved up here when Nancy was in high school because my grandmother wanted her to have a better education than she could in the South, thus providing her with the opportunity for a better life. But Nancy's bipolar made school a struggle, and holding down a job even more so. Her last job was as my father's secretary at his office in Drummond, when he was starting out as an investment advisor. Instead of firing her, he married her (he jokes that he proposed in order to avoid having to pay severance). After that, Nancy devoted her time to being the perfect wife and mother, and caretaker for my aging, ailing grandmother. She drove us all insane.

When I was entering high school and Coral had already left for college, Dad started splitting his time between the Drummond office and headquarters in New York City. But even though this upped our income considerably, and my grandmother had passed away, Nancy didn't want to leave Chatwick. She says she didn't want to uproot us, but I think she couldn't handle the lifestyle change of moving to a community where she didn't feel she belonged. She never settled into the idea that she no longer had to struggle for every little thing; being too comfortable made her nervous, because she was always waiting for the other shoe to drop.

It used to drive Coral up the wall, having old things and used clothes when we could have afforded the latest and greatest. But then again, what didn't drive Coral up the wall about our mother? It's lucky for Nancy it was me who was home when my dad was gone, and not Coral; Nancy would have ended up wrapped around a tree or in a ditch somewhere.

This morning, I'm grateful for Nancy's frugality. Despite my best efforts to deny my homesickness, I can't help but smile as I run my palms over the worn-out cotton that is somehow always cool to the touch, even after eight hours of sleeping on it. Perhaps my childhood was less than ideal (whose wasn't?), but in this bed, in this room, I was always safe. Just like last night, surveying my unchanged room makes me feel like Kathleen

Turner in that movie where she is suddenly transported from middle age back to her high-school years. As I sit up in bed, I half expect the mirror above my dresser to reflect a girl in a poodle skirt and letter sweater.

Along with the yellowing-white desk where I used to write atrocious poetry and maudlin short stories, the closet and dressers still stuffed with clothes that haven't fit me since high school, and the Eminem poster on my wall (which makes me cringe), my bed is exactly where I left it, flush against the wall with the double windows that face the street. This was the only true surprise about the state of my room, as Nancy always used to threaten to move it away from the radiator the second I left the house. She claimed to worry about it being a fire hazard, but really she just has a thing about everything in the room being perfectly centered. I've always had a thing about looking out of the window from my nice, toasty bed. It was a never-ending battle that I seem to have won.

It's a beautiful sunny morning, and when I peel back the lacy white curtain, the view is exactly the same as I remember, except perhaps everything is a little smaller. The Menkins' weeping willow tree is overgrown, and the yellow paint of the Flemings' house is peeling off in large chunks. These are facts Nancy no doubt laments every day on the phone to her sponsor, who reminds her that she must "accept the things she cannot change." I have to crane my head to look down at our front porch, where the half-sized whiskey barrels spill over with the impatiens that Nancy plants every spring. It's fall now, and soon they will be dead.

Dead. Like Danny.

The thought sucks all the nostalgic air right out of the room. Suddenly the charming view outside my window changes. Now it's nighttime. Little eight-year-old Danny is bathed in the light from the streetlamp, his fist full of rocks, minus the few he's expertly aimed at my window to wake me up. He holds his finger up to his mouth and points to the back of the house. This image has haunted my dreams for years, but especially frequently in the last couple of months. It was a sign that I ignored. Danny needed me, but I didn't answer the taps at my window.

I would give anything to rewind a few months. To pick up the phone and reach out to him. Maybe it would have made a difference to hear from me, to know that I had never stopped caring about him. Probably not. The time I really could have made a difference is when we were young. Thinking about it now, what I can't believe is how little we were. I shouldn't have known yet how to take care of someone's wounds. How to keep secrets that big. But I did, because I had already kept my mother's illness hidden for years.

"Hi, sweetheart," my mom's voice jars me away from the window now, where Danny's wounded face still stares up at me. I feel wetness on my cheeks and realize I'm crying. I try to wipe away the evidence, but Nancy doesn't miss a thing when she's sober, which she's been for eleven years next May, as far as I know. "Oh," she says. The sound seems to escape her mouth by accident. Her tall, slim figure makes a few jerky movements back and forth, as if she is arguing with herself whether to bolt or to comfort a daughter who has called her by her first name since she was sixteen years old. In the end I think she realizes she has no choice but to try. She sits on my bed and rests her hand on mine. My knees are tucked into my chest with my arms clutched tightly around me, my default position when I'm upset. She squeezes, hoping it will trigger me to unwrap and fall into her, like I did when I was a child. It won't work this time.

"How are you doin'?" she asks. Despite living in Vermont since she was fifteen, Nancy retains a hint of her southern drawl. I used to get embarrassed when she would ask my friends, "How are y'all?"

"I'm fine," I say.

"Sweetheart, you are not fine. How could you be fine?"

"Where were you last night?" I ask, my tone coming off more accusatory than I intended in my haste to change the subject. In truth, I was mostly relieved when she wasn't home when I returned from the nightmare at Danny's house; it gave me a chance to wander through the rooms on my own, examining old photographs and trying to determine from the poses who had just fought with whom before the flash went off. But I had also felt the familiar surge of panic at Nancy being out at night, which I tried to suppress by reassuring myself she's not my problem anymore.

She sighs, withdrawing her hand. "I wasn't at Margie's, if that's what you're askin' me."

"I know. I was there."

Her face falls. "Oh, Ruby, did you go lookin' for me? I think, after more than ten years of sobriety, I at least deserve the benefit of the doubt."

"I wasn't looking for you. I was with the crew."

She nods at this, but I see the slightest hint of a furrowed brow. Does she think I'm dumb enough to follow in her footsteps? "I was at Charlene's," she explains. "She called me after y'all got your letters. We crossed paths and I waved, but you didn't see me."

"No, I was a little out of it. In shock, I guess. It's . . . a lot."

"Do you want to talk about it?" I shake my head. And what I mean by that head-shake is, *I don't want to talk about it with you. You couldn't handle it. I can't even handle it.* But she presses on. "What did yours say? Your letter, I mean."

I work hard to make my face weary instead of angry, my default reaction to Nancy's pushing. "Nancy, I *really* don't want to—"

She raises her hands. "Fine. Fine. Sorry, you don't want to talk about it." She sighs, staring out the window. "It just so hard to believe he's gone. That someone could be here one day and gone the next."

"It's not too hard to believe, considering he spent his time shooting up in his basement and writing hate mail." Whoa! I don't know where that came from. A minute ago I was feeling guilty, making excuses for Danny, and now I feel like screaming. It might be that old default reaction wriggling its way back in. At least I hold back my comment on being familiar with the concept of here one day and gone the next, due in no small part to her and my father.

Nancy's sympathetic face falls into a frown. She is disappointed that I am reacting in anger rather than sadness. Sadness she can hug. Anger she must be cautious of, because she knows what it's really aimed at. Or rather, who. "Ruby St. James, I am disappointed in you. I raised you better than to judge people on their weaknesses."

This is true, although it was less a conscious instillation of values than a by-product of growing up constantly navigating the tumultuous waters of *her* weaknesses. "I guess I'm just a little tapped out on empathy. I know you've told me a million times that addiction is a disease, like bipolar or heart disease." Suddenly I feel nauseated, thinking that I now know people who have all of these conditions. "But people can make a choice to get better. Look at you! You've managed to control yourself."

"Well, I couldn't for many years, baby girl, and you know that more than anyone."

I cringe at the term "baby girl," which Nancy calls me only when she wants to put me in my place. What right does she have to remind me of those years? Of course I know better than anyone. Dad gave up trying to save her from herself when I was too young to realize I couldn't. And when he got really fed up, he left for a year while Nancy proved to him she could maintain sobriety after treatment. After the three months she was in rehab and I was boarding at Ally's, that left nine months of sheer terror that she would go back to her old ways. Nine months of lying awake at night with my bedroom door cracked, so I could better discern if the clinking of a hidden vodka bottle was real or imagined. Was that the cap of a pill bottle I just heard, or was it simply a tube of chapstick? The answer was consistently benign, hence my father's eventual return, but I didn't relax until the very morning he pulled his Beamer into the driveway and casually lifted his small leather Samsonite out of the back seat, as if he had only been gone for one of his business trips. Welcome home, Daddy, here's your perfect family. All fixed, without any help from you.

"So when is Dad back from New York?" I ask.

Nancy sighs. "I think on Friday."

"Hmm, well, I'll see him back in the city then," I say.

Her lips tense, but she doesn't say anything. I know she's annoyed that my father sees more of me than she does, although not by much. Twice a year she comes to the city with him. While he works, she goes to museums and wanders around window-shopping (never buying anything, because she has perfectly good clothes at home). She and I have lunch together in the same restaurant every time, and she always orders the exact same thing. Routine keeps her sane, Nancy says, when I encourage her to try some other delicious-sounding item on the menu.

Time has provided just enough healing for hour-long chunks of civil, if not personal, conversations over tea and sandwiches, but being back in my childhood home makes it much harder to ignore the ghosts of the past.

"Have you heard from Jamie lately?" Nancy asks, soft as an underhand pitch. I sigh. Jamie was my boyfriend when I lived in London. My mother is a treasure trove of topics I do not wish to discuss this morning. "Ruby, I'm just *asking* a *question*," she continues. "I'm trying to have a conversation with my daughter, is that such a crime?"

I guess not. "I got an email from him last week, actually. His first book is selling really well, and he's working on the final draft of his second one, so that will come out next year. And," I say, pretending to inspect and flick a speck of lint off my knee, "he sent flowers when he heard about Danny." When I had *called* him about Danny is more like it, even though Jamie didn't even know who Danny was. Despite my waking him up with my call, not an hour later a dozen pink roses were delivered to my desk with a note: *Love Always. J.*

"Is he seeing anyone?" She leans in closer as she says this in a conspiratorial tone, as if we are girlfriends, out getting pedicures or something.

I can't resist a smile, so I turn my head and then look out the window again. Danny's face is replaced by a young couple who must be new to the neighborhood, walking their dog and pushing a stroller. A brand-new baby Chatwickian, not yet affected by the oppressive small-mindedness of this town.

"Oh, fine, I give up," Nancy says when she realizes I won't say any more. "Get in the shower, I'll start breakfast. I picked up some fresh blueberries for your pancakes." Blueberry pancakes were my favorite when I was five. I'm told for six months that's all I would eat. When my mother wasn't in a black period, she was the type of mother who would actually cook breakfast for us every morning—eggs, bacon, pancakes—as opposed to my friends' moms who worked and barely had time to shove a cereal box and a carton of milk at their kids as they ran around the house with one leg in a pair of pantyhose and one hand applying deodorant. I guess I would rather have eaten cold breakfast, if I could have had a mother who wasn't completely mental about a third of the time. My friends were jealous my mother was always around, at least when they were too young to realize there was something wrong with her. We always want the *other* kind of mother.

"Anything else I can get you?" Nancy chirps, her hands poised in the air like a waitress about to write down my order.

"Coffee, please."

She perks up, glad to be doing something for me. "How do you take it?"

"Black." She raises her eyebrows before she stands and leaves the room. I know she's thinking I'm too much like my father. Living in New York, working too much, not bothering to sweeten my coffee. Next thing you know, I'll be married to someone with bipolar who uses Martinis as medication instead of lithium.

As I let the water bounce off my outstretched palm, my hope quickly dashed that she's replaced the water heater that takes a full five minutes to kick in, I think about Jamie. Unlike my connections here, even after Jamie and I broke up and I moved back to the States, we've managed to remain friends. It feels good to picture him with his yellow-lined legal pad, scratching out some prose before committing the words to his computer. It feels good to think about anything unrelated to Chatwick.

The smell of pancakes drifts up from the stairwell, and my stomach (which I realize has been empty for the better part of twenty-four hours) growls with anticipation. I hurry through my shower and shimmy into a pair of jeans and a T-shirt, tying my hair in a knot at the base of my neck and racing downstairs. Nancy clucks her tongue at me. "Sweetheart, I wish you would keep your hair down; you know pulling it back makes your ears stick out."

Blueberry pancakes and criticism. A fine way to start the morning.

"Coffee?" I remind her, not responding to the feedback.

She pours me a cup from the pot she was given as a wedding gift thirty years ago and starts prattling on in her usual fashion, quickly graduating from the weather, her flowers, and this summer's disappointing yield from the vegetable garden (too humid); to her sponsor, Harriett, her therapist, Louise; and my father's workaholism. She works a few of my father's worst qualities into every conversation we have. She's so used to her family pointing out her flaws, it's her passive-aggressive way of maintaining the balance. She needn't bother; my anger is pretty fairly distributed between the two of them already.

Nancy is in the middle of explaining why she thinks Louise is secretly working for Dad, and I am in the middle of mentally constructing my To Do list to make up some of the work I've missed, when the phone rings. Nancy picks up the receiver, not bothering to pause her diatribe. "—and if he thinks I'm going to edit myself so I don't hurt his feelings, he is crazier than I am. Hello, St. James' residence." Her voice goes from bitter and indignant to syrupy sweet in 0.3 seconds. "Why, Murphy Leblanc, is that you? How nice to hear your voice! How are you doing with, you know, this whole Danny business? What stage of grief would you say you're in? I think it's safe to say our Ruby is nestled stubbornly in anger. Surprise, surprise, right?" She lets out a peal of laughter, and I can hear Murphy do the same on the other end of the line. I wonder if there's ever an age when you cease to feel embarrassed by your parents. I try to pluck the receiver from Nancy's hand, but she blocks me as she tells Murphy it can take months, or even years, to get to Acceptance.

"Hi," I say, when I finally win the wrestling match.

"Want to come over?"

"I . . ." *What?* Come over? I thought we had an understanding, that last night was goodbye. "I can't. I have to work. I've got at least eight hours to make up from yesterday."

"Okay. Later then. I'm in the biggest of my parents' rental properties, top floor. You know the one?"

He hangs up before I can nod a confused assent.

# CHAPTER SEVEN

# RUBY

### *Back then*

I scan the cafeteria, deciding against the freshmen and moving on to the sophomores. A fifteen- or sixteen-year-old would be a good fit for Murphy. Young and innocent enough to find him cool and charming, but not so young and innocent it would be gross. After all, Murphy just lost his virginity, so the ship has sailed on having a PG relationship.

Ally sneaks up on me. "What's with you?" she asks as she plops her tray down beside me. Even though I'm the only one at the table, she sits beside me instead of across from me, because that's where she always sits. Tara, Emmett, and Danny sit across from us. Aaron sits on Ally's other side. Ally is always in the middle, that way she can have one ear in any conversation. Murphy doesn't have lunch this period, despite his most valiant efforts to arrange his schedule to align with the rest of ours. For the last couple of days I've been endlessly grateful to Mrs. Clasky, the guidance counselor, for being one of the few people immune to Murphy's charms. I used to be one of them, too.

"Nothing," I tell Ally.

"Why are you squinting over at the sophomores? Did one of them piss you off?" Her eyes gleam. She's ready to slay anyone who's done me wrong. She also, to be fair, wants a good story. I have one, too, I just can't tell it to her.

"No. I'm trying to pick out a girl for Murphy." I shouldn't have even told her this much—if I open the door, she'll kick it in—but I'm distracted. I don't know any of these girls' names, but I've seen them at parties, sipping on peach schnapps and wine coolers and giggling like idiots. Murphy would do well with an idiot. Not that you'd have to be an idiot to like Murphy. That's not what I'm saying. He just needs someone fun. Light.

Ally shakes her head. "You guys are so weird."

"Weird how?" I ask.

Ally sidesteps the question with another question. "Can't Murphy find his own girls?"

"Of course," I say. "He's just not as good at it as me."

She smiles. Ally likes it when I'm cocky. It gives her a specific quote to pinpoint as she's trying to figure out why she resents me so much. Tara and Emmett sit down and immediately start making out, which puts me off my tater tots. Danny joins the table, asks what's going on.

"Ruby is taking it upon herself to find Murphy a girlfriend," Ally informs him.

"Hey, no fair. What about me?" Danny asks.

We all look at him. "What happened to Jenny?" Ally asks. Danny's been seeing Jenny Albrecht for six months, a long time for him. When Danny actually brings her around, she doesn't talk much. Actually, she kind of hovers and stares. Actually, she kind of scares the shit out of me.

"I haven't seen her much since she dropped out of school," Danny mumbles. I wonder why anyone would drop out of high school, especially in Chatwick. I mean, what else is there to do in this town besides go to school? Hang out in Barnard Park? Work at the Quik Stop? If you're *lucky* I guess you could get a job at the Endless Power battery factory at the north edge of town and hang on long enough to collect your pension after forty years of standing on an assembly line. Personally, I'm getting as far away from here as possible, as *soon* as possible. I want to experience things—art, music, culture, living somewhere where things are open past 9 p.m. Closest thing you get to any of that in Chatwick is our high school's Miss and Mister Bobcat talent competition, which I will *not* be taking part in, no matter how much Ally begs me to do a duet with her. She's even got Nancy in on it, ganging up on me to discuss costumes. Since my dad's been back, Nancy's been on her best behavior, and tailoring is her distraction of choice. Lucky me.

"So you got dumped?" Emmett teases Danny, coming up for air.

"Shut up, Emmett," I say. I never miss a chance to tell him to shut up, but especially when he's shitting on Danny. He sticks his tongue out at me. Danny reaches around Tara to punch Emmett in the arm. Emmett tries to kick back under the table, but from the sound Tara makes, he missed.

"Cut the shit, guys!" she whines.

"So what's this about you finding a chick for Murphy?" Emmett asks, as if nothing had happened.

"It's been like four months since he dated that last one," I say. "What was her name?"

"Jenessa," Ally says.

"Exactly, Jenessa. And that only lasted a few weeks. He's over it. It's time he gets back on the bike. Or the horse, or whatever stupid expression it is."

"It's 'in the saddle,'" Ally says. We all look at her in amazement. Somehow Ally and I have momentarily switched brains; I'm sticking my nose into someone else's business, and Ally is correcting me on figures of speech.

"Are you sure he's not already in the saddle, Tuesday?" Danny asks. One eyebrow is raised. My heart drops. Oh, crap! He's looking at me like he knows something. Does he know something? Did Murphy tell him something?

"I'm sure, Danny," I say, raising my eyebrow back at him. His expression clears immediately. Maybe I was imagining it.

Emmett looks between Danny and me. I hold my breath when he turns to me, but instead of pressing the issue, he says, "So can you believe this governor? How does she plan on paying for this jobs program of hers when we've got a fifty-million-dollar deficit?"

The crew groan and roll their eyes.


I pull into my usual spot in the alley behind The Exchange, which just so happens to share a parking lot with Margie's Pub. When I open Blue's rusty door, I catch a whiff of cigarette butts and day-old beer. It turns my stomach, making me think of the nights I've been forced to inhale that smell as I wait for Nancy to finish her last drink. It's not like the smell isn't also associated with my friends, but somehow it's different when I'm with them. Maybe it's because we're *supposed* to be messing around with that stuff. And maybe it's because I know when to put the drink down. Well, except for those few times . . .

I lift my backpack and see the envelope. Inside contains my entire future, a.k.a. my deposit and commitment letter to New York University. I know for sure this is what I want, but I haven't mailed it in yet. I don't know what's stopping me. None of my friends know I was accepted. I try to pinpoint why I haven't told them, as I slam closed the metal gate and pull down the wooden doors of the ancient elevator that takes me up to the shop. I've talked before about going out of state for college, but I don't think any of them have taken me seriously. People who grow up in Chatwick generally don't stray too far. For example, Ally is going to cosmetology school about ten minutes outside of town; Aaron will go to Vermont Tech a few hours south; Emmett's going to Vermont University in Drummond to study business; and Tara will enroll in the nursing program at Arwell College in the Northeast Kingdom. The two schools are only about two hours apart, but in college that might as well be halfway across the country. They all have plans to come back to Chatwick on weekends. Danny is going to work at Borbeau's, the mechanic shop where he already works/sells pot most days after school. The most disappointing is that Murphy will work for his dad. With his talent, he probably could have gotten at least a partial baseball scholarship *somewhere*. He could get out, but he won't.

That's why I have to find him a girlfriend. If he doesn't have anything else to focus on, we're going to end up sleeping together again, and then who knows what mess will be made of my plans.

It was enough of a mistake the first time, although he claims he doesn't understand why it can't be an ongoing thing. But it cannot happen again. Murphy is my best friend, nothing more. Granted, before last weekend, we *did* kiss on two occasions. One was on a particularly rough night, about three months after I lost my virginity to Hardy Crane, when I realized Hardy was never going to leave Brandy for me. Trust me, I *know* how disgusting that is, on all levels. Hardy is the most grotesque being on the face of this planet, and I'm convinced the only reason I was into him was because of what was going on with my parents. Plus, the therapist my parents forced me to go to when they got back together told me about this bonding chemical that gets released in girls' brains when they have sex. It's the same one that gets released when you breastfeed. For a girl who's never experienced it before, the shrink says, it can be particularly overwhelming. So I blame that. Plus, I was drinking a little more in those days. Ironic, huh? While my mom was drying out?

Anyway, one night after Hardy canceled plans on me for, like, the *tenth* time, Murphy literally shook me by my shoulders and told me Hardy loved Brandy, not me, and I needed to get over it because I deserved better anyway. I was so grateful for the truth, I kissed him. But it stopped there.

The other time was after Murphy got dumped by Charlotte Bicknell. She is a year older, and all the boys were completely infatuated with her (or rather, with her enormous boobs). I didn't think Murphy even *liked* her all that much (at least above her chest), but he sat on my rocker, crying. Actually crying tears. I had never seen him cry before. I'd *heard* him cry, over the phone, those first few months after what happened with Danny and we started talking to each other because we couldn't talk to anyone else. But I'd never seen him do it in person, and I thought maybe he would want me to pretend like it wasn't happening. But when I stood up and said I was going to get him a glass of water, he caught my hand and pulled me onto his lap. He kissed me long enough that I forgot about the water. By the time he went home, he wasn't crying anymore.

Both times, we agreed it was a huge mistake. We didn't want to ruin our friendship. So when we woke up the morning after we had sex, I assumed we would be on the same page. Instead, when I said we couldn't do it again, Murphy seemed disappointed. He said he was thinking it should happen *more*. Well, *of course* he thought that. I mean, he *is* a guy.

It's not that the sex was bad. Not like I'm some expert, but it was miles better than the handful of times I was with Hardy.

It turns out Ally's right about sex being better when it's with someone you care about. But that's just it. Murphy and I care about each other, and bringing sex into the mix will only confuse things. I don't want to lose my best friend just because we had a hormonal teenage moment after a couple of drinks and a hit of Danny's new supply.

The worst part is, even though the exact details are kind of hazy, I can't shake something Murphy said when we were lying together after it happened. I was trying to make light of the situation, so I said, "You see? It's not such a big deal. I don't know why you waited so long."

And then he said it. "I think I was waiting for you."

Shit!

Well, maybe not. He could simply have meant he was waiting for me because we're friends, and he knew I would be nice, even if he sucked at it. That's probably what he meant.

Right?

As I walk into the shop I'm greeted by Shawna and Donna (yes, they rhyme), who are waltzing to Garth Brooks. The sight is funny all on its own, considering Shawna is five-foot-ten and quite robust in frame, and Donna, the owner, barely clears Shawna's elbow and weighs about 100 pounds when soaking wet after a hot-dog-eating contest. But the oddity is compounded by the fact that Donna is wearing a purple velvet monstrosity of a hat on her head, complete with rhinestones and fringe. I will excuse that the day's Ugliest Drop-Off winner has been chosen without our normal voting ritual, because I can't imagine anything could top this hideous thing.

I lean against the door frame, happy to be out of my head and overtaken by something silly. Donna tips her head back, and, finally able to see, spots me. She breaks away from Shawna and shuffles toward me, her hand outstretched. I smile and take it, and she shuffles me back to Shawna and positions our hands together.

"You need the practice, Ruby," Donna says. "Prom will be here before you know it!" Donna steps back and waves her arms in the air like the conductor of a symphony as Shawna and I begin to sway, me stepping on Shawna's toes every five or six counts.

Crap. Prom! I forgot it's only four weeks away. Of course Donna would remember. I think she and Shawna are more excited about it than I am. For months, every time I came to work, one of them thrust a formal-wear magazine at me, with the corners turned down on pages of dresses, hairstyles, and makeup they liked. Shawna arranged for the tailoring of the dress I finally selected, and she even spoke directly with Cecile, Murphy's mom, to tell her what to order me for a corsage. I think Nancy is feeling a little resentful that she's been boxed out of the process, which makes me feel guilty, and that leads to me feeling angry. Shawna stepped in last minute *last year* when she realized Nancy was out of commission and it was getting down to the wire. Excuse me for betting on a more reliable horse this time around.

The radio changes to a more fast-paced Dixie Chicks song, and Shawna and I break apart. The three of us jump and shake our hips and twirl each other around. As always, at work, I feel my burden lighten. With these ladies—Shawna in her early thirties and Donna well into her fifties—I feel my age, instead of the 100 years old I feel compared to my friends.

Halfway through a mock pirouette, I spot a customer standing in the doorway, looking hesitant to fully enter the shop.

"Come, come, dear!" Donna says, and leads her into the store. "You don't have to dance, but you must sing a tune for us!"

The girl indulges Donna with a smile and a laugh, but is clearly uncomfortable, and rightfully so. I recognize her as one of the giggling sophomores.

"She's kidding," I say to her. "How can we help you?"

"My mom sent me in to check if she has any money in her account." At this signal the dance party is over, Donna heads into the window to model her headgear, and Shawna starts straightening the rack of jeans nearby.

"No problem, what's her code?" We're a consignment store, so people bring us their old clothes and we sell them, splitting the profit with the consigner. It's up to the client to come in and check if we owe them any money, and we assign each account a code so we know the person checking the account is allowed to collect it. We've had a few cases where kids have tried to collect on their parents' accounts in order to buy drugs. I know because they show up at Danny's later.

"Seven-seven-six-two-one," she says.

I circle around the cash-out counter to punch the code into the prehistoric Mac computer and get the hourglass symbol on the screen. "It's going to take a couple minutes to pull up."

She smiles. She has a nice smile. Kind eyes, too. "No problem," she says. "I've never been in here before, so I'll look around. You guys have some cool stuff!"

"Absolutely. We actually just started taking summer stuff, and there's a bunch of cute sundresses right over there if you want to check them out."

"Thanks, I will!"

Shawna sidles up and plops down in the chair next to the computer. Just as Ally did earlier, Shawna notices me squinting to the back of the store, lost in thought. She whistles and waves her hand in front of my face. "What's with you?" she asks.

"I think I might have found Murphy's next girlfriend."

"Oh! You caught your reflection in the mirror, then?"

"Oh, Shawna, give it up!" She's been convinced Murphy and I are destined for each other since . . . well, I've worked here for two years, and Murphy came in to take my lunch break with me in my second week, so . . . one year, eleven months, and two weeks? When I mistakenly told Shawna he and I had made a pact to go to senior prom together, our "fate was sealed," according to her. I *told* her the only reason we decided to go together was because of our respective *junior* prom experiences. I went with Eddie Rodowski, who grabbed my ass about forty times before puking all over my dress. Murphy went with Ramona Sturgess, whom Emmett set him up with because she was rumored to be easy. She spent so much time complaining about her recent breakup with Jed Sanders that Murphy deposited her at Jed's feet and told them to work it out, because he didn't drop $100 on a tux to be a couple's counselor. After that, we thought it would be best to go with each other, so we could be ourselves and not have the huge romantic pressure that comes with the prom. We have the best time with each other anyway. Even knowing this, Shawna thinks we're secretly in love. Just because she's older than me, she thinks she knows everything.

"You listen to me, Miss Ruby. Your generation might buy into the whole 'men and women can be friends' thing, but it's a load of bull. Sooner or later something is going to happen between the two of you, and when it does, you're going to feel like a total idiot for waiting so long to see it."

I feel myself start to blush and get up to busy myself straightening the rack of yet-to-be-tagged clothes behind the computer. Once the sophomore girl leaves, I will stand on a stool and read the brand, size, and category of garment to

Shawna as she types it into the computer, and based on the condition and popularity of similar items in the store, we price it. Then we print the labels and tag them before we put them out on the floor. I look forward to the repetitiveness of this process. It will help me focus on something other than what I'm focusing on right now, which is the memory of Murphy's mouth on my neck.

"You little hooker!" Shawna cries out. My eyes shoot over to the sophomore, who whips around to see the commotion, smiles, and then returns to browsing.

"Shhh, Shawna—Jesus!" I whisper-yell at her.

She lowers to a whisper, but gestures emphatically at me to follow her to the dressing rooms, at the other end of the store. I do, but only to avoid a louder scene. "Something already happened between you two, didn't it?" she asks.

"No," I say, but I'm a terrible liar.

"Hooker!" she whispers at me, swatting my arm.

"Okay, okay! We . . . *accidentally* . . . had sex."

She does a happy dance, rattling the mint-green dressing-room station constructed by Donna's husband.

"Stop it. Stop it!" I say, grabbing her arm to get her attention. "Listen, it didn't mean anything, and it's never going to happen again. So there goes your little theory right out the window." I go to march back to the computer, and she stands in my way. I try to go around her and she blocks me.

"Ruby, you're eighteen, and you've had a pretty fucked-up couple of years. I'm sorry if I'm the first to tell you this, but sex *always* means something. You and Murphy have something special, and you know it."

I think for a second, my eyes stinging. "Murphy and I *do* have something special. It's called friendship. It's one of the few things

I've ever been able to count on, and *that* means more to me than any stupid sexual encounter. Now please, drop it."

She lets me pass this time, and when I get back to the counter, the sophomore girl is waiting. "Sorry for the wait," I say, plastering a smile on my face as I circle back to the computer. "It looks like your mom has forty-three dollars thirty-one cents on her account. Do you want to take those off that amount?" I point at the short stack of sundresses she's laid on the counter.

"No, I'll pay for those myself. I wouldn't want to do that without asking her," she says.

I smile. So she's cute, she's smiley, she's a sophomore, she's *not* a spoiled brat, and she's cool with shopping for second-hand clothes. I like this girl.

"You go to Chatwick High, right?" I ask as I open the cash register and count out her mother's money. She nods. "What's your name?"

"Taylor. Taylor Bishop." She smiles and extends her hand to me. Bonus points for using her last name and shaking hands, unlike most of my peers.

"Taylor, I'm Ruby St. James. Tell me, do you happen to have a boyfriend?"

# CHAPTER EIGHT

# RUBY

*Now*

I climb the stairs to Murphy's apartment, all five flights of splintering wood attached haphazardly to the back of the apartment complex. From the street, the building gives the appearance of a single-family Victorian mini-mansion. Chatwick's Main Street is lined with buildings like this—enormous, old, and audacious in color, with chipped paint and sunken front porches in varying stages of yard-sale preparation. I remember when I was little, imagining cavernous hallways and rooms, filled to the brim with antique items that little girls were normally not allowed to touch. It wasn't until Murphy started taking me with him on his maintenance trips that I realized most of these buildings were sectioned off into depressing two-bedroom units that his parents rented out. The staircase has the appearance of a fire escape, but it is actually the main entrance to the apartments, one on each floor. This one in particular is the largest one.

I hesitate on the landing before the final flight of stairs. What the hell am I doing here? This was not the plan. All day I threw myself into work, assuring myself I would *not* be coming here. Not only does Murphy's arrogant summoning deserve to be rebuffed, but the more I interact with my old friends, Murphy in particular, the more likely it is that the secret I've worked so hard to bury will be resurrected. And yet here I am.

What is wrong with me?

This is ridiculous.

I turn to go back down the stairs.

"Someone there?" Murphy asks. I remain frozen mid-step. Maybe if I don't move, he'll think he imagined the noise and just go back into his apartment. "Ruby, I can see the top of your head." I look up and see him looking down at me through the wooden slats of the stairwell, waving. "Hi. Quit being an idiot and get up here."

I concede, trapped.

"What were you doing?" he asks as I get to the top of the stairs.

"I wasn't sure this was your place."

He nods slowly, in a way that indicates he's not buying it.

I stand on my tiptoes, peeking over his shoulder. He remains still, sizing me up. "So are you going to invite me in or not?" I finally ask.

"I guess," he says sarcastically, stepping back and waving me inside.

"Jesus, Murphy, do you have to make everything so goddamn awkward?" I say as I move past him.

"Me?" he says innocently. "I'm not the one creeping around on the stairwell!"

"I told you, I—"

"Wasn't sure it was my place?" he mocks.

"*Yes.*" I feel my face flush, so I don't meet his eye. Instead, I survey the place he calls home. It's small, by Chatwick standards, but large by New York City's, a typical bachelor pad, complete with leather furniture and a neon beer sign over the kitchen sink. I'm surprised by how tidy it is, remembering the state of his childhood bedroom. There is a distinct smell of Pine-Sol, and it is no small consolation imagining Murphy spending the day cleaning in preparation for my arrival.

"Nice print," I say, pointing my chin at the canvas on the living-room wall. I'm lying again. It's a generic painting of a little bistro with café tables and barrels of flowers in front. Two people face each other, their silhouettes blurry, sipping coffee. The colors are muted. It looks like it was mass-produced for customers of Bed Bath & Beyond who are looking for something that will go with everything. I'm only saying anything about it to find out how it got there, because it's a sign of a woman's input.

"Thanks. Mom picked it out." I glance at him, and he is half grinning. Is he smiling because he's embarrassed his mother decorated his apartment, or because he's lying and he knows that I know it? This is ridiculous. It shouldn't matter to me. And it doesn't.

It doesn't!

"So," I say, running my hand over a plush blue blanket flung on the back of his black leather couch and adding it to my mental evidence locker. "Now what?" Oh God. Did that sound like what I think it sounded like?

"I don't know. You wanna go for a ride?"

"Sure," I say, thankful he didn't respond in the pervy way he would have when I last knew him.

Murphy grabs his keys and we make our way back down the stairs. "So I guess climbing these is the drawback to living in 'the penthouse' rent-free?" I ask.

He laughs, but with a hint of offense taken. "Have you *met* Cecile? Not only do I pay rent, I don't even get a discount for being the super."

When we get to his truck, I think back to yesterday and how I wanted nothing more than this ride. Part of me wishes I had hopped in and demanded he take off. We would never have heard Danny's suicide note, dripping with disdain. We would never have been handed our secrets in little envelopes like remotely operated bombs. The others could read them, but who cared? We would be long gone.

As soon as I buckle up, I kick off my flip flops and fold one leg underneath me. I reflexively reach for my purse, before I realize rooting around in it will not produce a pack of Camel Lights and a lighter. I quit before I went to college, just one of the many bad habits I decided to leave in Chatwick.

Murphy is eyeing me. "Feel free to make yourself comfortable," he laughs.

I flash him a sheepish smile. "Force of habit."

"Your feet stink," he says.

"They do not!" I protest, whacking his arm with the back of my hand.

"Some things never change."

"And some things do."

We're both silent for a few minutes after that. Murphy takes me through town, and it's so surreal I feel almost sick. As I drove through it myself yesterday, it was easy to keep my eyes safely trained on the car in front of me without seeing what I now see. The Burger King the crew would hang out at after Emmett and Aaron's hockey games. Margie's Pub, and the retail space where The Exchange used to be—it closed about five years ago, Murphy tells me as we pass. After I left, at their insistence, I used to send Shawna and Donna letters care of the store, actual handwritten letters on fancy stationery I purchased at the NYU bookstore. I told them the same pack of lies I told my parents during my rare calls home. That I was healthy. Happy. Thriving in my new life. After a while it got to be too hard, so I stopped. Had I kept up my correspondence, I probably would have known they went out of business. Suddenly the image of them closing up shop for the last time, without me, wrenches my heart almost as badly as Ally's call about Danny's death.

We pass the high school, that pile of ivy-covered bricks, which used to look so gigantic and frightening. There's my pediatrician's office, where I used to love going because, after dutifully receiving my shots, they would give me this weird kind of bubble gum with a cold, liquid center. Nancy tells me Dr. Bates is still practicing, despite the fact he was approaching retirement age when I was his patient twenty years ago. Murphy turns onto Lake Road, and we go over the tracks and pass Charlene's Deli, formerly Deuso's Deli.

*None of you bothered to try to help me when I was alive, when it counted.*

I stiffen, and Murphy squeezes my shoulder, only for one second, before returning his hand to the wheel. I close my eyes against the words repeating in my head. When I open them, I see we're passing Hardy Crane's old house. Neither Murphy nor I comment on this particular landmark.

Not far after the deli, the homes and shops become farther apart, and Murphy picks up speed. We're going into Chatwick Town, the countryside. We pass the old white church I used to feel a tug toward. I was not raised religiously, like Murphy. Instead I grew up worshipping Santa Claus and Bob Barker, so the source of the tug was more a sense of mystery and magic than of any type of real faith. The people spilling out of the cathedral doors on Sunday mornings always seemed so bright and happy, and I longed to belong with them.

After the church come the farms and the manure. I take a deep inhale and instantly feel more relaxed. This is the part of

Vermont I truly miss. The country. "Nothing like a little cow shit to remind you you're home," I say. I glance at Murphy and instantly realize my mistake.

"There's more to Chatwick than cow shit, Ruby."

I forgot the number-one guiding principle of this town. You can only talk smack about it if you're an insider. The crew and I used to bitch about this place all the time, but that was when we were in it together. The second I packed my bags and left, it became forbidden for me to utter so much as a syllable against it. It's like how you can criticize your own mother, but no one else better, except your sister. Even *then* it's only okay if your sister still *talks* to your mother (I know, because mine doesn't). Murphy, like Ally, like everyone I know here, is poised to attack anyone—including, or maybe especially, me—who talks shit about their proverbial mother.

"I'm actually serious, Murph," I say. "I really have missed this." It's the truth. The sensations I'm experiencing from riding around with Murphy are exactly what give me anxiety every time I think about coming home. They're exactly what I was afraid of feeling: Youthful. Yearning. Alive.

As we drive farther, I can see the sun starting to set over the lake. This used to be my favorite time of day to ride around, the light filtering through the leaves and branches of the 100-year-old maple trees. The promise this time of day has always held, the night stretched ahead so full of opportunity for mischief or excitement or even disappointment. Anything to make you feel . . . something. Now, just like back then, the moment is so romantic it feels sad. That beautiful, lonely kind of sad.

We pull into the parking lot of Chatwick Bay Park. We're not supposed to be here past dusk, but that's never stopped us before. I look out over the lake and remember all the times I came here with Murphy or Danny or Ally, or by myself to let the placid waters smooth out the clutter in my mind from the latest blowout at home. Murphy swings the truck around in the parking lot so the bed of the truck faces the water. We get out and Murphy opens the tailgate. He holds out his hand to help me into the bed. I pretend I don't see it and haul myself up on my own. He laughs. "Still a toughie," he says.

"I don't know what you mean."

"It just kills you to ask for help. Or even accept it, when it's right in front of your face."

"I didn't need it," I shrug my shoulders. He nods, looking at a spot on the lake way in the distance, smiling to himself.

We sit in silence for a while before he says, "So . . . should we talk about—"

"Emmett. We should talk about Emmett," I interrupt. I know he's going to want to talk about our secrets, and I can't lie to him. And I *definitely* can't tell him the truth.

"Right," he says, his face turning grim. He turns to face the water. After a moment, he whispers, "He could die. He could have already died."

As overwhelmed as I feel, I can only imagine what Murphy must be feeling. He could have lost them both—Danny *and* Emmett—in one fell swoop. And even though Emmett assures us he's fine, that could change at any minute, according to Steph. These people are part of my past—hell, they *are* my past—but to Murphy they are his present and future, too. And they all seem to be disappearing. "Are you okay?" I ask. He nods, staring off into the distance. "It's okay if you're not, you know," I say. I put my hand on his knee, and he covers it with his. I get a flash of us in this same position, Murphy's hand over mine on Blue's gearstick, on the way to dropping him off at baseball practice. I remove my hand and tuck both of them underneath me.

"Why was it always so hard for them?" Murphy asks softly.

"Hard for who?"

"Em and Dan."

I look at him in shock. "You're kidding, right?"

He shakes his head.

"Oh, Murph. You really don't know?"

"What?" he asks, his voice edged with irritation. "What the hell else don't I know?"

I ponder how to word this thing that has always been so obvious to everyone but him. "It was a competition."

"For what? They never dated any of the same girls."

"Not over a girl. Over you."

It's true. Murphy's mother, who was no great fan of Danny Deuso's, once confided in me while we watched Murphy pitch a no-hitter that she blamed herself for Danny's presence in Murphy's life. She and Emmett's mother were in the same birthing class—so Emmett and Murphy really were, as Danny so bitterly articulated, "friends since the womb." Their moms decided to separate them in kindergarten to allow them to develop more on their own. This didn't phase the affable Murphy, but painfully shy Emmett was miserable. At the end of their first day of school, Emmett's mother called Cecile to report Emmett coming home in tears. Apparently at recess time, he looked all over for Murphy and found him up the highest branch of the tallest tree, Danny by his side, both boys hanging from their knees and grinning like Cheshire cats. I don't think Emmett ever recovered from Danny's abrupt and unwelcome entrance into his life. He spent the remainder of Danny's life competing for Murphy's love.

"The thought never even occurred to you?" I ask.

"I guess I never really thought about it like that. I just thought they rubbed each other the wrong way."

"They are very different. Were." Truth is, the two couldn't have been *more* different. Where Emmett was well-behaved and liked to be in control, Danny was a troublemaker who went with the flow. Where Emmett was smart and liked by the teachers (despite his occasional smart mouth), Danny battled with paying attention and was constantly lectured by even the nicest of our instructors. What neither of them realized was that they balanced each other out perfectly, and that Murphy needed them both. They were like the angel and the devil, one on each shoulder. The good and the bad, the boring and the adventurous.

"We should probably talk about the other thing. You know, the secrets."

Surprised by the change of subject, I don't have enough warning to stop myself from tensing slightly, which I'm sure Murphy notices. He leans forward to reach into his back pocket and pulls out his envelope, already creased at the midpoint, and the ink spelling his name already faded, as if he's been carrying it around with him for years.

*Just remember that all things done in the dark have a way of coming to light.*

"All right. What's your secret?" I dare.

"What's yours?" he asks.

Simultaneously we shout over each other, "I asked you first!" which makes us laugh.

When it gets quiet again, I feel my heart seize with panic. How reckless of me to play Chicken with something this serious. If Murphy *does* tell me his secret, it's only fair I tell him mine, and, as I mentioned, that is not an option. If my suspicion is correct, Murphy thinks my envelope matches his. He thinks all he covered up yesterday with the crew was a simple indiscretion between two consenting, horny teenagers, and I want to keep it that way, without having to lie to his face. "We don't have to talk about it, Murph. I mean, let's not."

He seems relieved, and I wonder briefly if I'm wrong. Does the paper in that envelope say what I think it says? Or is Murphy's secret some other twisted, dark thing? Maybe it's something that doesn't have anything to do with me. It's been ten years. It could be anything. But no. It's about me. It has to be. Why else would he be pressing the point, now that we're alone?

"What about what Danny said?" he asks. "If we don't tell each other—"

"Oh, Murph," I say, smiling in that pitying way I know he hates. "Do you really think Danny Deuso—the guy who wanted to climb Mount Kilimanjaro but wouldn't even go for a walk on the Rec trail, the one who was going to find the cure for AIDS but failed science, the *King* of Big Ideas with no follow-through— do you really think he would have actually taken the initiative, as his last act, to *pre-arrange* some big, public reveal of all our deepest, darkest secrets?"

"Danny was a lot smarter than people gave him credit for," he says.

I purse my lips against the frosty mood that is suddenly in the air. "I *know* Danny was smart. Don't talk to me like I didn't know him." Murphy looks away. "I'm just saying," I continue, realizing I'm using one of Nancy's famous introductory clauses that Coral and I always mocked, "he wasn't much of a 'do-er.' He was smart about people, and, I hate to say it, about how to get them to do what he wanted. He's pissed at us and blaming us for everything that went wrong with his life, and in some drug-induced haze he wanted to get back at us. He's just *saying* he arranged for everything to come out because he wants to force our hands."

"Then why wouldn't he just put them all in his letter?" Murphy asks.

I sigh. "I'm guessing he liked the idea of us all squirming to figure out how to cover up whatever we didn't want the rest of the crew to know. I mean, how would it even work? Say he picked someone to reveal our secrets out in public, announce them at Margie's, or whatever he felt appropriate. What's the trigger button? How would that person know whether we already told each other or not?"

"You've given this a lot of thought," Murphy says. "And you sound a little panicked."

He's right. I sound like Nancy when she's manic. I take a deep breath, counting to ten before continuing. "I just think I knew Danny pretty well."

"And I didn't?"

"I didn't say that."

"But that's what you meant. You always mean what I think you mean, but you *say*, 'I didn't say that,' because you think I'm stupid and can't read between the lines." Murphy's words snap like a whip, and I look at him in shock. As much as he and I have bickered in the course of our friendship, I don't remember ever feeling such blatant hostility from him. There was a hint of it in Charlene's driveway, but last night with the crew he was . . . that's it. He's fine when we're in a group, but when we're alone the real feelings come out.

"You're angry with me," I say.

He snorts and folds his arms. "I see the great New York education has paid off."

"YOU'RE angry with ME?" I launch myself off the tailgate, spinning around on him.

"Well, I know that's impossible to believe, isn't it? That *I*, the asshole, the villain of every story, could be mad at the Almighty Ruby St. James, who is so high above everyone else that she thinks she knows *everything* about them. Even though she hasn't bothered to so much as pick up a phone in ten goddamn years!"

Well, that shuts me up.

I march around to the passenger side of the truck, slamming the door after hopping inside. I glance in the side-view mirror and see Murphy kick at a clump of dirt and storm off toward the water. I sit with my arms crossed, fingers tapping on opposite elbows, lips pursed. I know I look like Nancy when I do this, but I'm angry, and I can't help it.

A few minutes later, he wordlessly opens the driver's side door and climbs in, slamming it closed behind him. He looks over at me, and I look out the window. He sighs, starts the truck, and we rumble out of the parking lot. I remain in the defensive position, cursing Danny for dying and Emmett for having a heart condition, and Ally for looking at me at the funeral as if we were strangers for a millisecond before she hugged me. Most of all, I curse Murphy. It's because of him this is all so much harder.

When we pull into his apartment parking lot, I jump out of the truck practically before he even comes to a complete stop. As he bounds up the flights of stairs to his apartment, I rummage through my purse for my keys, coming up empty. "Shit," I whisper as I increase the intensity of my search. "Shit shit shit!" I go back to the truck, whose door is mercifully unlocked, hoping my keys fell out in one of Murphy's angry sharp turns on the drive back from the bay. Nothing on the floor, in the glove box, in the cup holders. Not between the cushions, or under the seat, or in the side panel.

I get out and dump the contents of my purse onto Blue's hood, but my search is futile. When I look up, Murphy is at the top of the stairs, dangling my keys over the banister. "Missing something?" he shouts.

"All right, Murphy, drop 'em." He raises his arm, and for one horrifying moment I'm sure he is about to throw them with his pitcher's arm into the woods beyond the parking lot. I get a mental image of how demeaning it would be to crawl on my hands and knees through the bushes to find them, especially as the sun sinks below the horizon and I, like many years ago in Danny's field, do not have a flashlight. Perhaps he gets the same image, because he lowers his arm and turns around to go back inside.

"Come get 'em," he calls over his shoulder.

I stand at the bottom for a minute, contemplating alternative solutions that don't involve spending one more second in this man's—scratch that, this boy's—company. I could walk home, but there's no spare key for Blue, so I'd have to come back anyway. I actually consider having Nancy call Cecile. That would serve him right, but I can't bring myself to sink to the same tactics I used when we were ten and he wouldn't stop yelling "mushroom!" every time I walked in the room for six weeks after I cut my hair short.

Finally, I give up. I take a deep breath and bang my way up the five flights again. By the time I reach the top, I'm huffing and puffing from the effort and the anger. Murphy has disappeared into his apartment, leaving the door open for me to storm through. I grab my keys from the counter where he's tossed them. I should just leave. I know that. I should leave right now and that would be the end of it. But I can't help myself.

"You know," I say, "you all think I'm some pretentious city snob, that I think I'm better than you. But it's not true." I'm so angry my voice breaks, and hot tears sting the corners of my eyes. "The reason I haven't been home, haven't kept in touch, haven't been here for friends who have needed me? It's too hard, Murphy! It's too hard because everything is associated with *you*."

His face changes then, understanding dawning on him. The thought actually hasn't occurred to him before, the idiot, and it's only in this emotionally collapsed state that I could ever admit it. He charges toward me, arms outstretched, and I know what he's going to do, and I know I should stop him, but instead I move to meet him halfway. We are like two freight trains about to collide. We know it will be messy, but there's not much we can do to stop it now.

He plants his hands firmly on my face and kisses me. A jolt goes all the way through me and back up again, and everything I've ever felt for or about Murphy Leblanc comes over me like a flash flood. I stop him from kissing me only long enough to lift his shirt off over his head, and he gives me the look I know well; he knows what's going to happen, but he can't quite believe how lucky he is. He takes my shirt off, kisses my neck and cups my breasts, and then he consumes me in a bear hug and lifts me so I can wrap my legs around him. He walks us to his bedroom, our lips never leaving each other, and we fall onto the bed, clumsily fumbling off the rest of our clothes until there's no more to remove. He looks into my eyes; his are pools of black. I nod and he reaches into his nightstand for a condom.

*They're both really good at ignoring problems.*

# CHAPTER NINE

# RUBY
## *Back then*

Murphy fake gasps and clutches his heart dramatically when I emerge from my kitchen, freshly made up and styled by Shawna, the queen of all things girly. He knows a big reaction is expected of him, from all the cheesy teen movies and TV shows where prom is like the be-all and end-all of life. Of course, instead of doing the genuine jaw-dropping thing (which I well deserve, I might add, with 300 bobby pins, a can of hairspray, a gallon of makeup, and four-inch heels), he makes it into a joke. Would a moment of stunned silence be too much to ask? I guess with Murphy, it would be.

It doesn't matter anyway, because he's somebody else's boyfriend. It's amazing how quickly Murphy and Taylor became a couple. All I did was point her out to him in the cafeteria, initiate a mutual wave, and pass along her number to him. It seemed like a nanosecond after that they were going out. It's not really like Murphy to rush into things, so she must be one hell of a girl. I mean, she seemed to be completely fine with us sticking with our original pact to go to prom together, so she's either awesome or a really good liar. I gave him an "out," told him if it made things awkward he could take Taylor and I would find someone else, but he insisted that we made plans long before Taylor was in the picture, and he wasn't going to go back on his word. I was secretly relieved, because there's no way I would have found an acceptable replacement on this short notice (even Eddie Rodowski has a date this late in the game), and after all the planning Shawna and Donna did, I would hate to disappoint them.

My parents take about a thousand pictures, in the foyer, on the porch, in the driveway. They're smiling and being all cheesy, and I go along with it because I know they so desperately want to forget that my father wasn't here for junior prom, and my mother was sleeping off a depression crash inside and was not even aware when Eddie picked me up on the back of his motorcycle. I'm sure neither of them would have approved, had either been present. To be honest, I didn't really approve, either. I had to put a helmet over my up-do and by the time we got there my hair was flat and I was covered in bugs that had met their death on my skin. To top it all off, Hardy Crane was the first person I saw before I got a chance to straighten myself out, and the way he smirked at me made my bug-splattered skin crawl. Later, he and Brandy McCallister were crowned prom King & Queen, which Ally complained shouldn't be allowed, since Hardy was a second-year senior by that time.

Murphy opens the door of his truck for me, which is a welcome change. Normally, if he's driving, he'll roll the car forward a little bit as I try to get in, laugh hysterically, promise he won't do it again, and then do it again. One time he did it so many times I went back in the house and refused to go anywhere with him. He's as stubborn as I am, so instead of apologizing he just left. When he called me later that night, we didn't discuss it.

We go to Emmett's house and take *more* pictures with the rest of the crew. It's weird not going to Danny's, where we always meet up, but he can't come to prom because he was suspended for smoking on school grounds. Again. Even if he wasn't suspended, though, he probably wouldn't have come. He and Jenny have been over since he caught her making out with Brad Lewis down by the tracks. After the dance we'll all go to Tara's house, because her parents are in Michigan taking care of her stepfather's mother, who just broke her hip. We're not allowed at Danny's because Charlene is in one of her rare "putting my foot down" modes, and is disgusted with Danny's smoking even though she herself smokes, and half the time buys extra because she knows Danny will steal them. Charlene must have attended the same School of Sporadic and Hypocritical Parenting that Nancy went to.

Emmett and I get in a fight over who gets to ride shotgun. Emmett thinks "the boys" should ride up front together and I should sit in the back with Tara. I say it's prom, and we should sit with our dates. Emmett says it's not like Murphy and I are on a real date, and I blush as much with anger as embarrassment. To my surprise, Murphy tells Emmett to get his ass in the back or he's going to have to beg a ride from Aaron and Ally, who have made it clear they want to have dinner alone, for once.

We go to a restaurant in Drummond, for no other reason than it's thirty minutes outside of Chatwick and it gives us more time in the car, more distance and independence. It gives us a one-up on the rest of our class, who are all congregating at one of the two restaurants in town, both of which have newsprint as placemats and coloring crayons as utensils. Our crew isn't afraid to leave Chatwick. At least not for one meal.

While we're waiting to be seated, an older woman on her husband's arm leans into Murphy and says, "Your girlfriend is stunning." He doesn't correct her about my title. He just nods, says, "I know," and then loops his arm around my waist. I can't help but smile.

When we arrive at the school gym we mingle a little, the girls all comparing dresses. Mine is royal blue, with little silver sparkles woven into the fabric. It looks like the sky right after the sun sets and, not to sound cocky, but I like it the best. I *should*, considering the vetting process.

Murphy drifts over to Taylor and starts dancing with her not long after we arrive. We talked before about this and I told him I didn't mind, but he's gone for so long everyone else starts to couple off and I'm left standing alone. I try to appear totally comfortable standing in the corner and watching, but I'm not. I feel lonely and stupid. I should just have gotten another date, or stayed home. *He* was the one who insisted we still go together. He said after all we've been through together, and after all I've been through in the past couple of years, I shouldn't miss my senior prom. Thinking back on the conversation we had, his words sound more like pity than solidarity of friendship, and it makes my stomach turn. I rush into the bathroom but don't throw up. I'm careful not to let the tears in my eyes actually fall, ruining Shawna's hard work.

I'm glad Ally didn't see me rush off. She was supportive of the idea of Murphy and I keeping our date. A little too supportive. "Ruby, who cares about Taylor, she's a *sophomore*. She doesn't even belong at prom." Ally is not so keen on Taylor yet; she doesn't trust that she'll be around for the long haul (the idea that the goal of most high-school relationships is not, in fact, to end up married is unfathomable to her). You wouldn't sense the distrust, based on how they gossip together when Murphy actually brings her around. But if Ally saw me upset, it would lead to drama. She would give Murphy a talking to, and then everyone would be talking about it.

As it is, I feel like a horrific cliché: the girl crying in the bathroom at the school dance. How pathetic. I stare myself down in the mirror and give myself a no-nonsense-style pep talk. I look pretty, and I should go out and find some other loser who doesn't have a real date and dance with him. I wish Danny were here. He would dance with me, *and* he would have snuck in a flask. *That* would make this whole thing more bearable.

When I finally come out of the bathroom, Taylor is lingering outside. I force myself to brighten, like nothing is bothering me, and ask her if she's having a good time. She smiles, either faking her warmth or genuinely tolerant of her boyfriend being at prom with another girl (for some reason I don't understand, I really feel like it's the latter). She says, "Murphy's waiting for you by the stage. Sorry I've been hogging him!" I feel guilty, and cover it by saying, "Of course not!" I am amazed at how good I've become at this fakey girl shit I've always hated, but if I don't play along, I end up looking even more pathetic than I already do.

I find Murphy waiting where Taylor said he would be. Wordlessly, we start dancing to a fast song, Murphy spinning me around and shaking his hips goofily. We dance to three fast songs in a row without stopping, laughing the whole time. I'm the one who taught him to dance, if that's what you call this. It was the first time he was the only one to show up at my house after school, and he confessed he didn't know how to dance and that's why he always sat on the bleachers at dances. I turned on music and made him show me. It turned out he wasn't a bad dancer, just a silly one, which made it all the more fun. When a slow song came on, I showed him where to put his hands for a slow dance—"No, not there, you perv," I had said.

Like then, the music slows now, and I shuffle backwards to make my exit so he can dance with Taylor, but Murphy grabs my elbow and pulls me close to him. His cologne, which he always wears a touch too much of, fills my nose. He's been wearing the same kind since we were freshmen—some uncle brought it down from Montreal for him. I got him a new bottle for Christmas this year, noticing the one in his bathroom was running low. He says, his mouth right up against my ear, making me shiver, "I'm sorry if I've been dancing with Taylor too much."

"Oh, stop it," I cover, pulling back slightly. "Don't worry about it. She's your girlfriend, you can't just ignore her! I'm the one who should be sorry. I'm feeling a little stupid now that we're here. It's like you're my big brother and our mom forced you to take me."

Murphy slows his swaying almost to a halt. "That's not what it's like," he says. "I brought you because I wanted to." When our eyes lock, I feel something shift inside me.

Before I can put a name to it, the fire alarm goes off.

Our look lingers for another second before a couple bumps into us on their way to the exit. I glance around to see if anyone noticed our little moment, but all I see is the blur of all my classmates making their way out of the gym. Murphy puts his hand on the small of my back and guides me through the crowd.

It's raining when we get outside. Of course. Mrs. Parizo, my Advanced English teacher, tells us the alarm was triggered by the fog machine, and we can't go back inside until the air has cleared out a little. I look around for our friends but don't see anyone, even in the stilts I'm wearing for shoes. They must have gone out one of the other exits. All the girls around me are freaking out because their hair and makeup are getting ruined. I look at Murphy and say in a mocking tone, "Do I still look pretty?", knowing full well my up-do is now both flat and frizzy and my makeup is smudged.

He shakes his head and pulls me in so that his lips touch my ear again. "Beautiful," he says. I shiver again, and he thinks it's because of the rain, so he covers me in his tuxedo jacket.

When we're given the all-clear to go back in, we decide to go have our official prom picture taken before we forget. The photographer positions us in the classic cheesy-couple pose—Murphy standing behind me with his arms around me, both of us facing the camera. I try to explain we're not a couple, but he says this is the best way to show off the dress, so I comply. Murphy holds me a little tighter than is really necessary and cracks a joke about the photographer's coffee breath, making me laugh just as the camera goes off.

After the King & Queen are crowned and it's not Ally and Aaron (which Ally refuses to admit she's been expecting and waiting for), we all disperse. Danny picks up Emmett and Tara, who are in charge of getting one of Emmett's brothers to buy us beer for the night. Aaron and Ally go to pick up snacks for later. Murphy says goodnight to Taylor, who has curfew and isn't allowed to come to Tara's for the after-party because she let it slip there wouldn't be parents there. I wait patiently, but feel a weird little twinge when he kisses her goodbye.

It's just me and Murph as we walk down the ramp to the parking lot. The rain stopped at some point when we were inside, so the air smells like fresh, damp earth, and the clouds are clearing to show the stars. The moment is too quiet, something I'm not used to when I'm around my best friend, so I complain about my feet hurting. He scoops me up without a word and carries me in his arms until we get to the car. I force myself not to ask him what's gotten into him. The answer might ruin everything.

We're the first ones to get to Tara's, so we use the Hide-A-Key under the frog statue, as Tara instructed. We head to separate rooms to change into the casual clothes we packed into overnight bags earlier. I feel sad changing out of my dress. It's the prettiest I've ever felt, and I'm not ready for that to be over. I sit at Tara's vanity and stare at myself, then lift a piece of the skirt to my nose. It still smells like Murphy's cologne. After a minute, I hear a soft knock on the door. I open it, and it's Murphy. He's in jeans and a T-shirt, and has two beers in his hand that he must have stolen from Tara's fridge. I make a mental note to replace them when our beer gets here, so Tara's parents are none the wiser.

"Just wanted to see what's taking you so long," he said, raising his eyebrows that my appearance hasn't changed at all.

"I couldn't reach the zipper." I'm too embarrassed to admit I'm already feeling nostalgic for this night, for senior year, for our crew as we know it, and it's not even over yet. He crosses behind me and starts unzipping my dress. I close my eyes and feel his breath on my shoulder blades. Suddenly I'm transported back to a few months ago at Danny's house. The rest of the crew in bed already, Murphy sneaking up behind me, whispering in my ear. Before I knew it we were kissing, and we barely closed the door to the spare room before we started stripping off each other's clothes. That was it. Nothing caused it—no sweeping romantic declarations or any special circumstances that brought us closer. It just was.

We hear one of Aaron's signature burps, signifying the crew's arrival. I've never been so grateful for his gas in all my life. I tell Murphy thanks for the help and he'd better get downstairs. He does.

The girls and I change into our normal clothes but leave our hair up and makeup on. There isn't much choice in the matter. Removing the clips and bobby pins now would leave a Bride of Frankenstein mess of our hair, and none of us feels like completely showering off our fancy looks yet.

We drink and get a little high and smoke Tara's mother's secret cigarette stash. We play Asshole and continue to dance, staying up most of the night. People start trickling off to one of the many bedrooms, but Murphy and I stay up, continuing to play cards, as if we have some unspoken agreement that we need more time for just the two of us. Finally I declare I'm ready for my last cigarette. Even though Murphy *never* smokes, and normally complains when I do, he comes outside to the porch with me. It's cold, so Murphy takes off his coat—this time his trusty blue flannel in place of the tuxedo jacket—and drapes it over my shoulders.

Once again the moment is too quiet, the crickets and my sporadic exhalations the only sounds. So I say, "What's with all the chivalry tonight, Murph?" I mean it to be funny, and I expect him to overcompensate by giving me a brotherly cuff on the arm, breaking the tension. But he's quiet. He opens his mouth, closes it. Opens it again. Closes it.

My heart starts to beat harder, because I think he's trying to figure out a way to kiss me, and I don't know what to do if he tries. I thought we were past this. No matter what I've been feeling tonight, Murphy has a girlfriend. After Hardy I swore I would never do that again, and I won't let Murphy become a cheater, either. Just because it's too soon for Taylor to give it up, doesn't mean I'm his automatic sexual consolation prize. Besides, all those feelings before—I was simply swept up in the whole prom mania. Twinkly lights, overplayed love songs, all that chiffon. Murphy's my best friend, and that's all. Right now, he's just trying to get into my pants. It's bound to happen; he's a dumb, horny boy.

Then he says, clearly but softly, "I love you, Ruby."

Oh.

# CHAPTER TEN

# RUBY

## *Now*

I lie in Murphy's bed, comfortable enough, considering I'm naked and slipping around on satin sheets. Murphy Leblanc—little Murphy, who was chunky until the tenth grade, whose proverbial cherry I am personally responsible for popping—now has satin sheets. It's nauseating and hilarious all at the same time. They positively reek of his cologne, or maybe my nose is just hyper-aware. They say scent is the most powerful of the senses, the one most tightly connected to memory. I catch a whiff of this smell or something similar in the city from time to time, getting off the subway, in a crowded theater, at the bodega across the street from the office. It never ceases to make me simultaneously anxious, aroused, and headachy.

We both lie on our backs, staring at the ceiling, catching our breath and our thoughts. Outside, it has started to rain, as if nature itself is displeased with our union. Neither of us knows what to say. At least I don't know what to say, and I'm not sure if Murphy cares enough to say anything. It's silly that I'm surprised when he breaks the silence with a joke. "So . . . .how you been for the last ten years?" he asks.

I laugh, clutching the smooth sheet in my hands. He laughs too, and it sets me off into a fit of giggles, like we're fourteen and on the phone until way too late.

He asks me about New York, and I tell him how mind-numbing my job is. I tell him I spend time in bookstores and cafés, hoping to be inspired by all the pretentious hipsters jabbing away at their MacBooks; but instead of inspiring me to write, the trips usually end with a return to my couch to eat potato chips in front of bad reality-TV shows. I tell him something I haven't yet said out loud, that I'm thinking of going back to school to get my Masters in Fine Arts, if for no other reason than to force myself to write something other than apologetic emails to clients who are annoyed their ads didn't get better placement. He likes the idea, he says, because then the countless hours I spent reading my short stories to him over the phone will have been worth it. I tell him about how much I love the city—MoMA, Central Park, the shops with freshly cut flowers on every corner. How you pass a million strangers and none of them know anything about you. I tell him about the monthly (more like quarterly) dinners I have with my father. Away from my mother's penny-pinching, he has his assistant book us at exclusive restaurants I wouldn't otherwise even be able to get a reservation in, let alone afford to split the check.

He asks me about my friends, and I tell him about some of my coworkers I occasionally have drinks with. He tells me they don't count. I tell him I live with my sister, but she's always away on shoots, so I only see her three or four times a year. I tell him about Greta, my roommate from the London years, who moves freely about the world as if things like working visas and health insurance are of no importance. I've gotten a free place to stay in Brazil, Vietnam, and (my favorite) Turkey as a result. When I mention that my favorite thing about Greta was how she didn't care what anyone else thought, that she slept with anyone and everyone and had no qualms about discussing the gory details, his interest is piqued. I especially loved when she talked about her conquests in front of Jamie. His princely manners disallowed him from any comment, so the best part was watching him squirm.

It's not the first he's heard of Jamie, Murphy tells me. Apparently Nancy and Cecile swap stories when they run into each other at Martin's, the grocery store. Nevertheless, he asks me more about him. I tell him: yes, Jamie's good-looking. Yes, as good-looking as you, but in a different way. Yes, he made me laugh, too, also in a different way. Murphy's cautiously satisfied with this answer, but still wants to know more.

So, I tell him how we met: Jamie was the professor's assistant in my Gothic Literature class when I studied abroad. He resigned halfway through the semester, and as the dozens of other lovestruck girls fawned over him after his announcement, I suddenly had this surge of panic that I might never see him again. So I asked him out. We went to a coffee shop and talked about books for hours; Jamie teased me when I tried to impress him by "casually" dropping in references to Chaucer and Hawthorne. He told me he had resigned because he wanted to "give writing a go." I found out later he comes from a pretty well-to-do-family, which is how he could afford this luxury. I hasten to tell Murphy that, beyond Jamie's impeccable table manners, you wouldn't have suspected he came from money. Especially with that sloppy hair and the corduroy blazer with the elbow patches, frayed at the edges, straight from the clearance bin at Professors 'R' Us. It feels important that Murphy doesn't think I spent three years in a relationship with a snob.

It took a while before I knew I loved Jamie. Instead of coming home and attending NYU graduation, I had (much to Nancy's dismay) skipped the ceremony, signed another lease with Greta, and took a job at *The Sun* in their sales department. I swore it wasn't about Jamie, that I loved London and my job and Greta and loathed commencement ceremonies (based solely on my high-school experience), but of course it was about him. It wasn't until about a year afterward that I knew for sure. It was when I read the pages of his first book. I remember how nervous he was to hand them over. We had been in bed, just like Murphy and I are now, when he carefully placed them on my lap. Instead of watching for my reaction as I read, which would have been vain and obnoxious, he simply got up and left the room. His writing was so beautiful, yet simple, just like we were. With each turn of the page, I knew, finally, that I was in love.

"So what went wrong?" Murphy asks.

I think for a moment. "Timing."

"Explain."

"I'd rather not."

He holds up his hand, his fingers clenched like talons. "Tell me or I'll give you the Aaron claw."

We both laugh. And then, because it's Murphy, and because before we fucked everything up we used to spend hours dissecting stuff like this, I tell him the truth. The only thing Jamie and I ever argued about was living together. He was approaching his thirties toward the end of our relationship, so all his friends were settling down and he was ready to take steps that I wasn't. He wanted me to move into his gorgeous flat, live off his family money, and start writing. What a prick, right? I should have *leapt* at the chance, but I couldn't make myself want it. I didn't feel comfortable not paying my fair share (and I *never* could have on my salary; even if I had kept my job, I could barely afford the crap-shack Greta and I stayed in), and I already had a good thing going with Greta. I liked living with her. She was entertaining and fun. She cooked things I still can't pronounce, and I cleaned up after her. I got to hang out with Jamie when I wanted to, and be on my own when I wanted to. It worked for three years. But then Greta, the bitch, decided to follow this guy she'd been seeing for just four months to *Ghana*, of all places, and it sort of held this giant magnifying glass up to our relationship. Jamie asked me one more time to move in with him, and when I refused, he ended it.

What I don't tell Murphy is that my reasons for not moving in, although true and valid, were only branches on a whole tree of excuses. The root of the problem was I was twenty-two, then twenty-three, twenty-four, and twenty-five, and I wasn't ready to move in with Jamie. With anyone. It wasn't Jamie. He was practically perfect. It was that the closer we got, the more I felt the weight of my past holding me back. I started to feel like I couldn't breathe. The better he treated me, the more I resented him for being overall better than me—a better writer, a better partner, a better person.

*I hate myself for what I've done. For what I am.*

Since Jamie, there's been no one of significance. Sometimes I meet someone interesting and go on a date. We go see a movie or comedy show, or for dinner somewhere trendy, a walk through Central Park, or to a museum. It rarely goes past the second date. I'm not very interested in third dates, the famous one where you're supposed to have sex with a person you barely know. The guys I've gone out with are attractive enough, it's just that none of them have made me feel as safe and loved and adored as Jamie. And none have made me feel as alive and excited and crazy as the guy lying next to me. I *definitely* don't tell Murphy that. And I don't tell him that, considering Jamie and Greta are still my best friends and neither even lives on this continent, I'm a little lonely.

I switch the subject to him, bracing myself for a report on the ins and outs of every girl in Chatwick. But instead he tells me more about his business, how happy he is to be building homes and running his own crews. "There's always a finished product, a good home for a family to be raised in, and it'll be there at least as long as I'm alive, if not forever." I picture him driving in his truck, a grandson in the passenger seat, pointing out the buildings he's responsible for. It's a nice picture, but it also makes me sad.

I ask about his mother, realizing she is another person once a part of my life and now all but forgotten. "She gets tougher with every sunrise," he says, as he's always said of her. Cecile *is* one of the toughest ladies around, but not many people have seen the soft side I've seen. After I got Blue but before Murphy got his first truck, (a gap of about a year, which felt like ten for him), I used to shuttle him back and forth from baseball practice, doing my homework in Blue in between. The first time I came to pick him up, Murphy had read his schedule wrong and I was an hour early picking him up from his house. Cecile's small but solid frame thundered in after dealing with a rat situation at one of their apartments, and she was in no mood to have "dead weight" hanging around the house (she actually used that term). She put me to work in the kitchen, chopping onions for the dinner she would heat up when I brought Murphy back from practice. Nancy was going through a black period at the time, which meant a frozen dinner on a TV tray on a *good* day, so the experience of chopping and chatting with Cecile felt blissfully normal and domestic.

After that first day, I started showing up early on purpose, and without any discussion Cecile would put me to work, instructing me in her low, firm voice and occasionally guiding my hands to show me the proper technique for a stir or a whisk. Her hands were always pleasantly cool, even when working over her enormous gas stove, and I secretly treasured the intimacy of it. Murphy, meanwhile, would pore over his schoolbooks, struggling to complete his homework, biting his tongue in concentration. Perhaps this is why we, and our friends, bought into our insistence that we were "like family" for so long. The picture of the boy doing his homework while the womenfolk busy themselves making dinner is like a goddamn Rockwell painting.

I gradually became less and less afraid of Cecile, and once I proved I wasn't totally useless in the kitchen, she displayed a sort of muted approval of my presence in her son's life, despite her skepticism as to the need for young boys to have female friends. I wonder now if she knew about Nancy and was doing her part to make me feel like I still had a mother, when things at my house were bleak. I was always invited to dine with the Leblancs when I brought Murphy home from practice, and many times I took her up on it. Except for when I was dating someone, and then I would just tell Nancy that's where I was and go off with him instead.

Murphy tells me that Cecile was diagnosed with Lyme disease, which I take harder than he seems to think is appropriate. It doesn't bother her much, as far as he knows. I point out that she wouldn't tell him if it did. He says he would know anyway, and I know that's true. One of the many things I know about Murphy that most people don't is what a mama's boy he is.

He tells me his father retired around the same time Murphy started his company with Aaron, but he still consults on some of Murphy's larger projects, and he and Cecile still run all their properties with the help of Murphy's older brother. His brother had "a few bad years" when he dated Jenny Albrecht, Danny's on-again-off-again girlfriend from high school, but they've been broken up for over a year. The only residual effect from the relationship is his need to smoke pot at the beginning of each day. Considering the stuff Danny was into at the end, both of us agree this is no cause for concern.

Murphy doesn't mention a girl, and I don't see any notches on his bedpost, but I suspect there's a lot he doesn't tell me as well. I don't press for the details of his love life, because I'm not sure I can, as he did, remain stoic as he talks about them. I wonder if I was imagining the tension in his jaw as I talked about Jamie.

We listen to the rain against the windowpane for a moment, our eyes drooping in the peaceful post-coital haze. A question floats into my head and I ask it, despite knowing it will make me sad. "Where do you think he is?"

"Who? Dan?"

I nod.

"I don't know. Heaven, I guess."

*Try to be happy I'm finally at peace.*

"Heaven," I repeat. It's a concept I haven't really contemplated in a long time, even when I first heard Danny was gone.

"You don't think so?" Murphy asks, rolling over to face me, his head propped in his hand. I roll to mirror his posture, which is a mistake, because from this angle I can see the sparkle in his eyes. The thrill of it is like a stab through my heart.

"I don't know," I say, looking away. "It's always seemed like such a nice idea, that we all go to this big pillowy cloud-place after we die. But then what?"

He laughs. "I don't know, I guess I never thought past that part."

"I mean, it seems kinda dull, doesn't it? We just float up there, strap on an unflattering toga, and stroke a harp all day?

I mean, that's why we work hard to be good people? That's our big reward?"

He's amused now. This feels like one of the conversations we used to have at night, after our parents had gone to bed (or Nancy had gone out), whispering into the phone so we wouldn't get hollered at to hang up and go to sleep. "There's probably more to it than that," he says.

"Like what?" I ask, collapsing my arm and lying back down, my hands clasped together. I look expectantly at him, like a kid waiting for their parent to tell them a bedtime story. He laughs at this.

"Maybe it's like this movie I saw once. You get to pick if you stay in heaven, or if you go back for another life. And if you choose heaven, you kind of create whatever you want it to be like."

"What do you think Danny would choose?"

"Well, given that he just topped himself, I don't think he'd be too psyched about the idea of living life all over again, or taking his chances on a new one. He's probably up in heaven dealing dope to all the angels," he says.

The mental image makes us both laugh, but after a minute it hits me what we're *really* talking about, and I start to cry.

"Hey," Murphy says, pulling me into him and speaking softly into my hair. "I'm sorry, I shouldn't have made a joke."

I shake my head. "No, it's not that. It's—everything. Danny and Emmett and . . . this."

"Was I that bad?" he asks, mock-offended and clearly trying to lighten the mood.

"No," I say, pulling myself together and giving him a little kiss on the forehead. "That's not what I meant."

"Was it better than . . . you know, before?"

I roll my eyes. "Murphy. The last time we had sex you were a newbie. If you hadn't improved your skills since then, it would be a problem."

He searches my face and must realize this is the highest praise he's going to get from me.

"What would *you* choose?" I ask him. I'd quite literally prefer death to talking about us back then.

"Heaven, for sure," he says, as if it's the most obvious thing in the world.

"And what would your heaven look like?"

"It would be like one endless night at Margie's. Cold beer. Good friends. Beautiful, easy women."

I groan. I can't help myself. This is what Murphy has become? A 'necker? Has he always been one, and I just never noticed because I was surrounded by them?

"Oh, and what would your heaven be, Miss Priss?" he asks, pushing pretend glasses up his nose with his index finger. "Sitting on the sofa with a glass of wine and a good book?" He says it in a mock British accent, and I wonder if he's taking a dig at Jamie. It's weird I even *told* Murphy about him, I realize. The two of them are completely separate worlds for me. It's like I'm not even the same person when I'm thinking about one or the other.

"Actually, that sounds kinda nice," I say. "But I would pick reincarnation."

He rolls his eyes. "Of course you would, Tuesday."

I'm taken aback. "Why 'of course'?"

"Because you're always in search of something better. Always have been, always will be." He looks into my eyes now, and I turn back to face the ceiling.

We're quiet for a minute.

"You know," he says, in a tone I recognize as his I'm-about-to-poke-a-bear/you-with-a-stick tone, "I really think we should just tell people. I mean, I'm guessing your secret is about us. It happened so long ago, and I think people will understand. What's the big deal?"

The words feel like shots to the kneecaps, even considering he thinks we're talking about two totally different things. "How would Taylor feel, if that gets out?" I ask. I know from Ally that they broke up years ago, but not so long ago that it had anything to do with us.

"She knows."

*All things done in the dark . . .*

I nod slowly, feeling the color drain from my face. "Right," I say finally, throwing off the covers and jumping out of bed.

"Hey. Where you goin'?"

I shimmy back into my clothes, my back to Murphy, so he can't see the hurt on my face. It was one thing for it to be our little secret, but for him to tell Taylor? And for it, apparently, not to have made a difference in their relationship? How he must have downplayed what happened. How little it must have meant to him for him to be able to explain it away. "Sorry, I gotta go. More work to do."

"It's Saturday night."

"Yeah, well, you know what they say about New York," I force cheeriness into my voice as I make a beeline for the door. "It never sleeps!"

"Ruby, wait," I hear him say as I let his screen door slam shut behind me, running out into the rain.

# CHAPTER ELEVEN

# RUBY
## *Back then*

I don't say anything for what probably seems like a long time. But I can't help it, I mean, he loves me? Murphy?

"You mean, as a friend, right?" I ask, glancing in his direction and then returning to stare straight ahead. I'm giving him an out, because it's prom, we've been drinking and smoking, and this has suddenly gotten way too serious. It's entirely possible that my freak-out radar is just oversensitive. We've always said how great it is to have a best friend of the opposite sex. You get the companionship without the commitment, the perspective without the pressure. What's not to love? I must be misunderstanding. Murphy must simply have forgotten to add the "man" and the punch in the arm.

"No," he says, "I've been *in* love with you. For a while."

So much for that theory. "How long?"

"Two years."

I take a puff of my cigarette to trap the gasp in my throat, then offer it to him. I'm not surprised when he actually reaches for it and takes a deep inhale. His confession is changing everything; it might as well change his stance on smoking. "Two years," I repeat when he passes it back. I try to calculate backward. Two years ago would be sophomore year. We had dated dozens of people, between the two of us, since then.

One of them being Hardy Crane. "All this time? Why the hell didn't you say anything?"

"You know why, Ruby. The timing was never right. Either you liked someone, or I liked someone, or neither of us liked anyone and we would kiss and then you would tell me what a mistake it was, because it would ruin our friendship."

"I thought we were in agreement about that. I mean, you're my best friend."

"I know."

"That's not something I've ever wanted to risk. Boyfriends and girlfriends break up all the time."

"I know."

I stamp out my cigarette on the side of the staircase and let it drop to the ground. I think briefly how much time we're going to spend combing the lawn for butts in just a few hours. We really should have put a can out.

"I can't believe you've been hiding this for so long," I whisper, letting my head—too heavy now—drop into my hands. Maybe I did see this, *feel* this coming. I guess if I'm completely honest, there have been times when I sensed Murphy might want more, and there were also times when I thought my feelings might tiptoe over the friendship line, but we never talked about it, so it always passed like a storm cloud over an otherwise sunny day. To hear it out loud like this? It's too real. I start to sniffle. Then, floating above us for a moment and seeing that my best friend is—for the first time—telling a girl he loves her, and wanting better for him than a tearful reaction, I make myself shiver to pretend the sniffling is from cold rather than emotion.

He puts his arm around me and I lean into him, even though my instinct is telling me to run away. I thought setting him up with Taylor would set us back on the right track. The friendship track, where we get to have fun and be ourselves and never fight. Not about anything real, anyway.

"I'm sorry, Murph, I don't know what to say." Because I don't. I can't say for sure I feel the same way, but I can't say for sure I don't.

"You don't have to say anything," he says, and I can tell he's trying really hard to sound fine with it all. But how can he be? The only desired outcome of telling someone you love them is for them to say they love you too, and immediately. Any variation from that is crushing. We wordlessly get up, creep inside and up the stairs, and climb into the twin bed of one of Tara's brother's rooms. At first, our backs face each other, but despite my good intentions I start to cry, and Murphy rolls over to hold me. He strokes my hair, peppering my hairline with tiny kisses, and whispers that it's all right until I fall asleep.

When we wake up the next morning, Murphy is still holding me, and I find I don't feel as sad as I did the night before. A little anxious, maybe, but not sad. And maybe even a little . . . happy?

It's absolutely gorgeous outside, and after I help the girls clean up all the beer cans and cigarettes (while the boys play with Tara's little brother's friggin' Nerf guns), Murphy and I go to his house right around the corner. I know I should go home, and I get a wave of guilt thinking about Taylor, who is sitting at home waiting for Murphy to call. But Murphy is the one who invited me over—hell, he's the one who started all this—and I'm not ready to go home to sift through this mess alone. Suddenly alone doesn't have the appeal it used to have. I feel like there's some kind of spell over us, and as soon as we part ways, it will be broken.

I change into Murphy's T-shirt and nylon athletic shorts, which are now designated as mine after so many post-field party visits when I demanded comfy clothes that didn't reek of bonfire. We grab a blanket and lie in the sun on his back lawn. I spend the time practically: trying to convince Murphy he doesn't really love me. If he cracks, I'll know he doesn't, and then it will all go back to normal.

"You hate the way I say 'orange,'" I remind him.

"Well, Jesus, it's 'oaringe', not 'arnge,'" he says.

"And you hate that I smoke."

"You'll quit. Someday. Right?"

"I've whored around for two years."

"No, you haven't. You've slept with two guys, and one of them was me."

"Yeah, and neither of them was my boyfriend. What do you call that?"

"You're independent. Unconventional. And awesome."

"I don't even know how to have boyfriends, Murph. I don't even know if I want one."

"Okay."

"And we've been best friends since eighth grade. Who would you talk to when I piss you off?"

"Good point," he says, smiling. "Probably the same person I talk to about it now. You. I'd say that gives us one-up on most of the couples we know."

I don't bring up the biggest question on my mind: *What about the crew?* These friendships, however flawed, are the only thing I've been able to count on through the whole mess with my parents. I don't want to risk losing them. Even when I didn't know what Nancy's mood would be like from one day to the next, when I didn't know if my parents were together or divorced or something in between, I've always *known* I can go to Ally and feel mothered; I can go to Tara and dance around in my underwear; I can go to Danny and feel like I'm taking care of someone who really needs it; I can go to Emmett and fight if I need to blow off steam. And I can go to Murphy and laugh and know everything will be okay.

But if they all know about Murphy and me, it will be weird and awkward. Suddenly we'll be a *couple*, and every bonehead comment Murphy makes will be a reflection on me. We'll be responsible for each other's actions in a way we haven't ever had to be. We've always just been able to enjoy each other, and now we'll have to defend each other. Our disagreements will affect the crew. They will be *owned* by them. Every touch and look and sentence uttered will be up for analysis. And I don't want to be a contestant in the relationship contest with Ally and Tara. They alternate between competing over who has the best boyfriend and who has the worst, depending on the drama of the day.

I bring up the question that *should* be the biggest on my mind, if I were a better person, anyway. "What about Taylor?"

His face clouds over, and he takes a moment to respond. "She'll survive." He doesn't explicitly promise to break up with her, and I don't ask him to.

After several hours of alternately dozing and indulging my neurosis, Murphy sits up straight, suddenly hard-faced. "Look, Ruby. I said what I said last night, and I meant it. If you don't feel the same way, that's fine. I'm not going to die. But I thought you should know the truth. Now let's just drop it. And maybe you should go home and shower, because you kinda stink." I give him a playful sock on the arm, and he pulls me close and gives me a quick peck on the lips. Uh-oh. I push him off and glance around frantically. What if Cecile sees?

"Okay, I'm going home," I stand up abruptly. "Listen, I don't think we should tell anyone—"

"—anyone about this, especially the crew, because it's none of their business and we don't want it to become 'a thing,'" he recites. It was the same thing I said to him the night I took his virginity.

The next few weeks are a blur of confusion, excitement, and despair. Murphy and I continue to hang out, but, just as I worried, everything is different. It's good and bad. The bad comes when we see each other in the halls or greet each other in front of our friends. We're both trying to make it seem normal, but suddenly we can't remember how we used to act around each other. The more casual we try to be, the more awkward it is. One time we even shake hands before heading into class. I'm really glad nobody saw that.

The good, and I mean *really good*, part happens when we manage to be alone. At first, tension crackles between us like an electric fence. It's the same spark and playful sense of humor that's always been there, but now I'm hyper-aware of it, and it's obvious that what we have—what we've always had—is more than friendship. Everything is amplified.

I drive Murphy to get his hair cut at Le Beax Cheveux (whose name implies a higher level of sophistication than Chatwick is capable of). Since I got my car, I've taken any excuse to leave my house, even if it's chauffeuring my friends to appointments like a soccer mom. It's a chance to sit in my car and smoke and read, and not worry about a tense conversation coming around the corner at home. But lately it's more about getting to spend any amount of alone-time with Murphy that doesn't appear sinister. This time, I don't sit in my car; I go in with him and sit in the waiting area. I pretend to flip through a magazine, but every few seconds we exchange flirty eyes in the mirror. The stylist makes a comment about what a cute couple we are, and we immediately stiffen. I go back to my magazine, and Murphy tells the stylist, "We're just friends." I'm not looking at him, but I can tell he's smirking when he says it.

Afterward, we walk down the gravel driveway and I risk contact by running my hand through his still impossibly thick hair. I tell him it looks great, and he looks at me with this gleam in his eye I've been noticing lately. Has it always been there, and I just didn't see it? He bends down quickly and scoops me up in his arms, like he did on prom night. I let him carry me a few feet, but squiggle out of his arms as we approach my car, which is parked on Main Street. Not ten seconds later do we hear a honk. A maroon SUV drives by, Taylor waving from the passenger seat of her mother's car. Murphy and I wave back enthusiastically, then avoid looking at each other on the ride home.

That's the other bad part. He still hasn't broken up with Taylor. I don't want to ask him to, not while I'm still unsure about taking her place. It occurs to me he hasn't made up his mind, either.

A few days later I drive over to his house to give him a ride to baseball practice. I haven't done it this year because he got his truck right before baseball season started, and since Dad came back, Nancy makes a big show of having dinner on the table every night. But Murphy's truck is at Borbeau's getting an oil change. It's another cover we don't discuss. Murphy knows how to change his own oil, and even if he didn't, an oil change doesn't require an overnight stay in the garage. I pretend it's out of habit that I'm here early, ready for my cooking lesson with Cecile, but when I find out she's showing an apartment, I'm not exactly crushed.

I pull up a stool and look over his shoulder at his homework. Murphy is *not* stupid, but school doesn't come as easily to him as it does to me, and besides the one class we have together, we aren't in any of the same classes. The work he's doing now is Pre-Calc, which I took last year. I point out a couple of errors in his work, and give him a few tips on remembering the formulas. I can tell he's a little embarrassed, and I scold myself internally for being such a know-it-all. After a few minutes, though, we're laughing about it and he's asking me more questions. My hand brushes his as I point something out in a textbook, and he looks at me. I feel myself blush, so I get up with the excuse that I'm thirsty.

There is so much tension in the room it feels like I'm trying to run through water as I cross over to the fridge. I can feel Murphy wanting to ask me if I've given "us" any more thought, and I'm sure he knows I want to ask him what's going on with him and Taylor. It's been so many days between his big confession that I'm starting to wonder if it was even real. And neither of us wants to bring up anything that might break the spell. Just being in each other's presence lately has been intoxicating. Our feelings for each other are forbidden, and wrong, and therefore incredibly hot.

After rooting around in the refrigerator for an impolite amount of time, I grab a Diet Coke and pop the tab. When I turn around, Murphy is there, and he grabs my face and kisses me with all his might, pushing me up against the fridge. His kiss is so full of passion I lose complete control, dropping my soda on the ground and wrapping my arms around his neck. The already infinitesimal gap between us closes, every cell in our bodies charged with heat. In one movement he pushes up my skirt and slides me farther up the fridge so I can wrap my legs around him, and I feel like I'm going to explode if I can't have him, right here and now.

But just as suddenly as it begins, we hear the rattle of keys from the side porch signaling Cecile's return, and Murphy drops me like a sack of potatoes. I hastily grab the towel from the fridge's door handle and act like I've been on the floor all along, diligently mopping up the spilled soda. Murphy darts over to the sink to retrieve the paper towels.

"What happened here?" Cecile demands.

"He did it," I say, pointing at Murphy, while he simultaneously says, "She did it," and points to me. We laugh. We continue sopping up the mess until Cecile taps her watch and tells us we're going to be late, that she'll finish cleaning up. Murphy and I make our way up to standing, hurriedly dispose of our towels, get a gruff kiss on the cheek each from Cecile, and rush out the door to my car.

We resume laughing once safely in Blue, and when I rest my hand on the gearshift, Murphy reaches over and covers it with his. In this moment, my questions about whether or not he really has feelings for me or is just a horny teenage boy disappear. This isn't only about sex. Not for him. Not for me, either. It's love. First love.


When Murphy's done practice and a warm bowl of his mother's tomato soup fills his belly, he calls me. I'm still so shocked by the realization that I'm in love with my best friend, I can hardly speak.

"What's with you?" he demands, after a silence longer and more awkward than we've ever sustained.

"I . . ." It's all that can come out at first.

"Yeah?"

"I wish things were different."

"Meaning?"

"You and Taylor."

"That's all I needed to know," he says, and hangs up the phone.

# CHAPTER TWELVE

# RUBY

*Now*

56 Main is packed, proving that Sunday brunch is not just hellish in the elitist bistros of New York, but in all parts of the world. I fight through the crowd, trying to spot my friends while simultaneously trying not to make eye contact with the people around me. The last thing I want is to run into my third-grade teacher or one of the families I used to babysit for before I realized my general dislike of children under ten. I very much want to avoid a conversation with a kid who doesn't remember me changing their diapers, and is now all awkward and pimply and gives off the sticky scent of puberty. "My, how you've grown!" and "I remember when you were this big" are platitudes I would very much like to keep out of my vernacular.

I spot the crew at a long table at the back of the restaurant. I take a deep breath, telling myself this is the last thing I have to do before my mother drives me to Drummond, where I will board a plane and put everything that's happened here back into the little Chatwick box I keep buried deep, deep inside my emotional closet. Yesterday was the only day I was able to successfully hide in my room, feeling guilty that I wasn't visiting Charlene or trying to get together with Ally, or even talking to my own mother. So when Steph called to invite me to this last-minute gathering, sweet as can be, I couldn't say no.

Now that I'm here, I wish I had said my flight left much earlier than it does. The table my friends occupy is huge, and peppered with outsiders I wasn't expecting. Steph is seated at the middle of the table, next to Emmett. They are turned away from each other, speaking to people on either side of them—Emmett to his parents, Steph to a girl I don't recognize, who is sitting next to Murphy. Two older people sit across from Steph and Emmett, whom I assume are Steph's parents, and another couple our age sit next to them. At the far end of the table are Aaron and Ally. They are both frowning, but Ally brightens when she sees me, waving me over.

"I saved you a seat," she says. I smile and sit in the empty chair. Something about Ally has always made me seek her approval; that's probably why even when we were kids, I struggled to share things with her. Looking back, it was less because she was a gossip than the fact that I always wanted her to like me, and telling her all the awful things I thought or felt or did risked her thinking poorly of me. But times like now, when she saves me a seat and goes out of her way to make me feel included, in a situation where I am clearly an outsider, makes me feel the same way I did when I was in fourth grade and Ally wanted me to sit next to her at lunch. Cool. Special. In.

I survey the room. 56 Main is a new restaurant, at least since I've been gone. When I lived here, it was called McAlister's, and the room we now sit in was an ice-cream parlor where I worked illegally the summer I was fourteen, earning $3.50 an hour under the table plus half the tip jar (anywhere from twenty-five cents to two dollars). I made sundaes and ice-cream cakes and covered everything edible in hot fudge, sneaking it into my mouth between customers. The brass bars I used to polish every night and the garish rubber-rimmed maroon area rugs have been removed, but copper fans still hang from the multicolored beveled ceilings.

Ally reads my mind. "Remember when I used to come in, and you would charge me for a small but give me an extra-large?" she asks. I smile in the conspiratorial way we always smile. I do remember.

I say hello to Emmett's parents; his mother says how good it is to see me. It is nice to see her, too, although I'm not entirely sure why they're here. It seems kind of formal to have your parents present at a brunch with all your friends, but maybe this is how things are done when you all live in the same town, once you're adults? Should I have asked Nancy to come along?

Steph notices me and gets out of her chair to greet me. She introduces me to her parents, and to the couple sitting next to them, who are Steph's friend Elizabeth and her husband, AJ. Elizabeth smiles and waves, too far across the table to shake hands. AJ nods his head at me and goes back to laughing with Murphy about something. My inner twelve-year-old wonders if they are laughing at me, like the day Emmett pointed out to the cafeteria that I was wearing a bra. Jesus, I really need to get out of here.

Steph introduces me to the girl sitting next to Murphy, Krystal, and tells me that she, Elizabeth, and Krystal grew up together in our rival town of Branton (pronounced around here as Bray-in, the "n" and "t" in the middle skipped over like a waste of time). Krystal smiles and says it's nice to meet me, but the warmth does not reach her eyes. She has acrylic nails, an orangey hue to her skin that can only be attributed to self-tanner, and her hair is highlighted to within an inch of its life. Despite her somewhat cool attitude, I try to project friendliness and full acceptance of the fact that she is sitting in what would historically be my seat, the empty one next to Murphy.

We all hold our menus without reading them, distracted by our individual pockets of conversation. My end of the table is oddly quiet, especially considering I'm next to Ally, so I follow the conversation of Emmett's and Steph's parents, laughing politely in the pauses of well-polished childhood stories, most of which I was present for. Every so often I risk a glance down the table at Krystal and Murphy. I notice that whenever she speaks, she puts one hand on Murphy's arm. Whether she's claiming him as her own or just trying to make sure he realizes she's there, I'm not sure. I also notice, as she does it, that Murphy tenses or shoots her a warning look.

"That girl, Krystal?" I ask behind my menu to Ally. "What's the deal with her?" I am as casual as I can possibly be, considering I'm starting to get a sinking feeling about the relationship status of the man I slept with just days earlier.

*When it comes to things that really matter, you guys barely even know each other.*

"They're 'special friends,'" she says with air quotes, rolling her eyes.

I knit my eyebrows, plastering an artificial smile on my face to keep up the pretense for any onlookers. "What does that mean?"

"Well, everyone knows they're sleeping together, but Murphy insists they aren't a couple. I can't blame him—she's really obnoxious."

"Hmm." I can feel the patches of furious red hives start to spread on my chest, and I adjust my cotton scarf to cover them up more completely. Girlfriend or not, Murphy's been sleeping with this girl, and he didn't even see fit to mention her to me? Preferably *before* we had sex?

Krystal looks down the table then and catches Ally's eye. I

worry that she overheard us, but she calls down, "Hey, Al! Are we on for Zumba class tonight?"

"Of course," Ally says, as if they are best friends. When Krystal looks away, I raise my eyebrows at Ally. She whispers, "Well, she asked me to go with her, what was I supposed to say?" I can't help but laugh. Ally will never change. She could hate your guts, but she couldn't be mean to your face if you kicked her in the shin.

After we put in our orders, Emmett clinks the side of his mimosa glass to get our attention. I wonder briefly if he should be mixing alcohol with the blood-thinners he told me he has to be on. It used to be I would never question his stringent following of doctor's orders, but in light of his self-prescribed anti-anxiety treatment, I can't be sure.

"I have an announcement to make," he says and he looks at Steph, who blushes and shrugs her shoulders up, ducking her head slightly.

I suddenly know what he's about to say, the reason we are all here, the reason both of their parents are here. I feel dumb for not figuring it out the second I walked in.

"Steph and I are getting married," he says. "We've decided New Year's Eve will be the big day." Krystal, Elizabeth, and all the parents immediately squeal in delight, leaping from their chairs and surrounding Emmett and Steph. The rest of us are on a five-second delay. In those five seconds, my mouth goes dry and I forget how furious I am with Murphy as my eyes automatically search for his. I know we are thinking the same thing. Emmett used to say he planned to hold out on marriage as long as possible. Has he just grown up and fallen in love? I mean, I can't imagine anyone more worthy of the change than Steph. But is this his "as long as possible"? Why so soon? New Year's Eve is less than four months away. Is he not telling us something?

I feel Ally's hand squeeze mine under the table. It's both a reassurance that she's as scared as me and a reminder we're supposed to be enthusiastic, too. I feel us mentally put our hands in the center and break with a "Go team," as we jump up in unison to congratulate the happy couple. I'm either noticeably stiff as I hug Emmett or he was just as much a part of our psychic huddle as the rest of us, because he whispers in my ear, "It's not what you're thinking. I said I'm going to be fine, and I am. I promise." I relax, sending out vibes to Ally and Murphy to do the same. After the week we've had, our reaction isn't out of doubt that Steph is the one; it's out of fear that another of our friends will disappear.

The food arrives and we all take our seats. Krystal, Elizabeth, and Steph's mother start chattering about the logistics of planning a wedding for this winter, with a family as large as Steph's. I hear Krystal faux-whisper, "How are you going to pay for a wedding? I thought you had all that debt from the operation?"

"Krys," Elizabeth says sharply, shaking her head. Emmett shoots daggers at Krystal and then at his fiancée. He may have been successful at keeping his situation from the crew, but I'm not sure how much of it was *ever* a secret from Steph's friends. And good for her. Why should she have to bear that burden on her own?

Krystal straightens her posture as if she hadn't asked the last question. She asks in a sing-songy voice I'm instantly annoyed by, "So, Stephie, who's going to be your maid of honor?" She shoots Elizabeth a competitive look, which I would probably chalk up to being for show if I hadn't disliked her from the moment we met.

"Actually," Steph says, "I would love it if you would be my maid of honor, and if Elizabeth would be my matron of honor."

Well played, Mrs. Soon-to-Be McDowell. Krystal's mouth

drops for a half second into a little pout, before realizing she's being watched closely by the rest of the table. "Of course!" she says, hugging Steph to her and managing to conjure up some happy tears.

"That's right, I forgot you can have both of us, since Krys isn't married," Elizabeth says, seemingly without harmful intent, although I'm starting to see that the nature of their friendship is a little more overtly rivalrous than that of most girls, who are the exact same way, only they are better at hiding it. Krystal purses her lips and shoots a meaningful glance at Murphy. He doesn't seem to notice.

"And Murphy will be my best man," Emmett says, grinning.

"What? No courting process? You're not even going to ask me if I want the job?" Murphy cries in mock offense. The rest of the table laughs.

"No," Emmett says, to more laughter.

"What about your brothers?" Ally asks.

"They'll be groomsmen, but they live too far away," he shrugs. I know that's not the real reason, it's just a convenient excuse. Murphy would be Emmett's best man even if his brothers lived next door to him. He asks Aaron and AJ to be groomsmen as well.

"We're going to ask Charlene to do a reading," Steph says. "One of Danny's poems." A quick glance at Ally reveals I'm not the only one touched by this. "We had to find some way to honor him. He was so helpful to us before he died."

Emmett puts his hand over Steph's, and her eyes widen as she realizes she's said something she isn't supposed to say. I don't look at Ally, but I know her radar must be up along with mine. Danny? Helpful? To Emmett? How? By selling him weed?

"Of course we're not sure we'll find one that's appropriate," Emmett laughs, glossing over it.

"You will," I assure him. Danny had notebooks and notebooks full of poems, and while most of them were dark and haunting, he let me read a few that radiated love from every drop of ink. He would never tell me who they were about. I can't imagine Jenny Albrecht inspiring that kind of prose.

"Ally, would you be one of my bridesmaids?" Steph asks.

"I would be honored." The way she says it is practiced, and I wonder how many brides she has stood up next to over the years. She was probably maid of honor at the wedding of Tara, who (Ally had informed me at Margie's) married a soldier in college and had a baby six months later. Ally is little Wyatt's godmother, and when she showed me pictures on her phone I nearly choked. Tara, my old friend, mother to an eight-year-old boy. Emmett refuses to acknowledge his existence, even though they broke up years before Tara and Wyatt's father got together. Ally doesn't understand his inability to let it go, but she's *married* to the first person she fell in love with. We always feel like our first love is ours forever, far beyond the point when they're no longer in our lives.

"And, Ruby," Steph says, "Emmett and I have talked about this, and I know you live in New York, so if you want to say no, we totally understand, but I'd love for you to be one of my bridesmaids, too."

I'm stunned. "Me?" I can't imagine she's serious. I only met her less than a week ago, and she wants me to be a bridesmaid? A moment ago I was wondering if I'd even be *invited*. If it weren't for Danny dying, I might not have been.

"Yes," she says, linking her arm with Emmett's and exchanging the kind of smile that makes single girls feel all the more single. "Emmett has always said he thinks of you as a sister, and family is the most important thing in the world."

My eyes sting, and I take a second to swallow back my emotion before I say, "Yes, of course. I would love to be a part of your wedding."

And just like that, my graceful exit from Chatwick disappears, and I am a member of the crew again. Full-fledged.

We remain stubbornly at our table long after our plates are cleared and both sets of parents drift off. We stir the dregs of our coffee, order another round of mimosas, and toast to Emmett and Steph. We talk about where to have the events leading up to the wedding. Without thinking, I offer to host everyone in New York for the bachelorette party. After it comes out of my mouth, I worry it will sound like I don't think Chatwick is suitable, or that I don't want to be bothered traveling back, but Steph squeals in delight, and Elizabeth says something about reenacting scenes from *Sex and the City*, and the deal is sealed.

We toast to Danny. We reminisce about high school, the last time we were all together. They reminisce about other things that happened while I was in New York or London. I suddenly ache to be a part of those stories somehow, or at the very least for my absence to have been felt. It's selfish, I know, given that I was the one who left; and it would have been impossible, given what I was carrying around. But I even wish, just a little, that I had never left. That I had made different choices. It makes no sense. Growing up, all I ever wanted to do was get out of here, and now that I'm back and surrounded by my friends, I'm wondering what was so wrong with it in the first place. I knew this would happen when I came home, and perhaps, more than anything, this is why I've stayed away so long. This place, these people, these feelings. They're intoxicating. I'm as much an addict of Chatwick, and the pain and the drama, as Danny was of anything that numbed him. I've relapsed after a ten-year run at sobriety.

*And now I'm nothing but a junkie.*

"Well, I really don't want to steal you guys' thunder, but there's something I'd like to say before Ruby disappears again," Ally says, looking pointedly at me, before squeezing Aaron's arm and smiling. Aaron's eyes widen, and I'm surprised to find him shaking his head at her. She doesn't see; she's already turned back to the group. My eyes connect with Aaron's, and I narrow mine in concentration. It's no use. Aaron grew up in Chatwick Town and didn't join our group until high school. The telepathy doesn't extend to Townies.

After a pause that allows sufficient anticipation to build up, Ally says, "We're pregnant!"

Everyone stands and another round of excited hugs is exchanged. The boys clap Aaron on the back, making lewd comments about sperm and masculinity, but Aaron remains grim. A feeling of panic courses through me, just as it had when Emmett made his announcement. Why isn't he more excited? Why didn't he want Ally to tell us? Did he feel like it wasn't the right time, or is there something wrong with the baby? I think back to the night we spent at Margie's, when I could tell Ally was lying. It was when she said her secret was nothing bad. So is there impending doom accompanying this happy news?

Ally reveals nothing as she is questioned about when the baby is due (in the middle of March) and if they are going to find out the sex of the baby (no). Every inch of her is a proud mama. She takes a sip from her glass, and I realize she's been drinking water while everyone else has been sucking down breakfast cocktails. Thinking back to the night of Margie's Pub, I remember Ally holding a clear fizzy drink with a straw. I had assumed it was a vodka soda, but it must have been just seltzer.

"Wow! So, Ally, was that what Danny had on you? Was that your secret?" Steph asks.

"Steph, please, let's not bring all that up again," Emmett says, more polite in his request than he had been the day of the reading at Danny's house. He must have learned his lesson about what happens when you tell Steph to shut up.

"Secret?" Krystal asks.

"Oh, it was the strangest thing," Steph says, turning toward her friends. "Danny had an envelope for each of them, with secrets he knew about them. He told them they had to reveal them to each other 'or else,'" she says. I am disappointed in my new friend, the way her eyes glisten with the power of information. She is not above the Chat. None of us are.

"Ooooh, what a fun little game," Krystal says. "Well, let's hear 'em!" She looks at me as she says it. The feeling that she has it in for me strengthens. Whether Murphy told her about our little rendezvous or she's just the type of person who is distrustful of new women, I don't really care. Either way, I don't feel the need to deal with her attitude any longer.

"I think the key words you missed are 'reveal them to *each other*,'" I say, forcing a smile that matches Krystal's, in that it doesn't reach my eyes. I want to say more, like "It's none of your fucking business, and keep your orange nose out of it," but I don't want to ruin the happy mood. Krystal and I remain smile-snarling at each other, neither of us looking away until Ally speaks.

"Yes, to answer your question," she says, breaking the dense air. "That was my secret. I ran into Danny at the pharmacy when I was picking up my prenatal vitamins, and he noticed. I was just too excited to make something up."

"That's fucking bullshit!" Aaron suddenly explodes. He shakes off Ally's hand and launches out of his chair.

"Aaron—" Ally starts, bewildered by her husband's sudden outrage.

"That's not your secret, and you know it," he says, fuming down at her. I've never seen Aaron look at Ally like that. Ever since high school, even when the two of them had their stereotypical adolescent squabbles, his eyes always held nothing but patience and admiration when they were trained on her. It was something I was always jealous of, something I *thought* I saw in Murphy's eyes, something I definitely saw in Jamie's. I wonder for a second what Jamie would think of this little crew, and of me suddenly reclaiming my place in it, but the combination of the champagne and my two worlds mentally colliding makes my head hurt.

"What are you talking about?" Ally says.

"I read your secret," he says. "You wouldn't open it in front of me, and then you just told me it was about the baby and wouldn't show it to me. I found it in that compartment in your purse you think I don't know about, the one with the cigarettes in it." He stops at this point and gives an aside to the group. "She hasn't had any in there since we found out she was pregnant." I'm relieved, not because Ally has finally given up her occasional secret smoke, but because despite Aaron's fury, he is still clarifying his own anger in order to defend his wife. It's a good sign.

"Oh, Aaron, you don't understand," she says, visibly deflating.

"How could you not tell me you had an abortion?" he bursts out. I can practically hear the sound of a record screeching to a halt as the rest of the dining room falls silent.

Ally's face drains of all color. "Aaron," she whisper-yells. "Please sit down, you're embarrassing me."

"I'm *embarrassing* you?" he yells. He grabs his keys from the table and storms out of the emergency side exit.

Ally turns to the group and says, with tears in her eyes, "It's not true. I mean it's true Danny wrote that, but I didn't do it! Aaron is the only man I've ever been with, and I *never* would have done that without telling Aaron about it. I would never have done that, period." She puts one hand on her stomach, reassuring her fetus of its safety. "I don't know why Danny wrote that." Tears spill onto her cheeks, and I put one hand on her back, rubbing gently.

"Come on, I'll bring you home," I say. I hug and say goodbye to Emmett and Steph, nod a "nice to meet you" at AJ, Elizabeth, and Krystal (even though the latter was a bald-faced lie), and give Murphy an aggressive slap on the back, saying I will see him at the wedding. It's a hint that I'm angry, which I hope the rest of the crew doesn't pick up on. Krystal looks from me to him, searching for signs of threat. I just smile back at her. I put my arm around Ally, who leans into me as we exit the restaurant. It should be the last thing on my mind, but I wish with my whole body that Murphy would come after us, to stop me from leaving. To tell me there is an explanation for the horrible girl sitting next to him. To tell me I mean more to him than Krystal ever could. That he wasn't simply using me for sex. It seems I've been waiting for him to do that for ten years.

Just like before, he doesn't.

# CHAPTER THIRTEEN

# RUBY

## *Back then*

"So, Murphy, have you talked to Taylor, since . . .?" Ally asks Murphy.

We are on our way to the gym for the stupid end-of-year assembly, the one where they hand out awards for things none of us have—perfect attendance, school spirit, Best Hair (well, Ally's in the running for that last one, but rumor is it's going to Gwyneth Grant and her white-girl dreadlocks). Murphy gives me the side eye and then returns to looking straight ahead, not meeting Ally's gaze or mine. He shakes his head. My heart stops. What is Ally talking about? Does she know something about Murphy and me? Is there some rumor circulating out there that I'm not aware of? Does everyone know; have they known all along, and I've been drifting along, thinking Murphy and I are in this secret bubble of shame?

"Well, is she doing okay?" Ally persists.

"I don't know, Al. I just said I haven't talked to her," he says through his teeth.

"What are you guys talking about?" I burst out. I don't want to have this conversation here, in the hallway outside the gym, with the entire student body milling around us, but I have to know.

Ally looks at me, then at Murphy, her entire face a question mark. "Murphy broke up with Taylor. Last night." She looks between us again, searching. "How did *you* not know this?"

I feel my face turning bright red, and I know Ally is already starting to be suspicious, so I tell them I forgot something in my locker and make a break for it. It only takes about five seconds to get lost in the crowd. From time to time, I shoot a look over my shoulder to see if Murphy is following me. I hope he isn't, because then Ally would *definitely* know something was up. But when I look back and don't see him, I'm disappointed, because I want to pull him into a deserted classroom and talk. Or not talk.

I can't sleep. Murphy is free. There's nothing standing between us now. Well, there's *no one* standing between us. Which means, of course, that I need to figure out what to do. Murphy is still my best friend. I'm still feeling a little guilty Taylor is hurt. I'm still going to NYU, and Murphy is still staying here.

But suddenly all these barriers don't mean as much as they did before. Now, all I can think about is being with him. Laughing with him, kissing him, making love to him. My heart is racing. I am so happy just at the thought of being with him, I feel like I'm going to burst. I can't contain it for one more second. I have to go to him. I have to tell him.

I glance at the clock. It's after midnight on a Thursday. I pick up the phone, but almost immediately put it back in its cradle. There's no way I can call him. First of all, the last time Cecile slept through a ringing phone in her house was the night Roger died. She never confirmed Murphy had snuck out of the house that night, but afterward, every time Murphy tried to steal the portable from her room, Cecile was wide awake and waiting for him. As much as Cecile and I have bonded, she is still one frightening woman. If I call her house in the middle of the night, my house had better be on fire. Even then, I think she would be displeased with my judgment to call her son instead of the fire department.

Still, I can't wait to talk to him. I can't sleep, or stop thinking, or even breathe until I get the words out. I launch out of bed and dress as quietly as possible in sweatpants and a hoodie. Then I change my mind and put on jeans. I'm about to go tell Murphy Leblanc, my best friend since seventh grade, my friend since kindergarten, that I love him. The moment calls for more than sweats. Although we *are* talking about the guy who once held me down and farted on my head until I threatened to throw up on him. So I keep the hoodie.

I creep past Coral's room; she is home for the summer only because her recent break-up left her without a place to stay. I'm more worried about her waking up than my mom. My dad is in New York this week, and my mom's bipolar meds make her sleep like the dead. I know Coral won't stop me, but seeing her will be my reality check. I don't want to think about reality right now. I just want to be happy.

I decide not to drive. I don't want the sound of the engine starting to alarm Coral—and Blue rolling into the driveway would *definitely* wake Cecile. Plus, the walk will give me a chance to work out exactly what I'm going to say. Unfortunately, it also gives all the doubts I've been pondering for a week a chance to creep in. I stop in the middle of the road. I have a scholarship to NYU. Murphy's not going to come to New York. But he could, right? Or, if he wants some time to think about it, we can do long-distance for a while. It's not like we don't have plenty of experience talking on the phone. We live in the same town, see each other almost every day, and we still manage to fill up hours every night with phone chatter. It could work. I mean, we *love* each other. What's more important than that? I keep walking.

I stop again. What if I wake up the Leblancs? Or what if they discover me trying to sneak into the house? What if I can't wake Murphy? It's a risk I have to take. I have to try to see him right now, before I chicken out. I keep walking.

Right before I get to Murphy's driveway, I stop again. What if I misunderstood? Prom night is kind of hazy, and maybe Murphy was just drunk and trying to get laid. I mean, he didn't tell me he broke up with Taylor. Why wouldn't he tell me that? But I remember the look in his eye when he danced with me at prom, when he whispered in my ear that I was beautiful out in the rain, when he picked me up outside his barber shop, when he put his hand over mine on the way to baseball practice. I keep walking, and this time I don't stop until I get to Murphy's house.

I tiptoe down the gravel driveway, sending up a thank you that his bedroom is on the ground floor of the big brick house. His window is slightly open, and I press my ear against the screen. It occurs to me, somewhat irrationally, that Taylor could be in there with him. Maybe she *had* to see him in the middle of the night, too, to try to get him back. Maybe it worked. But I don't hear anything but the fan Murphy needs to have on in order to sleep.

"Murph," I whisper, barely audible. I try again, a little louder. "Murphy." Nothing. I wonder if I should throw stones or something, like Danny used to. Like he still does sometimes, when he has nightmares and can't sleep. I think of Danny. What is *he* going to think of all this? Will he approve of his friends getting naked and falling in love? Or will he think it a disaster, like I did up until tonight? I decide against throwing stones, mostly because I would feel like an asshole throwing stones when his window is within arm's reach. I give a light knock on the sill and hear an immediate rustling of sheets. My heart is pounding so hard I temporarily can't hear or speak as Murphy's face appears in the window. On the way over, I imagined the conversation would go something like this:

*"Ruby. What the fuck?" he would say. (He's very grumpy when he gets woken up.)*

*"I need to talk to you," I would whisper.*

*"Now? Are you insane, woman?" he would demand.*

*"No, tomorrow. I just thought I would deliver an in-person twenty-four-hour notice," I would start to yell.*

Then he would meet me at the side porch entrance and we would have a very awkward conversation about our feelings for each other.

Instead, without saying a word, Murphy lifts his screen, reaches down, grabs me under my armpits, and pulls. He knows why I'm here, in the middle of the night, and it's certainly not to deliver *bad* news. I use his force to help me scale the short climb and topple into his room. Thankfully his bed is pushed up against the window, like mine, or my leg or arm or face would be broken.

He kisses me, and before I know it my shirt is off, and then his shorts are off, and then everything is off. His mouth moves all over my skin, and I bite my fist to keep from moaning too loudly. I kiss him everywhere, too, and he lets a groan escape. He fumbles through his nightstand for a condom, and I realize this is the first time we'll have had sex completely sober. But I don't feel sober. I feel high, like I'm flying. He enters me, his arms framing my head, his hands in my hair. We lock eyes as we make love. Making love. I'm not a virgin, but this is a first.

When we're finished, we lie next to each other on our sides, looking into each other, not able to stop touching one another. I know I haven't yet said what I came here to say, and I know I have to, in order to make this real. In order for us to move forward, and stop the game-playing and the secret-keeping. The words spread inside my chest, looking for an escape. It's painful. I can't say them. Saying them will kill me for sure.

"Murphy," I finally say, tentatively.

He doesn't say "What?" or "Yeah?" He just waits. He waits for several agonizing seconds.

"I love you."

"Duh, Ruby," he says, gathering me up and rolling me on top of him, my heart feeling like it's going to explode.

The next day at school, Murphy and I keep our distance until our friends are out of sight. Last night we didn't really talk about what comes next (we didn't really talk about much of anything, although I did manage to squeeze out of him that he didn't tell me he broke up with Taylor because he didn't want to put pressure on me). We can't exactly start making out in the hallways without sitting our friends down for one of those after-school special-style talks. He manages to sneak my books into his pile on the way to class, prompting me to ask him if we're going to split a milkshake before the sock-hop later. Then, once we're in class Murphy passes me a note. "Do like I did," it says. "Tell the crew you can't hang out this weekend."

"Okay," I scribble back, giddy as . . . well, as a girl in love.

The weekend is amazing. We spend most of it at my house, since Dad decided to stay in New York for the weekend and Nancy is in a milder version of a black period, which means she stays in her room and watches TV until the storm passes, instead of going out drinking. Coral is off hanging out with high-school friends, and keeps out of our hair on the rare occasion she is home. She was not a bit surprised when I filled her in on my own and Murphy's Big Feelings. "I wondered when you were going to figure that out, dummy," was all I got from her.

Murphy and I snuggle and kiss on the couch, jumping away from each other when we hear Nancy's footsteps on the creaky staircase. When she descends, she suggests we all watch a movie together and I make up an excuse to leave the house—that I'm teaching Murphy to drive standard. We decide it's not the worst idea for him to learn anyway, so we go down to the parking lot of Chatwick Elementary to give it a try. Murphy is hopeless, and we end up laughing too hard to drive. Instead, we have sex in the backseat. Famished afterward, we pick up fast food and bring it back to his house, snuggling and kissing on *his* couch now, the one in the basement, until late into the night. We fall asleep watching a stupid movie where all the actors are dressed up like apes, and wake up in the middle of the night to make love again before I sneak out to go home.

Since the warm weather has come early but my parents aren't physically or emotionally present enough to do it, Murphy spends most of Sunday morning giving our pool a final cleaning so we can take a swim. We splash around for most of the afternoon, me riding around on Murphy's back. We've done this a million times, me enjoying the weightless feeling and the close contact with another human that doesn't feel threatening; only now, I occasionally spin around to face him, and he carries me to the part of the pool that's blocked from the house's windows by the deck and presses me against the side, kissing me. As the sun starts to go down, we wrap ourselves in towels and sit close together on the rocker. I am happy and warm.

So naturally, I have to fuck it up.

"God, Murphy, what are we doing?" I ask, breaking away from a kiss.

His eyes, just a moment before full of desire and love, suddenly look panicked. "What do you mean?" he asks.

"I *mean*, you love me, I love you—now what?"

He frowns, shakes his head. "I don't know."

"Well," I say, resentful at having to pull his teeth, "are we a couple? And if so, what happens next year when I'm at NYU?"

He pulls away from me, his whole energy stiffening. "I don't know," he says quietly.

Now I panic. This is not the answer I've been expecting. As fun and wonderful as Murphy is, he's not the type to do something without thinking. Case in point, he's been in love with me for two years and hasn't said anything because he couldn't be 100 percent sure of how it would all turn out. I guess, knowing this, part of me assumed Murphy already had some kind of plan about how to move forward.

"Ruby, we're having a nice day. Do we have to talk about this now?"

I look at him, exasperated. How is this not an important conversation to have? And why is he so caught off-guard? I mean, did he *forget* I'm going away to school next year? We sit in silence for several minutes, questions racing through my mind like the ticker tape at the bottom of the CNN Money channel my father always has on in the background when he's home.

My frustration turns on a dime to regret. We *were* having a nice day, and now there is a frost in the air that I'm unsure how to thaw. True, we *do* need to have this conversation, but it doesn't need to be right now. We just began to enjoy each other, and now there is a physical space between us that hasn't existed in over thirty-six hours. I have a fleeting feeling the gap will never again be closed, but I dismiss it as silly.

"No. We don't have to talk about it now," I say, forcing a decidedly chipper tone. "Come on, let's go get a snack." Although the last thing I feel like doing is eating. Suddenly I feel like I have ten pounds of lead in my stomach.

"Actually, you know what?" Murphy says, standing and drying off vigorously with his towel and pulling his shirt back on. "I forgot I told Emmett I'd help him and his dad finish their deck. I should probably go. I said I would be there an hour ago."

My mouth falls. Murphy's lying. Even if I *didn't* already know he had told the boys he would be out of town until Sunday night, I would know he's lying to me. It's not that he's obvious about it; it's just that I know him. I'm the only one who can beat him at poker, not because I'm such a skilled card player, but because I can always call his bluff. But I want to believe him now, even though I know I shouldn't, because if I don't, it means he's blowing me off. It means that, as suddenly as I've come to have him, I'm losing him.

"Okay," I say, again with forced nonchalance. "Call me later?" I cringe inwardly as soon as I say it. I'm becoming everything I hate about girls with boyfriends: purposely ignorant, clingy, dependent.

"Yeah," he says, forcing a smile, "of course." He stoops to give me an awkward kiss on the cheek, and then hightails it through the gate.

He doesn't call me later. He barely looks at me the next day at school, and he doesn't return my calls the next day, or the day after that, or after that. And even though something in me *knew* from the second he pulled away from me on my deck that it was over, that he had changed his mind, I'm still not prepared for Friday morning, when I see him headed down the stairs at school. Just as I'm about to call out his name, to confront Murphy then and there and make him tell me what the hell is going on, I notice he's not alone.

He's holding hands with Taylor.

Over the weekend I hide from my friends, too shocked and hurt to trust myself around them. Murphy doesn't call to explain what I saw, even though we made direct eye contact for long enough that he almost fell down the stairs. He doesn't even call to see how I'm doing.

It's not until Monday, when I'm alone at our bank of lockers, that he walks up and says hello, casually, as if it were any other day. In response I hastily swap my paper-bag-covered Calculus book for my Journalism notepad and slam my locker door. He dances around to block me from leaving. "You're just not going to talk to me?" he demands.

He looks hurt. Legitimately hurt, as if *I'm* the one in the wrong. "Why should I?" I shoot back. "You didn't talk to me before getting back together with Taylor."

"Tuesday," he starts.

"Don't call me that. Don't call me anything. I don't want to talk to you."

"You have to let me explain," he says, pleading, his eyes watering.

"It would have been nice if you had 'explained' before I had to see the two of you together, like you and I—" I wave my finger between the two of us, and then falter. The lump in my throat prevents me from saying, "like you and I never happened."

"Look, I'm sorry, okay? I didn't mean for it to happen like that. I was trying to figure out how to tell you, and then Taylor came to talk to me before I saw you, and it . . . sorta happened."

I feel like I'm going to be sick. I'm looking at a boy I've shared everything with, whom I love, who I thought loved me, but he's explaining himself as if he had smoked my last cigarette, instead of stomping on my heart in the middle of the hallway.

"It's just, when I thought about you going away to school, and being without you, I'd be so miserable when you were gone. And then you would come home for a weekend or for Christmas and I'd be so happy, and then you would just leave again. I don't think I could handle it."

The million questions that have been simmering for days burn in my throat. *Why didn't you tell me you were feeling this way, so we could work it out together? Why didn't you think of this before you told me you loved me and ruined everything? Why does that mean you have to get back together with Taylor? Did you just tell me you loved me because you wanted to sleep with me, and you thought you were safe, because it was so unlikely I would end up feeling the same way?*

Before I can decide where to start, Ally and Aaron round the corner. I want to scream, to tell them and everyone else in the hallway what is really happening. Ally would be on my side, and at least then I wouldn't be alone in this. Murphy wouldn't just get away with it. But I can't. I don't want everyone knowing that Murphy Leblanc has, essentially, played me. That I'm a complete idiot. That I'm heartbroken and weak. I lean close to him and growl, "You're a coward, and you make me sick. Don't talk to me."

I hug my notebook to my chest and turn to go to class. Of course I don't really mean it. I want him to know that I'm about to be out of his life forever, and I want that to be enough for him to chase after me and tell me he's made a mistake.

He doesn't.

# CHAPTER FOURTEEN

# ALLY

## *Now*

I never understood what is so friggin' great about New York City, and I still don't get it as our bus pulls into the station. I mean, sure, the buildings are cool. They're super-tall and shiny and there are more windows in one skyscraper than in all the homes in Chatwick put together. Back home, actually in all of Vermont, I'm pretty sure, there's a law against building over a certain amount of stories. I think it's like five or six. Not that there's much call in Chatwick for buildings with more than three or four floors.

Don't get me confused with a country bumpkin. I've taken my fair share of trips to Boston for Red Sox games, and to Montreal for bar-hopping and shopping. In grade school, Ruby and Emmett and I were part of the band (Ruby played clarinet, I played trumpet, and Emmett played flute, believe it or not; he had a crush on Addie Helsley, who played the flute, and he thought it would be a good way to get close to her), and we took band trips to Washington DC and, yes, even to New York.

I mean, a city's fun for a visit, but to live? No thanks. All it is is a billion people crammed into a small space, living on top of each other, breathing in the revolting smell rafting up from the sewers. What *is* that smell anyway? It's like sour breath and dirty socks, with a hint of urine. I'm not looking forward to it, with the increased sense of smell the baby has brought on.

And why are cities always so grey? It's not just smog, it's like the *weather* is always cloudy. It's like the sun can't shine on a place with so many miserable people living in it. Ruby talks about the museums and the theatre and the restaurants, dropping the names of them like I'm supposed to be impressed, but if you ask me, you can get all of that in Vermont, there's just less choices. I don't think that's the worst thing in the world. Sometimes too many choices make people pick nothing at all, and if I'm going to pick nothing and just sit at my house, I can do that in Chatwick for a third of the cost, and I'll be able to find my way around and get a parking spot a hell of a lot easier, thank you very much.

But fine, we're here. Steph is excited to be having her bachelorette party in the Big Apple, and it's all about keeping the bride happy. (I don't know that I was given the same courtesy; it seemed to me to be more about what everyone else wanted to do, but I didn't know these girls then, so it's not their fault). I reach across the aisle to shake Steph awake. She is wearing a bachelorette sash I got at the party store, and sleeping on the shoulder of Elizabeth, who is snoring up against the window. I guess the "super-secret" Nalgene bottles filled with boxed wine that Krystal packed might not have been the best idea. They got all rowdy and obnoxious after an hour, and then they passed out for the rest of the ride. I guess if I weren't pregnant, I would be in the same boat. But I'm a mother now, so I have to be the responsible one. Who am I kidding? I would have had to be the responsible one anyway. I always have been. Emmett *thinks* he is, because he's all upstanding citizen-y, but all he cares about is himself. I'm the one who has to think about everyone else.

The girls and I get up and stretch. We're at the back of the bus at my request (near the bathroom, since I have to pee every ten seconds), so we have to wait until all the other passengers file out. I hear a knock on the side of the bus, and when I look, I see Ruby standing there in a blue peacoat that probably cost more than my first car. Her hair comes down in long waves from a cable-knit hat. The curls have kinks at the bottom, and I know I will have to fix them for her. The girl never did get the hang of a curling iron. It's cute that she tried, though.

She waves one mittened hand at us. The other is holding a sign in Ruby's computer-neat handwriting that says "Chatwick Bitches." I laugh when I see it, glad she is still the same old potty-mouth Ruby and not some proper city snob. She laughs too, and when she does, a little puff of fog fills the air. It's early December, and it hasn't snowed yet back home, and it doesn't look like New York has gotten any, either. Usually we've gotten at least a dusting by Halloween. The smart parents order their kids' costumes one or two sizes larger so they can fit over a parka. It's funny to watch the neighborhood fill up with puffy little witches and Supermans. Anyway, I wish the snow would come. I'd rather it snow than simply be cold and dead and grey. God forbid we have a White Christmas and start and end winter on time.

It's been a l-o-o-o-o-n-g fall. The shitstorm Danny unleashed with his little team-building exercise back in September still hasn't settled down. I mean, it's great we know about Emmett. It's better in the long run that we know. It's not being nosy, it's just that I think it's always better for stuff to be out in the open. How else can you deal with it? But then the little fucker—Danny—makes up a secret for me that isn't even true. I'm all for women making their own choices and all that, but it's not a choice I could ever personally make. The only reason I can possibly think for Danny making that up is to cause trouble for me and Aaron, because we're happy and he was miserable. But if that were his point, wouldn't telling my real secret probably do enough damage?

The worst thing is, it's working. Everyone is taking the word of a heroin addict over me, including my own husband. I've tried everything to get Aaron to believe me. I even offered to get him a copy of my medical records, but he said I could have gone to Planned Parenthood under another name. He even accused me of cheating on him! He says that's the only reason he could see for me not telling him about the baby—that it wasn't his. The man I married, the man I've loved for half my life, thinks I am capable of that. After that conversation I gave up on trying to get him to believe the truth and started being angry right back at him. So, yeah, my second trimester has been *great*, thanks for asking.

Notice also that Murphy and Ruby haven't said Word One about what's in *their* envelopes. If you buy that load of bull about Danny's secret being theirs, too, you are a fool. Now, Murphy is one thing. You can't ever expect Murphy to take responsibility for anything he does. But Ruby? I expected more from her. I'm not sure why. I mean, she *did* basically chuck our friendship (and all our friendships) the minute she pulled out of her driveway for college. And *perhaps* I'm a little bitter because all she has to do is show up at Danny's funeral and everyone acts like she's some hero, simply for gracing us with her presence. Meanwhile, she wouldn't have even come if it hadn't been for me.

I was so mad about how she expressed her condolences when I called to tell her the news, as if it were *my* loss and not hers. Like I was telling her my grandmother or my dog had died. In that minute I left open for her while I was crying, she put up the wall that separated herself from me, from us. Sure she'd been away for a while, and God knows why. The girl already missed my wedding, and I didn't make a peep. I just wrote her a nice thank-you card for the champagne flutes she sent from London. But there's no registry for people who have lost a son or a childhood friend. I wasn't going to let her just send flowers, throw some money at the problem and bury it like Danny was about to be buried. She needed to be there. She needed to come back to help fill at least a little bit of the space Danny left open. And I'm glad she did, even though it's been nothing but a rollercoaster ride ever since.

The wedding is only four weeks away, and we're having the bachelorette party now instead of a week before the wedding (like most people do) because of Christmas. It's just too hard to get everyone together. Planning this has been like being a dentist. I feel like giving birth is going to be easier than being a bridesmaid in this wedding. Every time there's a decision to be made, I make sure to text Elizabeth, Krystal, and Ruby all at once, because if I start with just one person, Krystal or Elizabeth give me attitude about being left out of the loop. Of course, when I text everyone, the only one who responds is Ruby, and she always says, "Whatever you guys think is fine with me!" which is *so* helpful, especially when Krystal refuses to respond because she is offended I've included Ruby, who she considers to be a bridesmaid "in name only," whatever that means. But if I do something based only on Elizabeth's response, Krystal throws a hissy fit, to make sure I know Elizabeth and she are equal to each other but above everyone else, and just because Elizabeth and I are married doesn't mean we should be the ones deciding everything. I feel like Jerry friggin' Springer with these girls.

We get off the bus and Ruby hugs all of us. Me, because it's me; Steph, because you have to hug the bride, even if you've only met her once before; and Elizabeth and Krystal, probably because she doesn't want to be rude, although those hugs are awkward. Elizabeth is surprised by it, and Krystal makes a big show of hugging back with both arms, like the two of them are the best of friends, even though Krystal has decided to hate Ruby just like every girl Murphy dated in high school did.

Ruby takes my luggage, even though it's a rolling suitcase and I'm perfectly capable of handling it. We cross the street after waiting like ten hours for the pedestrian light to give us the go-ahead. We have a couple of lights like this in the busier intersections of Chatwick, but no one uses them. When there's two lanes of traffic instead of these six, it's pretty easy to tell for yourself when you have enough time to cross. Ruby hails a cab without breaking conversation, and I can't help but feel a little proud of her. I remember her being kind of awkward, especially in groups of girls. She was always quiet and let others take the lead, except when she and Emmett would get into it about politics, or whatever smarty-pants shit they were talking about. Here she smiles a lot, she leads us around like it's nothing, and she chatters with us excitedly about our trip and our plans for the weekend. Her eyes shine. Her skin glows. I don't know if it's because she's older and more confident or if New York brings out the best in her. Maybe there's something about the grey of everything that makes her more colorful. At any rate, I'm starting to rethink my opinion that Ruby has stayed away so long just to be stubborn and prove us all wrong.

After a terrifying cab ride to a place she tells the driver is called Murray Hill (I don't know if that's the name of her building or what; I thought we were in Manhattan?), we are finally at her apartment. She apologizes once for every flight of stairs we have to carry our luggage up (so about seven times). It's amazing that in New York City they haven't heard of elevators. Isn't it a law that you have to have them in buildings with multiple stories? How do handicapped people get around in this city? It's hard enough just being pregnant and having to hike up all these stairs. Now I see why Ruby has designated herself as my bellhop, and I'm grateful for it.

She shows us into her apartment, which she's decorated with streamers and balloons and a *lot* of penis paraphernalia. Steph is excited, and I can tell she feels special that Ruby went to the effort. It's weird, Ruby's never before shown any signs of her mother's homemaking skills, which is fine, because that means she hasn't shown signs of her mother's crazy, either. I remember Ruby's birthday parties growing up: there was always a theme and her mother would make these elaborate cakes and decorations. It was the one thing Nancy could be counted on, to make a big deal of her children on their birthdays. More birthdays than not, anyway.

Some of that must have stuck to Ruby. Not only did she go all out with the bachelorette decorations, but underneath all the fluorescent crepe paper and penises there's a pretty decent apartment, decorated simply and comfortably. Unlike her mother's house, there are no pink flowers or girly prints of any kind, but it's clean and cozy and well lit and there are a couple of throw pillows and blankets. There are no dishes in the sink or cockroaches on the floor or rats scurrying through, so right away it's more than I was expecting. (Tidiness was never Ruby's strong suit as a teen. I suspect being messy was her way of rebelling, since she didn't drink much. Well, being messy and her whole Hardy Crane phase.)

The place isn't huge, but there's a decent living space with a small, modern kitchen and bathroom. I'm surprised at the second bedroom, as from what I hear it's impossible to afford a two-bedroom apartment in this city. Ruby explains that her sister lives here on and off when she's not traveling for her job. Coral is a photographer, and I guess her work is kind of unpredictable but pays well enough when she can get it that she can afford to pay rent at a place she doesn't actually live. Must be nice. Right now I think she's in Argentina. Or Armenia. One of those.

I put my things in Ruby's room. We worked out ahead of time that I would sleep in her bed, because she knows me best. Then Steph and Krystal and Elizabeth will sleep in the spare room on either the double bed or the small blow-up mattress that looks brand-new; Ruby must have purchased it for our stay. I get the feeling she hasn't had visitors before, and I wonder for the first time what her New York friends are like. Does she have a tight group of friends like the crew? Is there a New York version of an Ally, an Emmett, a Danny? Or does she keep to herself, without anyone forcing her not to? I can't decide which scenario makes me more sad.

I pick up a picture on her nightstand of her and a man I don't recognize. He's handsome in a nerdy kind of way, glasses and all. I show it to her. "Holding out on me?" I ask. It would be just like Ruby to have a boyfriend all this time and not tell anyone about him.

She shakes her head. "That's Jamie."

I remember the name. He's the reason she stayed in London, although she said it was for "a job opportunity." He's the reason she wasn't home for my wedding.

"That was actually taken last year, I spent Christmas with his family in Bloomsbury."

"Didn't you guys break up when you moved back to the States? That was at least two years ago."

"Yeah," she shrugs. "We're still friends. He's kinda my best friend, actually."

I look at her like I'm always looking at her, like she's got snakes coming out of her ears. But that answers my question. If Ruby's best friend is an ex-boyfriend who lives on another continent, how happy can she *really* be here?

"Just because Jamie and I didn't work as a couple, it doesn't mean we don't care about each other. Besides, I've done enough cutting people out of my life simply because they've hurt me."

"Or sometimes for no reason at all," I say before I can think. She winces. "I'm sorry," I say, even though I'm not. Not really.

"It's okay." She starts to say something else, but our conversation is interrupted by the girls in the spare bedroom. Krystal "calls" the bed, but Elizabeth points out that Steph should get first pick because she's the bride, and Steph is trying not to piss either of them off by pretending not to care. These girls. I wonder if Ruby had never left town and the two of us still hung out all the time, would we still act like we were in high school?


"Do you need anything before I turn out the light?" Ruby asks. It wakes me up. We only got back to Ruby's place about twenty minutes ago, but I was asleep before my head hit the pillow. I actually fell asleep in the cab on the ride home, despite Krystal and Steph screaming the lyrics to an old Britney Spears song at the top of their lungs. I must have gone deaf and passed out. Or maybe it's just the weekend that's exhausting me. Cities are tiring enough as it is with all the walking, but being pregnant is a whole other ball of facts.

I hate to say it, but I can't wait to go home tomorrow. Don't get me wrong. It's been fun, and Ruby's been great. She took us to this restaurant last night where you sit on the floor and eat with your hands, which was . . . different, although the baby didn't seem to enjoy the food. Then to see *Mamma Mia* on Broadway, which was really fun. She says she got the tickets free from a "hookup at work." I don't know if she meant a connection from one of her advertising clients or a coworker she's hooking up with. When I asked, she just giggled like I had told a joke. Either way, it was nice to do something where I could sit down and not feel left out because I can't drink. I think Ruby planned this on purpose because of me, which was nice of her.

Even though I've known her all my life, there have been times this weekend when I feel like I'm getting to know Ruby right along with Steph and Elizabeth and Krystal. Who knew she was such a considerate person? I mean, she's always been *nice* and friendly to people, at least until they give her a reason not to be. And I remember she was always good about offering to share. Like if she was using lip gloss or eating gum, she would always offer it to me, too. And we almost always shared cigs, even if we had more than one. There was something about the passing of it back and forth that made us feel connected, I think. Like with each puff we were taking on a bit of the other's pain—the fight she escaped from at home, the worry that Aaron would cheat on me like my dad always did on my mom. Damn, I miss smoking.

Today we went shopping, which was a *huge* ordeal. Krystal insisted on going to stores like Prada and Manolo Blahnik, just to say she'd been there, but we would get in there and the sales associates would give us the stink-eye because we're so obviously not rich, making us all feel like shit. Then Krystal would shout about how expensive everything was, making us all embarrassed to be seen with her. She also insisted on taking pictures in front of the signs of each store and every landmark we went to afterward, and she would always ask Ruby to take the pictures, like it was a Chatwick girls' trip and Ruby was the tour guide instead of part of our group. Ruby didn't complain, but by the end of the day I could see the little wrinkles around her lips that mean she's irritated.

I don't know what's gotten into Krystal, either. I mean, she's always a bit much, but you'd think she was the *bride* this weekend with the amount of attention she's demanding. For example, at lunch Steph asked Ruby to tell the mushroom story again, which was a big hit. Everyone's laughing, even me, who's not only heard it before but actually *lived* it, and Krystal cuts in and starts talking about how she knows what we mean about Murphy's deep sleep, and how she practically has to slap him awake "every morning," (as if that was the point of the story). Steph and I make eyes at each other; we know very well she doesn't live at Murphy's, and as far as we know she only sleeps over on the nights he can't find anyone else to take home from Margie's. But for the rest of the day, it was Murphy this and Murphy that. "Oh, Murphy would love that shirt, I have to go in and get it for him," and "Murphy told me he loves it when I wear black, so I really want to find a sexy black dress for the rehearsal dinner." It's like since Murphy's out of earshot, she's given herself free rein to pretend he's her boyfriend. But trust me, she is a girl playing make-believe. Murphy hasn't settled down with anyone since Taylor, and if you ask me he never really settled down with her, either, if you know what I mean. And Krystal? He's just using her for sex. I'm not saying it's right, but it seems to be their understanding.

It's obvious Krystal (like every girl who's ever been dumb enough to like Murphy) feels threatened by Ruby, and hearing that they slept on the trampoline together probably triggered her competitive instinct. It's funny because, even though we all wondered if something more was going on between the two of them, them sleeping on the trampoline together was the one thing that *didn't* raise a red flag. The real couples always took the bedrooms (for privacy), and Ruby and Murphy slept *outside* where anyone could see them. Plus, they were on a squeaky trampoline. We would have heard if something was going on.

But this is what's always happened between Ruby and Murphy and their significant others. I can't say I blame people for getting jealous when the person they're dating is on the phone with someone else of the opposite sex for hours on end. Even though Ruby was always overly nice to Murphy's girlfriends, some of them would draw the line with Murphy. It was them or Ruby. Most of the time he dumped them. Sometimes, if the girl had particularly large breasts, things would get chilly between him and Ruby for a few weeks. But that never lasted. Part of the reason Murphy and Taylor lasted so long is because Ruby moved away and stopped talking to all of us. Ruby's boyfriends didn't stand a chance, either, with Murphy being so "protective" of her. He would either get all Puffy-Chested Tough Guy about it or freeze the guy out entirely. He used to say if they weren't man enough to stand up to him, they weren't strong enough to handle a girl like Ruby, and it was better she find out sooner, so she didn't get hurt. The one guy who did stand up to him was Hardy, and we all know what good that did her.

So anyway Ruby did a good job at being super-polite with Krystal, but her lips got more and more wrinkly as the day went on. By the time we got to the male strip club where she had reserved us a table, she was drinking double vodka tonics. She didn't have a lot of them, but as she sipped I couldn't help but think of Nancy rattling the ice in her glass, to scare up every last trace of alcohol after a particularly hard day.

Now I know this might sound bad, but when Ruby went to the bathroom, she left her phone on the table next to mine, and when it vibrated I picked it up. *For the record*, I thought it was mine at first. But when the notification said, "Text Message from Jamie Wells," I pressed the button to open it before I could stop myself. It said, "Reading Steinbeck and thinking of the time we had a row over his merits. Years later, I'm finally giving him a second chance. You were right, it's gorgeous. Xoxo J." Best friends, my ass. Like she and Murphy were best friends? It's like she has a permanent blind spot for the men in her life.

Tonight was less fun for me, not that it matters. Steph had a great time, and *that's* what matters, stuffing singles into G-strings and getting lap dances. But do you know how *weird* it feels to be pregnant in a *strip club*? From the looks I was getting, I felt like a hooker in church. I kept trying to cover my swollen belly with my coat, but it still didn't feel right. So when Ruby asks me if I need anything, all I can think is that I want to be at home. Not the home that exists now, but the one I had before Danny died, when I had a husband who loved and trusted me, who was excited to bring the baby growing inside me into this world. And because I'm exhausted, and because it's Ruby, I tell her that's what I want.

Ruby isn't facing me, but her posture slumps. She hangs her head, and then rests it in her hands. "I'm so sorry, Al," she says.

I roll up to my elbow and reach out to touch her back. She gives a little start. She doesn't like being touched unexpectedly, even now. "Thank you, but it's not your fault," I say.

She nods and turns to me. "Yes, it is." I watch her, not understanding, as she opens the drawer to her nightstand and pulls out the envelope labeled "Ruby" in Danny's handwriting. "It's my fault," she says, "because I think Danny mixed up our secrets."

# CHAPTER FIFTEEN

# RUBY
## *Back then*

Today is a day I'm supposed to feel happy, accomplished, joyful, hopeful. At the very least proud.

I feel nothing.

After the ceremony, my friends gather behind the gymnasium for group pictures in our caps and gowns. I smile through gritted teeth at the other end of the row from Murphy, who gets to enjoy this day. Then Taylor, who sat with the Leblancs during the ceremony, jumps into the photo session as if she's been a part of the crew all along. I step out of frame, letting myself get swallowed up in a sea of cheap green polyester. For a moment I stand in the same spot where Murphy told me only weeks earlier, as we stood in the rain in a gown and a tuxedo, that I was beautiful.

Each of us has our own family graduation celebration before we're supposed to meet up at Tara's house later for the big party. My parents and Coral and I are going to Rick's Seafood for dinner, and that leaves a few hours to kill. I can't decide if it's worse to be alone with my thoughts or endure the exhaustion of pretending I'm happy for my family's sake.

At home, Nancy hands me a card with Murphy's name on it and instructs me to run it over to his house. I hold it up to the light. There's money in it. Nancy is sending me to the boy who broke my heart with a cash reward in hand. Because he's "part of the family." Meaning: he was the one who was there for me when my parents weren't. Also meaning: he would sometimes carry Nancy to bed after she passed out on the kitchen floor, and was polite enough never to bring it up again.

I could refuse, or even pop it in the mail, but as much as I hate Murphy, I want to see him, too. I want him to see me and feel awkward because I'm there. I want him to feel the same discomfort I feel, as if he could even handle it. I want him to have a chance to realize he made a mistake.

I pull up to see Murphy's entire family, including his extended family from Quebec, milling around the yard. Murphy's back is to me, playing volleyball with his cousins, occasionally hollering out a swear word in French to make the younger ones giggle. Before I can take so much as a step toward him, Taylor spots me. She waves enthusiastically and then bounds up to me like she hadn't just seen me hours ago.

"Ruby! I'm so glad you're here. Everyone's speaking French, and I have no idea what they're saying." She lowers her voice. "I think they might be talking about me."

My annoyance at her presence softens. It isn't her fault what Murphy's done, as much as I want to blame it on her. If anything, I'm the one to blame. "I know how you feel. I used to think that, too. But it's more likely they're talking about snowmobiling or hunting." I somehow manage the energy to smile.

She exhales, relieved, and then a light bulb seems to come on. "Murphy said you weren't coming," she says.

"Oh, I can't stay. My mom just wanted me to drop this off to him." I wave the envelope.

"Wow, your mom is giving Murphy a graduation present? And I saw one on the counter for you, too. You guys really are like family." It seems she is reassuring herself more than looking for confirmation.

"Speaking of which," she says, "I'm really sorry about, you know, your family situation."

I stare at her blankly. "Excuse me?"

"Well, Murphy told me about your mom and how she's a little," Taylor circles her temple with her finger, "and how your dad moved out for a while until she stopped," and she simulates glugging a bottle. "That must have been really hard for you. That's why, when he told me he worried about breaking your pact to go to prom together, I was like 'Oh my God, I totally understand. The poor girl has been through enough, without getting *ditched* right before prom!'"

I want to burrow into the ground and never come out. Not only did Murphy share the personal details of *my* life with this little tween, but he actually made it seem like he felt *sorry* for me? And now this little *toddler* is in on the pity party?

"Yeah. So, look, I really have to get going. Can you give this to Murphy for me?" I shove the envelope in her hands and turn to leave, but not before Cecile catches my eye. It looks as though she's been watching me and Taylor. She points to the side entrance of the house and waves me over. I consider ignoring her, but she starts to wave me over emphatically, so I obey, following her into the kitchen.

Handing me the envelope with RUBY printed in block letters on the front, she pulls me into a hug and says, "For the daughter I never had." For Cecile, this is an emotional scene of epic proportion. Maintaining her firm grip, she says, "I'm so glad you came into Murphy's life, and mine." Just as the tears start to line my eyelids, she whispers into my hair, "And I'm so, so sorry."

I pull away, looking at her eyes. Pity. A less patronizing pity than was in Taylor's eyes moments before, but pity all the same. Cecile knows. Of course she knows. Of course Murphy would share our story with his mother. Of course her opinion would carry the most weight with him. Suddenly his words, *you would come home and I'd be so happy, and then you would just leave again* float through my head in the low, gravelly tone of Cecile's voice. It was her who advised against the heartache of a long-distance relationship. She can say she thinks of me as a daughter, but the long and the short of it is: I'm not. Murphy is her son, her baby, and she has to think about what's best for him. No matter if she's actually right. No matter who gets hurt.

I can't think of anything to say back to her. When I try, nothing comes out but a pathetic little squeak. I hold the envelope up to her to make sure she sees it, before dropping it on her kitchen counter with a thwack. Wordlessly, I exit the kitchen and climb into my car. As if sensing my presence, Murphy's eyes connect with mine before I press down hard on the clutch to shift into reverse.


The ringing phone pierces through the scene playing on the backs of my eyelids. It is an unwelcome sound, at once vanishing the streets of Paris and the harmonica and Murphy and I dancing in our prom-wear. I wince my eyes open and quickly reach out to pick up the portable from my bedside table.

"Hello?" I croak.

"Ruby St. James, where the hell have you been?" Ally's voice comes barreling through the receiver.

"Um," I start, unsure how to explain. I haven't spoken to Ally, or anyone from the crew, since Graduation Day, two weeks ago. And if it hadn't been for the knee-jerk reaction of being woken from a sound sleep, I wouldn't even have answered the phone now.

"And why do you sound like you're sleeping? It's two o'clock in the afternoon!"

*Is it?* I glance over my shoulder at my clock radio to confirm. It's across the room, strategically placed to force me out of bed to turn off the alarm each morning. The clock is another thing I've neglected since graduation. I've actually rearranged my shifts at The Exchange to afternoons, so I can wring every possible second of unconsciousness from the day. I panic for a second, thinking I am late for the second time this week (after assuring Donna I would never let it happen again), before I remember it's Sunday. The Exchange is closed, because everyone in town is at church instead of shopping for sweaters priced at $7.95.

"I must have dozed off reading," I lie, trying to force some cheeriness, or at the very least normalcy, into my voice.

"Oh yeah? Must be one hell of a book to forget about your friends for two weeks."

"I'm sorry, Al, I haven't meant to ignore you. I just have all this summer reading to do." I clench my teeth after I say it. Not only am I lying, but I'm bringing up a sore subject to deflect attention. Ally found out I was going to NYU from Murphy; I didn't tell her myself. She was hurt and confused that I kept it from her, or at least that's what she says. She's really just offended I'm going away at all. To her, it's a comment on her own choice to stay in Vermont.

She is quiet.

"I've missed you," I say, placating her. "What's new?"

"Oh, not much. Aaron is spending more time playing basketball at Barnard Park than with me. I know we're not going to be *that* far away from each other next year, but it would be nice if he wanted to spend some time with his girlfriend."

"That sucks . . . And how's Murphy?" I try to ask casually. I don't want to know, but I desperately want to know.

A pause, then, "You don't know?"

"Don't know what? What happened?" I ask. Did a tree fall on him? Did Taylor dump him? Is he in New York City, trying to figure out if he could live there with me? I don't have time to contemplate which one would be preferable.

"Nothing," she rushes to say, "I don't mean something happened. I mean, he's been kind of a prick lately. I think he's bummed that Taylor is away at horse camp, or whatever. I just mean, you don't know how Murphy is? I figured you were at least keeping in touch with *him*." Resentment drips from her voice.

"Horse camp?" I say, ignoring her jab.

"Yeah, you know, she's riding horses and shit. Aquarium camp, or whatever."

"Equestrian?" I offer, a smile beginning to twitch at my lips.

"Yeah, that's what I said." We both laugh. I bask in the thought of Taylor being away and Murphy being miserable. Then I have a sudden, wonderful thought—maybe Taylor dumped him before she went away; or better, maybe he dumped her, realizing he made a mistake when he chose her over me. Maybe that's what he's been calling to tell me, and I should have picked up the phone when I saw his number appear on the caller ID, just once out of the sixteen times. Suddenly, I have to know. But I can't ask Ally or she'll know something's up, especially considering my hibernation. And I can't simply call him. If I'm wrong, what kind of conversation will that be? I can't imagine anything more painful or humiliating.

"So there's a party at Luke's tonight. In his field," Ally says.

"Luke?"

"Danny's friend, from the garage?"

I murmur acknowledgment, even though I can't find Luke's face in my memory. I'm too occupied with thinking of all the things I want to say to Murphy.

"We're all going. It would be nice if you could take a *study break* long enough to see your oldest and dearest friends."

Suddenly it feels like that's exactly what's in order. A nice, big party with lots of people around. I can put in some face-time with the crew to alleviate my guilt. Plus, a bonfire is an easy enough setting to pull someone into a cornfield for a chat. Lots of shadows.

I ride to the party with Ally and Aaron, deep into the countryside. I'm quiet in the back of Aaron's pickup, the nerves from being out in public again, being around the people I no longer belong with, pulsing under my skin. The sun went down hours ago, leaving only a vague outline of the trees flying past my window. I wish I could jump out and hide up the highest one, so high that no one could see me.

Most of our graduated (or not graduated) class is there. Danny hugs me and Ally and slaps Aaron five, asking him to be his beer-pong partner. Aaron is known as King Pong in some circles. Murphy and Emmett haven't arrived yet, but Tara sees Ally and me and extricates herself from a crowd of rising senior girls. She drags us off for a half hour to strategize about how to act around Emmett, now that they have officially broken up. I try to be sympathetic, but I know they'll be wrapped around each other by the time their fifth beer is popped. Not that I'm in a position to judge anyone on their self-control.

When Emmett and Murphy pull in, Emmett unloads the bright-orange cooler, fishes out a cold one, and makes a beeline for the group of basketball players that just so happens to be at the opposite side of the field from me and the girls. I think he's avoiding Ally more than Tara, since Ally is the one who will call him a dickhead for the way he broke it off. Even though they had previously discussed ending things at the end of the summer, unceremoniously showing up at Tara's house with a box full of CDs, books, and clothes she left in his car was not the proper way to end a four-year relationship. Meanwhile Murphy struggles to balance the tent bag, tarp, and sleeping bags. He spots me, looking surprised. As if in two weeks he's forgotten I existed. I remind myself of the sixteen phone calls, but it doesn't help. "Tuesday, lend me a hand?" he calls out.

"No," I reply, in what I hope is a cool tone. Suddenly the idea of being even semi-alone with him makes me panicky. But when I turn back to Ally and Tara, they are both looking at me in surprise, so I sigh inwardly and go.

I grab the sleeping bags and follow him out way past the fire, almost to the corn. We are silent as we try to get the poles to come together through the little loops in the burgeoning darkness.

"You and Em looking for a little alone time tonight?" I ask, noticing how far away we are from the other tents. These are the first words I've spoken to him since that day at our lockers. The day my heart shattered.

He laughs. "I doubt Emmett will be bunking with me tonight," he says, tilting his head to a spot a little way away from the fire, where Tara and Emmett now stand arguing. "First step: fight; second step: get drunk; third step: fuck each other's brains out."

I want so badly to laugh, for everything to be back the way it was just a few months ago. But it isn't, and I can't. "So why do *you* need so much privacy?" I can practically taste the acid dripping from my words.

He tosses the rain guard over the peak, even though there isn't a cloud in the sky. "I just wanted to talk to you. You haven't answered any of my calls."

"Well, I don't understand why you're calling."

He looks genuinely taken aback.

"Because—"

I interrupt him, knowing this is my chance to ask the question I came here to ask. "Is it because you grew a set and changed your mind? Is it because you and Taylor aren't together anymore?"

He sighs deeply. "No."

Of course not. How is it possible I had hoped for anything else? Has the part of me who's grown up with my parents' fucked-up version of love learned nothing? "Well then, what's the point? You made your decision. I'm not going to beg you to be with me, if that's what you're waiting for."

"That's not what I'm waiting for."

*But why?* I want to ask. *How could you not want that? After what you said to me? After what I said to you?*

"I'm waiting," he continues, "for my best friend to come back."

"Hold your breath until she does," I say, dropping the edge of the rain guard and spinning to leave. With every step back toward the crowd, I force myself to calm my breathing, to stand up straight, to not let them see the effect Murphy's had on my heart. Despite my best efforts to appear casual about it, I believe later they will say I stormed up to where Emmett and Tara are fighting. I walk directly between them and pull Tara away. "Come on," I say to her, "you don't need this bullshit. Let's fill up, before the keg is tapped."

After filling a red Solo cup to the brim and losing Tara again to her drama with Emmett, I spot Danny sitting alone, his legs dangling from the deck of Luke's ranch-style house. The flames from the bonfire barely reach his face, but I can tell he is sulking. "Aaron's off his game tonight," he says, shaking his head as I hoist myself up next to him. He's drunk. And what's worse is, tonight he is Sad Drunk Danny instead of Fun Drunk Danny. And I'm fixing to be Stupid Drunk Ruby. This is not a good combination.

"It's just a game, dude," I say, forcing a casual air to my voice to lighten the mood. nudging him with my elbow.

"I know!" he says. "I'm not stupid."

"I never said you were s—"

"Where you been?" he cuts me off. He slugs down the rest of his beer, crushes the empty cup in his hand, and lobs it angrily at a small group of lacrosse players gathered about fifteen feet away from us. They give us the finger and move along when Danny stretches out his arms, challenging them to do something about it.

I take a sip from my cup to buy some time. As usual, the taste makes my stomach turn a little, but I'm determined to push through it. "I've been around," I say.

"Bullshit."

"Seriously! I've been getting ready for school. Driving to Drummond to get stuff I need for my dorm, doing my summer reading." I haven't done any of these things. I should be more ready than ever to get the hell out of here, but thinking about New York makes me feel sick now. "Plus, you know, hanging out with the girls before I go," I throw in for good measure, even though he knows as well as anyone that the girls of the crew haven't ever been my first priority.

He snorts lightly. "The girls," he says. He looks at me, and I see my lie in his eyes. "And what the hell is going on with you and Murphy?"

My pulse quickens. "What do you mean?"

"The only time I've seen you in the same area since graduation was right over there," he points to the cornfield where Murphy's tent is set up, "and you were fighting."

"Oh," I said, waving my hand dismissively. "That. He said something insensitive about Hardy being here tonight. You know Murph."

He nods, still looking at me like he knows I'm full of it. I don't know if he knows the truth about what happened between me and Murphy, and I can't ask. I can't hear the disappointment in his voice that I snuck around behind his back. That I kept such a secret from him, when he's always told me even the worst of the things he's done. That I'm now choosing to nurse my heartbreak alone, rather than share my misery with him, as always. As long as these things remain unspoken, maybe I can keep up the illusion that we are all just good friends, that I am an excited upcoming college freshman, ready to bust out of this wasteland of a town.

So we sit in silence until Ally and Aaron approach us, followed by Emmett, then Murphy. One by one, each of them hoists themselves onto the side of the deck, their legs dangling off the side like mine and Danny's. Just as always, we are sequestered from the outsiders, creating a wall of friendship we're all too afraid to admit is crumbling.


After my second keg stand, Murphy pulls me aside.

"Ruby, what the hell are you doing?" he demands, as if he has any right.

"What?" I ask, lifting my hands. "I'm having fun." My speech, I notice, is slightly slurred. I didn't sink any of the cups in my three beer-pong games, which means I had to drink all the ones my partner didn't sink himself.

"Yeah, well, the last time you had 'fun' like that with Hardy Crane," he lowers his voice now, realizing he's treading on dangerous territory, "it didn't end well for you. Remember that night?"

I poke him in the forehead, which, after I do it, seems like quite a silly thing to do. He grabs my finger, gently, and doesn't let go. I rear back from him. "Actually, I don't really remember. Do you remember . . . when you told me you loved me?" I hiccup at the end of this, my eyes filling with tears.

"Tuesday—"

"I told you not to call me that anymore. Only my friends can call me that."

"Oh, like your good friend Hardy?"

"He's just my beer-pong partner. What happened with us was a long time ago."

"Yeah and you worked really hard to put him behind you."

"What do you care, *Murphy*?" I hiss at him. "It's none of your business who I do and do not fuck."

"Why are you being like this? What the hell happened to you?"

I'm so angry my vision actually blacks out for a moment. Although, to be fair, the beer might have contributed to this effect. What *happened* to me? *You* happened to me, you fucking prick. You happened. To my horror, my entire body starts to shake. I'm afraid if I try to speak, a rage unlike anything I've ever known will be unleashed, and I won't be able to stop myself from strangling him.

"What's going on over here?" a voice says. Hardy appears by my side.

"Stay the hell out this, Hardy," Murphy warns.

"Ruby, are you okay?" he wraps his arm around my waist and pulls me to him possessively.

"No," I say, looking straight into Murphy's eyes. "I wanna get outta here. Where's your truck?" The look in Murphy's eyes is at least in the same ballpark as what I've been feeling for the last month, but as I walk away with Hardy, I'm nowhere near vindicated. Not yet.

# CHAPTER SIXTEEN

# RUBY
## *Now*

I didn't think it was possible to be more nervous about going back to Chatwick than I was for Danny's funeral, but as I maneuver my rental car onto I-89 in Drummond, only thirty minutes away, I hold the steering wheel in a death grip to steady my shaking hands. I rented a car this time, so Nancy won't have to drive all the way to and from the airport twice; and because the universe has a fantastic sense of irony when it comes to me, the only car available at Hertz was a Nissan Sentra. This one, about fifteen years newer than the one currently rusting in my parents' garage, has nothing on Blue. Sure, it has power steering, but that only serves to jerk me wildly off-course with every surge of nerves. I do have to hand it to the winter tires, though. Blue's tires are more suited for a bike ride on a flat, even surface than a drive on Vermont roads, with their frost heaves and black ice.

Ally and I have spoken just twice since the bachelorette party. The first time was the day after she left New York. I called to apologize *again* for not claiming the secret earlier. To be fair, I wasn't sure what had happened until Ally told me in earnest the secret wasn't hers. I suspected, and I suppose the reason I never opened my envelope is so I didn't have to know for sure. I insisted on getting on the phone with Aaron to tell him as much. It was the least I could do. To Aaron's credit, he accepted my apology graciously. I could hear a hint of curiosity, but he did not—as Ally had—demand details like when exactly it happened and how could I not have told anyone, and who was the father, anyway? I remained vague. I told Ally it was a really difficult time for me, right before I left for college. I told her the father of the child was not someone I was proud of, and that he never even knew about it, so I didn't feel right telling her, either. All that was true. But just like with Danny, I didn't tell Ally the whole story, and she drew her own conclusions.

The only thing Aaron put me on the spot about was Ally's real secret. She still insists Danny outed her pregnancy—her completely planned for, and very much wanted, *first* pregnancy. I told him the same thing I told Ally: that I hadn't read it. But based on the way she snatched the envelope out of my hand and inspected the seal for tampering, I'm guessing she's hiding something a little darker. I did not voice this suspicion to Aaron. They've been through enough, and I'm not going to play any further part in straining their marriage than I already have.

*Just remember that all things done in the dark have a way of coming to light.*

The second time Ally and I have spoken since the bachelorette party was her call to invite me to her annual Christmas party. Could I come home a couple days early in order to make it? Just like when we were young, I was so happy she seemed to have forgiven me that I immediately agreed. I had already taken the days between Christmas and New Year's Eve off for the pre-wedding festivities and, of course, the wedding itself. But I asked my boss if I could have a few extra days, with my fingers crossed behind my back for him to refuse. The fact that he allowed it is my karma for letting Ally take my fall, because it means I will be spending Christmas with Nancy and my father.

I've gotten out of coming home for every holiday season since college by scheduling a trip to see Greta or Coral, wherever in the world they are living or working at the time. I cite limited vacation time to Nancy, but she's not stupid. She knows I don't want to come home. Just the thought of spending the holidays in the place I grew up brings on a flood of images: Nancy in a black period, too depressed to get out of bed and prepare the fancy Christmas Eve dinner she planned, a ham spoiling on the counter while Dad hid in his den. Nancy still drunk in the wee hours of Christmas morning, while we opened presents and pretended not to listen to the veiled insults she and my father traded. My parents screaming at each other on New Year's Eve after coming home from a party where she drank too much and he flirted with someone else's wife.

But I can't blame my white knuckles *completely* on my family. Some of it lies with Danny, and some with me. Mostly, it's the unknown. When I came home in September, I knew it would be awful—an overwhelming mess of grief, awkwardness, and nostalgia. Not great things, but I could anticipate them. This time, I have no idea what to expect. Ally assured me she wouldn't tell anyone that the abortion secret was mine, but how can I trust a girl who cares more about what people think than anyone I know?

*All things done in the dark . . .*

And then there was that missed call I got last week. It was from an 802 number, Vermont's one-and-only area code. When I saw it, my mind instantly flashed to Murphy's face, and I didn't answer it for fear of a confrontation I was not yet prepared for. It could have been anyone, but I have Ally, Emmett, Steph, her bridesmaids (including the dreaded *Krystal*), and my family saved as contacts in my phone. Who else would be calling me from a Vermont number? The thought both thrills—*does he miss me?*—and scares me—*is he calling because he knows?* As angry as I am at Murphy, and as many times as he's let me down, I still think of him as my best friend. Like it or not, his opinion of me matters.

Even if Ally *has* somehow managed to keep quiet, I still have this feeling. It started a few days ago. A constant, chilling bubbling of nerves, making me feel like my body is made up of ice-cold lava. Every unexpected noise launches me out of my skin. Every night's sleep is filled with images of Danny, sometimes memories resurfacing from the past, sometimes things that will never be, conversations that will never take place. When I'm awake, it's like I feel him watching me. Something tells me he will make good on his promise. That, somehow, the whole truth will come to light. And when it does, despite Ally's assurance that she'll always be my friend, I'm not sure if she, or anyone, will ever be able to forgive me.

*Please don't hate me.*

I've thought about canceling. Oh, believe me. I've had the phone in my hand a dozen times, poised to dial Emmett's number and tell him I got pulled into a shitstorm of work to wrap up before the end of the year, and I'm not able to come home for the wedding after all. But then I picture his face. Emmett, my brother. The pain-in-the-ass boy who grew up to be a man with a heart that will kill him before his time. And Steph, sweet Steph, who has welcomed me into her family, despite knowing nothing about me. I can't disappoint them.

And even if I could be that horrible, something tells me I'm in this now. That I have to see it through to the end.

I pull up to the house, hesitating before I park *this* Sentra in the same spot I used to park Blue, and I sit for a few moments before I get out. Twinkling lights rim the roof and shine through the snow-covered cedar bushes. The two thin white pillars that support the front porch roof are wrapped with red ribbon (one ruby red, one coral red, my mother used to say), giving them the appearance of candy canes. Through the sheer curtains of the living room, I see the artificial tree that's overseen our Christmas proceedings for as long as I can remember. We always begged for a real tree, but my mother wouldn't hear of the money wasted each year on a tree that would only end up on the curb at the end of the season.

I walk up the steps and through the back door that leads into the kitchen, inhaling the scent of baking bread, and I remember that not all the days of Christmas were so tense and melancholy. There were the days when the lights first went up, when Mom would take our picture in front of the newly decorated house for the annual Christmas card. There was the party at my father's company at headquarters in New York, where all the employees' children got an age-appropriate toy that we then played with obsessively on the trip home. There were the Christmas hams she *did* manage to serve, with all the trimmings; and the sugar cookies we helped her frost, as we stood on stools and donned aprons our mother had hand-sewn, our tongues poked out in concentration as we tried to copy her intricate frosting patterns.

I feel suddenly sick with guilt and nostalgia. Nancy has been on her medication and off the hooch since I was seventeen years old, and yet every year I make an excuse to stay away from her, on a holiday that is so centered around family. I wonder if this is the first time she's even made the effort to put up the decorations since both her daughters left home. And in punishing her, we're punishing ourselves, because we've missed out on ten years of the best of our mother.

How much it must break her heart for me and Coral to withhold our love, year after year, and still she stays sober. Still she remains committed to treatment for her illness. It occurs to me that Nancy is not the only one I've shut out of my heart rather than forgive, and it's about time I change that. The realization freezes me to the spot in the kitchen. I drop my bag, my body racked with violent sobs. Just like the evening in Murphy's bed, it's too much. Too many memories, too many old feelings. Too much regret

And then my mother is there, enveloping me in a hug. I fall into her and cry, telling her how sorry I am, and she is shushing me and stroking my hair and telling me everything is going to be okay. She smells like vanilla, without even a hint of wine. It's going to be a sugar cookies and ham kind of Christmas.

But first. "Mom," I say, using her proper title for the first time in twelve years, "I have to tell you something."

# CHAPTER SEVENTEEN

# RUBY
## *Back then*

I sit with my knees hugged to my chest, a blanket wrapped around me, watching the bursts of light explode over the lake, miles and miles away. It's chilly for the fourth of July, even by Vermont's standards, but I'm not sure that has anything to do with my shivering. Lately, I feel an almost constant chill. I think of the crew, arranged in a semicircle in their camp chairs down at the park, sipping from their Burger King cups that are secretly filled with liquor. Surrounded by thousands of Chatwickians doing the same. For the first time, Murphy will be among them. And Taylor will be beside him. For the past four years he's watched the fireworks with me, here, on the flat part of my parents' roof. He and Danny both. But we're no longer the unit of three we once were. Perhaps we never were.

It's been another two weeks of deep hibernation, only leaving the house to do shifts here and there at The Exchange. I've been training Lacey, my replacement, a rising sophomore who is painfully chipper against my canvas of torment. Another person who's shown me how easily replaced I am among the people I love. Shawna and Donna love Lacey; the crew has embraced Taylor since her return from "horse camp;" and I have been forgotten. This time around, there have been no phone calls to dodge. Ally, Emmett, Murphy—they all saw me leave the party with Hardy Crane, and none of them have the strength or the sympathy left to drag me through that again. Danny is the only one I still talk to, although we don't talk about me and Hardy. We don't talk about me at all. He mostly just comes over and watches TV with me.

I'm startled by the whoosh of a screen opening. Before his feet even appear through my parents' bedroom window, I know it's him. The tears that spring to my eyes dissipate the image of Murphy and Taylor holding hands from adjacent nylon chairs. What is he doing here?

"Jesus, Tuesday, it's not *that* cold," he says, craning his head to see me.

"Go away, Murphy." I bat at my eyes with the back of my hand before he can see I'm crying.

"No." He navigates the slope of the roof carefully and joins me, mimicking my posture. We sit in silence for a moment, watching the fireworks.

"What are you doing here?"

He looks at me in surprise. "It's the fourth of July. Where else would I be?" I don't answer. "Where are your parents?" he tries.

"In Jamaica. Another 'reunion' trip." He nods. Every time my parents fight now, they make up by going on a trip together, rather than (metaphorically) traveling apart. Their therapist is very supportive.

"Where's your girlfriend?" I ask. "How are things with Miss Teen Vermont, by the way?"

"Don't do that," he says. "She's actually—"

"I don't *actually* want to know, Murphy."

He sighs. "I miss you. I really fucking miss you, Tuesday. I know I'm the bad guy here, but you're not the only one whose heart is broken."

I don't even know how to express my inability to understand this. How can he be heartbroken and happy in a relationship at the same time? What kind of sociopath can compartmentalize his feelings so ruthlessly? The word that appears in my brain every morning when I wake up flashes like one of the fireworks I'm pretending to care about: *Why?* But I don't ask it.

"I'm sorry, Tues. I don't like the way this all happened. I shouldn't have—"

"Lied to me?"

"What did I lie about?"

"You should never have told me you loved me. I'm your best friend, and you used the oldest trick in the book to get me back into bed."

"Is that what you think?"

"Of *course* that's what I think, Murphy! How could you love someone and then just cut them loose without any explanation?"

"I told you, I didn't think it would work out."

"Yeah, I know, I remember. You didn't want to have to miss me. Genius plan—clearly it's working wonders."

"It wasn't just that."

Again, I don't ask what else it was. I'm afraid any more weight on my shoulders will topple me right off this roof. But he tells me anyway.

"Ruby, look at me."

It takes me a second to gather the strength, but I do. He's the same old Murphy, but now that I know I love him, it feels like staring into the sun.

"We would have the summer, then you would leave. For New York, where you've always dreamed of living. And you'll change there. You're *supposed* to. And I'll be here, doing what makes me happy, and pretty soon the gap between who we are now and who we become will just be too big."

In his eyes is something I've never seen before. A maturity, but also a sorrow.

I sniff, and my voice cracks with every word. "But we could have tried, Murph. I think, with all that we mean to each other, we should at least have tried."

"And what would the best-case scenario have been, for us as a couple? That you would miss me so much you would come home, live in Vermont forever? Then what?"

"Then maybe we could have been happy."

He takes my hand. "Maybe for a little while, but how could I do that to you? How could I hold you back from the life you've always wanted? How could I be happy, knowing what you gave up to be with me?"

I watch as the words come out of his mouth, but it sounds scripted, like something a boy would say to a girl in a Lifetime movie. Like something a boy would say to a girl because he thought that's what she wanted to hear. And suddenly I'm angry again. "That's a real pretty speech, Murphy. Tell Cecile she should have been a writer."

He looks as if I'd slapped him, and it feels good to see him hurt, to have some of my power back. So I look away, and just let my comment hang there.

"Fine," he says. "All right. You want to know why I didn't go through with this? With us?"

"I do, but I don't think you're really going to tell me."

"It's this! This right here. You make everything so hard! You never let me get away with *anything*. You know every secret and everything I'm thinking and feeling before I can even put a name to it."

"And that's bad?"

"It's fucking annoying! Maybe I want to have some secrets. Maybe I want to be with someone who doesn't have debates with Emmett that make me feel stupid and small."

"I don't make you—"

"Someone who doesn't tell me how I feel. Someone who wants a simpler life, like me, who isn't going to spend her life being disappointed in me and resenting me for what she could have had. With Taylor it's..."

"Easy," I say.

"What's wrong with easy?"

At first I can't think of an answer. What *is* wrong with easy? I don't know, I've never known what easy feels like. And Murphy, aside from keeping Danny's secret, has never known what hard feels like. He's not built for it. He's not strong enough. I look him in the eye, mustering all the fury and all the pain I've felt in the last few months. "You are such a coward," I say. His face turns cold, and he stands up and scales the roof to climb back inside.

I follow him, not ready to let him leave without a fight. "That's what they call people who do the easy thing instead of following what's in their hearts. You go ahead and build your simple little life with your adoring little puppy dog girlfriend following you around and doing whatever you say, but you'll be bored to tears. You'll always have me in the back of your mind. And I won't be there. I'll move on. I'll get over it, because at least *I* tried. But you'll regret this decision for the rest of your life."

He looks at me, the anger fading from his eyes as he sees the tears stream down my face. He knows what I'm saying is true, just like I know what he's saying is true. If we were to be together now, we would destroy each other.

Murphy puts his arm around me and pulls me to him, and

with my head buried in his shoulder I hear him sniff, and sniff again. I put my hand up to his face, and then we are clutching onto each other, crying. Then kissing. Kissing kissing kissing. He stands up and holds out his hand, so we can shuffle down the slope of the roof and back in through my parents' bedroom window. We're barely inside when we start fumbling our clothes off, tasting each new revealed fragment of flesh like it's our last meal. We fall onto the bed, naked, desperate for each other.

"Are you sure you want to do this?" he asks me.

I nod, pulling his face toward me, so he can't see the doubt in mine.

Afterward I whisper, "I love you" into his ear. He says it back to me. Then I watch him as he gets dressed and walks out the door. His shoulders are pinched, and I know if he turns around I will see tears in his eyes. So he doesn't turn and say goodbye, or offer any lame platitudes like "Good luck in New York." He just walks out the door and out of my life, forever.

"Goodbye, Murphy," I murmur.

The pain will kill me. I'm sure of it.


The doorbell rings, startling me enough that I knock over one of the sky-high towers of books that surround me. I've spent the entire morning sorting books into piles: to bring to NYU, to leave at home, to give to Danny, to donate to the Salvation Army. I leave in three days, and I don't think that's enough time for me to get through them all. Nancy occasionally peeks her head into my room and clucks her tongue in disapproval. "Ruby St. James, if you don't stop messing around with your books and start in on your clothes, you are going to be one well-read, naked college freshman."

Things have gotten better in the six weeks since I said goodbye to Murphy. Not great. Not good even. But better. I've remained in hibernation, licking my wounds. Danny still comes over to watch TV with me, not talking about anything important. I take an occasional phone call from Ally, but list any number of excuses why I can't hang out. Work. Family obligations. Trips to Drummond with Nancy to fight in Bed Bath & Beyond over the price of linens for the extra-long twin mattress NYU insists I need special sheets for. The trusty "summer reading assignment." The crippling pain has settled into a dull, constant ache, but I fear that an in-person visit with anyone connected to Murphy will turn the intensity back up.

"Aaaaally, darlin'!" I hear my mother exclaim from the door in that sugary-sweet southern hospitality way that makes me cringe. "Ruby! Ally's here!"

I freeze. This was inevitable, I know, but still I'm unprepared.

"I'll just go up and see her, Mrs. St. James," I hear Ally say. I stand up amongst the rubble of my books, actually contemplating whether I could hide in my closet without being found. But who am I kidding? It's Ally.

So I go on the offensive. "Hey, Al! I'm sorry I've been so busy—it's been forever," I say brightly when she opens the door, moving toward her with my arms wide. But she's onto me. Instead of returning my embrace, she holds her hands up in front of her.

"Don't," she says. "Don't. You. Dare."

I step back, shocked by the bumpy but measured tone of her voice. I have never seen Ally this mad, and that includes the time Emmett called her the C-word when she wouldn't let Aaron go to a strip club in Montreal for his eighteenth birthday.

"Al—"

She ticks off on her fingers. "You have ignored my calls. You have blown me off every chance you get. You missed my birthday party. Thanks for the *card*, by the way. That was real *swell*."

"Ally, I'm sorry, I've been—"

"—busy." She nods, her lips pursed. She looks around at my piles: linens, clothes, toiletries. For such a frugal spender, in the end Nancy sure has stocked me with a year's supply of literally anything I could possibly need. "I don't know what the hell is going on with you," she says. "You won't talk to me. And Murphy, for once, doesn't seem to know what's going on, either. Not that he would tell me."

Just the mention of his name flares up something inside me.

"And you know what?" she cries, flinging her arms up in surrender. "I don't even care anymore. My oldest friend is leaving, and she doesn't even care enough about me to try to . . . see me before she goes." She falters and walks over to my nightstand, where a (miraculously full) box of tissues sits, and blows her nose. "It was bad enough the first time, Ruby."

"What are you talking about?"

"With Hardy. The sneaking around. The lying. But I excused it, because you were going through your parents' separation, and I knew you were hurting. But now . . . I mean for God's sake, Ruby, you're going to *college*. Why are you wasting your time on that scum, instead of hanging out with the people who love you?"

Oh my God. She thinks . . . she actually thinks . . . Well, never mind. Let her think it. Let them all think it. It doesn't matter anymore. In fact I might as well stop pretending things can ever be the same.

"Ally, you really need to grow up."

She reels back as if I've slapped her.

"I'm sorry, but this whole loyalty-to-the-crew crap you spout off . . . don't you think we're a little old for it? Maybe it's important to you, since you're sticking around, but I'm going to *New York* next week. I'm getting the hell out of here. And I don't plan on coming back." I hope she doesn't hear the falter in my voice at the end. I feel a wave of nausea, knowing exactly what I am doing to my friend. To our friendship. All because of something that isn't at all her fault.

She inhales sharply through her nose, finally resigned that this is the way it will be. "Well. Good luck, then."

I want so badly to stop her, to go after her as she leaves the room. But in her haste to escape the venomous bullshit I'm spewing, she knocks into a stack of sundries my mother has piled on my dresser, and a huge box of tampons falls to the ground.

Tampons.

When's the last time I used one of those?

Oh. Shit.

# CHAPTER EIGHTEEN

# RUBY

*Now*

My hands search behind my back for the support of the wall and I lean against it, trying to recover from the kiss Murphy has just planted on me. We are in a dark hallway outside Ally and Aaron's bathroom, where he has followed me. I look to him, eyes wide. "What was that?"

"Mistletoe," he breathes into my ear, his hands still on my hips.

I look up. "There's no mistletoe in here!" I exclaim.

He pulls back, but only slightly. Shrugs. "We were both under it in the living room, but I couldn't kiss you like that in front of everyone. Might cause some confusion," he says. His eyes twinkle with the mischief of days long ago, and I wish I didn't have to push him away.

"Why have you been ignoring me all night?" he asks. It's a fair question; every time I've seen him coming toward me, I've made a beeline in the other direction. Now that I've told Nancy the truth, I know I also have to tell Murphy. But not yet. Not tonight.

"Because I don't want to deal with your crazy girlfriend, honestly," I say, copping out.

He points to himself. "I'm dating someone in the living room?" With mock interest, he adds, "Is she hot?"

Now I'm working not to smile. Trying to have this much control over my face is exhausting, not the way I ever used to feel around my best friend. "Don't play dumb, Murphy. You know I'm talking about Krystal." I hate myself for adding, "And no, she's not, in my opinion." What is wrong with me? This guy doesn't just make me *feel* like I'm sixteen; he makes me act like it, too.

Murphy slaps his palm against the wall, genuinely angry. "Krystal is *not* my girlfriend," he says firmly.

"You might want to tell her that," I say, my arms crossed against both his bullshit and his sexual advances.

He rolls his eyes. "What now?"

I point to the opposite wall, indicating he should go stand over there and keep his hands to himself. He puts his hands up in surrender and obeys. I tell him about all the obnoxious conversations I've witnessed over text messages and about Krystal's behavior when she was in New York. As I talk, a familiar calm settles over me. It starts to feel like before we messed everything up with sex, and Murphy was just the person I complained to about stuff. I'm not talking to a man I'm sleeping with about a woman he's sleeping with. I'm talking to my best friend about a girl who pisses me off. He is listening intently, laughing in places where I add dramatic storytelling flair, his jaw tensing during the parts where my feelings were hurt.

"I'm sorry, Ruby," he says when I finish. "I guess she thinks we're a little more involved than we are. But it's not my fault. I've always been clear with her that I'm not interested in a relationship."

He has either chosen his words carefully or lucked into them, but I find myself wondering whether he's not interested in a relationship in general, or just not with Krystal. How ridiculous that I even care. "Why not?" I ask, hoping this will encourage him to clarify his point without sounding like I'm fishing for a relationship myself.

He considers this for a few seconds. "She's just not the one."

I arch my eyebrow at him and his face lights up with recognition. He tries unsuccessfully to arch one back at me, resulting in a look like he's trying to poop. It's an inside joke from ninth-grade studyhall, when I had tried to teach him how to control his brows individually, alternating between serious instruction and uncontrollable giggling. Frustrated, I had used my fingers to help guide his right eyebrow up. It was the first time I had ever touched his face, and I remember the way he looked at me when I did it. Was that when everything started to change? After that day, whenever I arched my eyebrow at him (which was quite often), he would do the same little wiggle, and it made me laugh every time, no matter how angry I was at him. Unable to stop myself, I cross the hallway to touch his eyebrow and guide it upwards. This time we're not giggling.

*They're both really good at ignoring problems.*

"What are you guys doing out here?" Krystal's voice pierces through the bubble that surrounds two people with history when they are left alone. I draw my hand back, but not sharply. I don't care if she sees. Murphy will always feel more mine than anyone else's, and, in Krystal's presence at least, I'm not going to apologize for it.

"Just trying to teach this old dog a new trick," I say without looking at her, and duck into the bathroom to sidestep whatever hissy fit Krystal is about to throw. When I come out, the hallway is empty.

"I swear, Rube, I didn't tell anyone it was your secret," Ally whispers to me in the same hallway where I was pressed into a corner by Murphy not an hour ago.

She doesn't really need to whisper; our conversation is more than disguised by the volume of the Christmas music and the whoops of laughter coming from the living room. We are the only two not drunk, although I have had two of my allotted three glasses of wine and am secretly wishing Ally wasn't pregnant just for this one night, so we could sneak out to share a smoke. But since neither of us *is* drunk, there's no justification for being outside in this particularly brutal December night, the kind where it's too cold to snow. People think that's a myth, but it's not.

"What?" Ally asks, offended by my knit eyebrows and pursed lips.

"But . . .?" I prompt her.

"But what?" She has one arm across her body, one hand in the crook of her opposite elbow, one forearm raised, as if we were indeed outside sharing that smoke. I half expect her to flick the butt, scattering ashes to the wind. I remember the way she was always able to flick ash out of the window at the precise angle that prevented any from flying back into the car. I never possessed this skill, and Blue suffered from frequent burns in her upholstery as a result of stray embers.

"Al, I love you, and you know I would understand if you told everyone what you know. I can't expect you to take that hit for me."

Ally's face turns to a pout. "I swore to you I wouldn't tell anyone about your secret, and I didn't. How could you think I would lie about something like that?"

"Maybe you didn't tell people it was my secret, but you must have told them the secrets got mixed up. How else would they believe it wasn't you? And how hard would it be to figure it out, once they knew the secrets were switched? I *am* the only other one of us with a uterus, in case you haven't noticed."

Ally's face hardens as I speak. "First of all, I would like to think the people I'm closest to in this world believe me when I tell them the truth. That goes for you—" she jabs a finger in my direction, "and for all the assholes out there," she jabs her finger toward the living room. "If they don't believe I didn't have an abortion, then I don't really care. They can think what they want. And if *you* don't believe I can't keep a secret to protect one of my oldest . . ." her voice breaks, "friends, then I don't know what to tell you." She starts to move past me.

"I'm sorry," I say, catching her arm. And I mean it. I realize I'm treating Ally like a person she clearly isn't anymore. A person she maybe never was. She looks into my eyes and must know I am sincere, because she softens. I pull her into a hug. "I didn't mean to accuse you of anything," I say. "I'm acting crazy."

She lets me hug her for a moment before I feel her stiffen. When she pulls away, her face is quizzical. "Why *are* you acting so crazy?"

I freeze. In that instant, I know she's got me.

"Seriously," she continues, "if *I* don't care that much what people think of choices I made in high school, why would *you* care? You've never cared what anyone thought about you. Except . . ." her face goes to a faraway place, remembering, calculating, watching as my eyes widen, ". . . Murphy," she finishes. "Oh . . . my . . . God. Hardy wasn't the father."

I stare into her eyes, my breath caught in my throat.

"It was Murphy. Wasn't it?" she asks.

I don't move.

"Ruby!"

Slowly, I nod my head. This isn't how it was supposed to go, but this is how it's going. I wait for Ally to scream at me, to scream for Murphy, but she doesn't. Her face wrinkles. She shudders.

"Ewwwww!" she cries. She starts hopping around, flicking her hands as if trying to shake off the visual image. "You let Murphy see your boobs? And you, like, did it?" She shudders again and continues to jump.

I can't help myself, I break into giggles. She starts to laugh, too, and before we know it we're clutching our bellies; hers swollen, mine empty. It's not until she starts to sing, "Ruby and Murphy, sittin' in a tree, K-I-S-S-I-N-G" that I stop laughing.

"Ally, shhhh. Shhhhh," I say, covering her mouth with my hand. Just like when we were kids, she licks my palm. "Jesus, Ally," I say, wiping my hand on the back of her dress. "Listen, you can't tell anyone."

She stops playing then. "Really, Ruby? More secrets?" She says it like she's disappointed in me.

"I'm going to. I decided today that I would. But not until after the wedding, okay? If he's mad, I don't want it to ruin the wedding. After I tell him, you can tell—"

" —no one. Then I'll tell no one. It's a secret between you and Murphy. It's no one else's business."

I want to kiss her with relief. "Thank, you, Ally." I think back to the night in the field by her house, flashlights at our feet that we had brought for one last game of tag, our hands in a circle. Reeling from her parents' divorce, Ally's impossibly tortured face as she made us vow to fight for our friendships and always to be honest with each other. She had needed us to do what her parents could not. "I appreciate you understanding. I know how important honesty is to you."

I did not mean it sarcastically, but I realize after I say it that she is, of course, lying to us all, too. Something strange appears on her face. "Yeah, well," she says, "some things are better left in the past." She looks beyond me, beyond the walls of the beautiful house her husband built for her. What are you hiding, Ally?

*When it comes to things that really matter, you guys barely even know each other.*

Even without knowing what her secret is, I suddenly understand something about Ally that I never did before. Behind each of her backhanded whisperings there is a little girl desperate to confirm that her beliefs are right, her choices are beyond reproach. When Ally makes snide comments about New York, or looks at the bookcases of my apartment and asks me where my Great American novel is, she's really looking for confirmation, if only from herself, that she was right to stay in Vermont, to marry young, to pursue the career she's in. She deals with the fear of judgment by going on the offensive, so she never has to play defense. I, on the other hand, have chosen to sit out of the game entirely.

She turns back to me. "Is that why you didn't come clean and say the secret was yours? You knew Murphy would figure it out, because obviously *he* would have known if Hardy had knocked you up." There is so much pain in her eyes—the old pain that I always favored Murphy's company over hers, the pain that I lied again. The pain of knowing how little trust I've placed in the girl who always saved me a seat.

I nod. "I never even slept with Hardy. I mean, I did, junior year—all that happened. But the night of that party, the one after we graduated? I was just trying to prove a point to Murphy, but when I got in the car I realized I was taking a giant leap backward and asked him to drive me home."

"And he did? Just like that? You're lucky he didn't—"

"He might have, but I was so drunk I threw up in his middle console. He dumped me at my house pretty soon after that."

We share a laugh, conspirators in the systematic destruction of a boy who treated us both badly.

"Let's get back to the party," Ally says, brightening in preparation for her audience. "It's time for the group photo. Maybe we should ask Krystal to take it. Would that cheer you up?"

I move to protest, but am ashamed to find myself nodding as I follow her back into the living room.

It ends up being a four-glass night.

I lie awake all night, every memory I have of Murphy running through my head. At seventeen, watching him hit home runs in his starched white baseball uniform, feeling a confusing secret thrill when he winks at me after crossing home plate. At ten, telling me my haircut makes me look like a mushroom, or a boy, and he's not sure which one is worse. At fourteen, confessing in a whispered late-night phone call that he's been having nightmares about Danny stabbing Roger in the chest. At twenty-eight, the pressure of his hands, now calloused from his work, on my bare skin.

*I hate myself for what I've done. For what I am.*

Now I remember Danny, the way he looked that first night he came to me for help. Roger had practically yanked his arm out of his socket, and Danny hobbled toward me in the dark like a wounded bird. If I had been smart enough then, or had trusted Nancy not to break under the stress, if I had called out for her instead of keeping Danny's secret, would everything be different? Would Roger have been sent to jail? Danny freed from his abuse? Could Danny have had a better life? Gone to college with me, even? If Murphy and I hadn't shouldered the weight of Danny's secret together, would we ever have become best friends, and then lovers? Would Danny still be alive? And what if things had gone differently when he came to New York? I could have saved him one last time. Or, really, for the first time.

*None of you bothered to try to help me when I was alive, when it counted.*

# CHAPTER NINETEEN

# RUBY
## *Back then*

It is way too early for my buzzer to be going off. I groan awake, resentful that my roommate, Lisa, has undoubtedly left her keys and ID behind in some fellow pretentious drama major's dorm room—again. Security at NYU is strict; even if they know your face, they don't let you up without your ID. Then I remember Lisa requested a room transfer and moved out yesterday. She swears it's to be closer to the theater where all her classes are, but I have a sneaking suspicion it's because I've been crying for two weeks. I guess it's hard to soak in New York when you're already drowning in your roommate's used tissues. I don't really care. In fact, it's nice to be able to experience my sorrow without the pressure of trying to appear normal. Besides, I have enough drama to carry me through freshman year without a roommate who majors in it.

I drag myself up, glancing at my alarm clock on the way to the door. It's 5:30 in the morning. I press the brass button, "You've got the wrong room." There's no other explanation for it. Who would be visiting me? I haven't made a single friend here, due in no small part to my complete lack of effort. I'm about to flop myself back into bed when a voice crackles through the speaker. "Ruby St. James? There's a young man here to see you. Are you expecting him?"

A young man? I haven't had a single interaction with a male since I've been here. I've barely left my dorm except to go to classes, and there I just sit silently in a cavernous lecture hall among hundreds of other students. But what if . . .? My heart stops. If it's not someone I've met here, there is only one young man who might be looking for me.

I press the button again. "Let him up."

Oh my God. The words echo in my head: *Are you expecting him?* No, not expecting. Fantasizing, yes, in my darkest and weakest moments, but not expecting. This is too much like a movie to be happening to me. Girl is homesick and alone, thinking the man she loves doesn't care about her. But now that she's really left, and the reality of her being out of his life is too much to bear, he drives all night—and he must have driven; there are no red-eyes from Drummond airport—to rescue her from her heartache.

My heart is pounding so hard I have to sit down on the bed, but I pop back up almost immediately when I realize I cried myself to sleep last night and haven't showered since the day before yesterday. I hastily spritz perfume, tie my hair back in a ponytail, and pinch my cheeks like I really *am* a girl in a movie, before there's a knock on the door. I force myself to wait a few seconds before I open it.

My face falls.

"Try not to look so happy to see me, Tuesday," Danny says.

I try to rearrange my face from obvious disappointment to pleasant surprise, but as with so many things, I fail.

"You look like shit," I blurt. It's true. His eye is swollen, his nose looks broken, and there are flecks of dried blood in his goatee. I thought I was done with battered Danny showing up at my door in the middle of the night.

"Thanks," he says. "You too."

I laugh. It's the first time in weeks that I've laughed. And then I realize this is *Danny* in front of me. Danny who knows me, who's known me for as long as we both remember. I don't ask him what happened to his face. Perhaps I should, but I've learned my lesson about asking questions I don't want to know the answer to.

"I'm really, really glad you're here," I whisper. My eyes water despite my best efforts. It's like they're defective or something; they're a goddamn faucet I can't turn off.

"Hey now," he says. He drops the backpack he'd slung over one shoulder and pulls me into a hug. "No tears. My face will heal, I promise."

I laugh again, and a fresh wave of tears comes after it. He squeezes me tightly, and I inhale his unique mixture of menthol cigarettes and Old Spice deodorant and home. He pulls back and puts his hands on either side of my face, wiping my tears away with calloused thumbs. "I was hoping to find you here with some trust-funded film major, smoking flavored tobacco from a hookah and wearing a beret."

I knit my eyebrows together. "Why would you hope that?"

We both laugh. "Okay, maybe not exactly that. I just mean I was hoping to find you happy. I wanted to see Ruby St. James in her grand new life. The one you always dreamed about."

I pull away from him, under the guise of clearing a space on Lisa's old bed for him to sit. It's piled high with clothes I haven't had the energy to deposit into the hamper, let alone wash. "Yeah, well, I guess it takes more than two weeks to build a new life," I say.

"Especially when you're in love with someone from your old one." He says it softly, gently, but it's not a question.

I almost laugh. He, like Ally, thinks I am in this state because of Hardy Crane. That I am broken by such a sack of scum. It would be easier if I let him believe it, like I let Ally believe it. But it's Danny, and he's trusted me with much worse than this, so I say, "That night, at the party, it wasn't what it looked like. Nothing happened with Hardy and me."

"I wasn't talking about Hardy."

"Then who—"

"Same asshole who gave me this," he says, pointing to his black eye. "Murphy."

My mouth falls open, my tongue lying heavy like lead. I'm not sure which revelation is more shocking to me: that Murphy and Danny came to blows, or that Danny knew something about me and Murphy. I decide to start with the less selfish line of questioning. "*Murphy* did that to you?"

He nods, then waves me off, apparently deciding the same thing. "But I don't want to talk about it. Let's talk about what he did to *you*."

I wait a beat. Maybe if I don't speak he will elaborate on his thing. No such luck. "What did he tell you?" I finally ask.

He shakes his head. "Not a thing, I swear."

The gratitude I feel towards Murphy for respecting my privacy is quickly replaced by disappointment that he didn't find it worth talking about to his best friend.

"It was the fourth of July," Danny continues, and my heart thuds into my stomach, remembering what had happened that day. "You went MIA again after Luke's party, and yeah, I figured you were hanging out with Hardy again. But we always watched the fireworks from your roof, so I thought I would take a chance and stop by. Murphy's truck was parked outside. I had asked him earlier if he was going to your house, like always, but he said he was going to Drummond with his brother. The fact that he lied about it, combined with how weird you guys have been with each other . . ." he holds up two fingers on his left hand and two fingers on his right and then connects them. He put two and two together.

"So if you knew about it since July . . . I mean, that's not what caused *that*, right?" I point at his eye, wondering if Lisa might have left her icepack behind in my mini-fridge. Although it's probably too late for ice at this point.

"Not exactly."

"Dan."

"I said I don't want to talk about it!" He turns away from me and picks up a book of short stories lying next to my bed. As he flips through, he says casually, "So you're in love with him?"

"It's not that simple."

"But you are." I don't confirm or deny, but he takes my silence as his answer and whistles. He whistles. "You're in love with Murphy Leblanc, and I never want to see him again. *This* calls for a smoke."

I start to panic. How to handle this?

"Come on," he says, elbowing me. "I finished my pack in the car. Can I bum one?"

"Non-smoking dorm," I say. "Sorry."

"Duh, Tuesday. I meant we should go outside."

"I don't have any."

"You don't have any? Seriously? You always have some. Well, whatever. This is New York, I'm sure we can find a place that's open."

"I quit."

He looks at me for a long moment. Eerily long. "You quit smoking after moving to a new place, where nothing's familiar and your heart is, clearly, broken?" He waves his hand at the moat of wadded-up tissues surrounding my bed.

"Seemed as good a time as any," I say, avoiding his eyes.

He jumps off the bed. "Holy shit, Tuesday. You're pregnant!"

Danny goes with me to Planned Parenthood for the initial appointment. They assume he's the father, and this doesn't seem to bother him. They ask a lot of questions about my mental health and ask me like 400 times if I'm sure about my decision. They pull me into a room separate from Danny, to confirm this is *my* choice and I'm not being coerced into it. I wonder if this is standard protocol, or if the state of Danny's face has something to do with it. Although, if they were taking that into account, they would probably assume that I am the one in charge. I try to schedule my appointment—the big appointment, the one for "the procedure," or "the termination," as they kindly call it—for tomorrow. But I am ten weeks pregnant, and since I have two weeks before I *have* to make a decision, Danny thinks I should give it a few days. "You can't undo it, Tuesday. I'll support whatever you want to do, I just want you to be *sure*."

I tell him I already am, that after two weeks of crying about it on my own and a few days talking it over with him, I'm finally sure this is the right decision. But I take his advice and schedule "the procedure" for early next week. The truth is, I'm *not* sure. I change my mind every other day. But when I strip away the hormones, and the voices, and the feelings I still have for Murphy, and the logistical questions about how this should be handled, all I have left is a screaming, pulsing fear. I am one large, exposed nerve. Everything hurts. Every single moment.

Meanwhile, Danny is a good distraction. I order take-out, or sneak food from the dining hall to feed him. The dorm is so big, even his massacred face doesn't stand out as a non-student's when he uses the men's bathrooms. He sleeps in Lisa's old bed. While I'm at class, he spends his time wandering around the city or critiquing my writing assignments while he hangs out the window smoking cigarettes. I tell him he can't smoke (cigarettes or otherwise) in my dorm, but every time I come back from class the windows are open and it smells like air freshener. He can't enter the building without an ID, which means he can't really pop out for a smoke unless it's timed with my return from class, so I let it slide. A smoking Danny is preferable to a non-smoking Danny, and what difference does second-hand smoke make, really, at this point?

It's surreal to have someone here from the life I've been mourning. We don't talk about Chatwick, or any of its residents, but having him here is a connection to the place I am disgusted with myself for missing. All I ever wanted was to get out of Chatwick, and here I am, in the most exciting city in the world, but still every bit as stuck there as I always was. Danny is too, I think. He seems to be heartbroken but refuses to talk about it, and I still don't know what caused the bruises that have started to transition from blue and purple to yellow and brown.

I'm not sure what his plan is. I've dragged him to some of my classes, and because he's read my assignments, he raises his hand and gets in debates with my professors and the other students. I don't know why Danny isn't in college himself; he's so smart. I tell him I think he should enroll, to which he scoffs or rolls his eyes. I'm not sure if I'm thinking in his best interest or mine. It's not like working at Borbeau's and selling weed is some great five-year plan, and as he pushes me out the door to explore New

York with him, I notice a boundless energy I've never attributed to him before. It's his first time in New York, but he's better at it than I am. While the areas I've come to know through my father are shiny and safe, Danny leads me to Chinatown, where we're not sure exactly what we're ordering (and my insatiable appetite keeps me from asking too many questions); to the second act of an off-Broadway show, by sneaking in with the smokers; to Coney Island, where I load up on chili dogs since I can't ride the rides. Despite the cloud of anxiety that radiates from every pore, I'm falling in love with this city. It's everything Chatwick isn't—loud, anonymous, and full of diverse strangers and new experiences. And if Danny is falling in love with it too, is it so crazy for him to stay? Maybe it's his chance to get out of Chatwick. And maybe it's mine to have someone to cling to, when all this is over. Would it be so bad? Isn't it my turn to lean on someone?

Tonight, our plan is to see a movie, at my request. I am, after all, for however short a time, pregnant, and my feet ache from all the walking we've been doing. But on my way home from class, someone hands me a flyer for a new underground jazz club, and I smile because I know this is just the type of thing Danny will want to try, and I will get to be the one to suggest it. He's been introducing the crew to new things since our ages were in single digits. Granted, most of them have been drugs, but not all of them. When we were little, he always found the secret hideouts in the trails behind Emmett's house, and he was always the one to get us to cliff-jump at the granite quarry—offering gentle encouragement to Ally and Tara and me, bullying to Emmett and Murphy. Even since he's been here, in "my" new city, he's the one pushing me toward adventure rather than allowing me to drown in my crisis. Perhaps there could be something more between us, if I could just get him to stay.

Despite my aching feet, I practically skip back to the dorm, giddy at the thought of finally being the one to introduce him to something new. This has been happening since Danny's been here, these waves of normalcy, even happiness. Small, merciful moments when I know everything will be okay. Maybe not now, but eventually.

But the thing about hormones, and the thing about Danny, is that in an instant, everything can change.

When I get to my dorm room, Danny isn't alone. A guy I've seen in the dining hall is sitting on my bed, holding a small bag of white powder and watching Danny thumb through a stack of money. The only sound in the room is the thwap, thwap, thwap of each bill as he shuffles it from the uncounted to the counted stack. Danny's buying drugs—bad drugs, not just a little harmless herb. But no; the visitor hastily clenches his fist around the bag and hightails it out the door, and Danny folds the money and tucks it into his cargo pocket. It's worse, somehow. He wasn't *buying* bad drugs. He was selling them.

I slam my bag down on my desk; the flyer for the club flutters to the linoleum floor.

"How was class?" he asks, as if nothing happened.

"What the hell was that, Danny?" I know the answer, but I just don't see how it can be true.

"I'm sorry. You usually don't get back from class before five."

"The professor let us out early. That doesn't answer my question!"

He picks up the flyer from the floor. "Hey, did you want to go to this? Looks cool."

"You're *selling drugs* out of my dorm room?"

"Ruby, don't play dumb. I've been selling drugs since tenth grade, and you know it."

"Yeah, *weed*, Danny. Not . . . not . . . I don't even know what that was, but I know white powder is not weed!"

"It's just a little blow. It's not a big deal!"

"Just a little *blow*!" My voice is approaching the screech Nancy makes when she finds her spices out of alphabetical order. "Do you know how much trouble I could get in? I could get kicked out of housing just for having you here for so long. If they found out you were selling drugs? Jesus, I could get kicked out of school!"

He's quiet, but his face reddens.

"And are you actually *doing* this shit now? How long has *that* being going on?"

He speaks evenly, pointedly. "Well, I see you have your priorities straight. Your first concern is for how much trouble you could get in. Your second is for me."

I'm so mad I can't even see his face anymore. Ten minutes ago this boy was my life raft.

"But that's always been the problem, hasn't it?" he continues, mistaking my silence for guilt and taking the opportunity to get in one more jab. "I always come second. With you, with my mom, with everyone!"

"Oh, spare me the song from the world's tiniest violin, Danny. You have *never* taken responsibility for anything in your life, and look what good it's done you! You're not in school. You have no job beyond *this*." I wave my arm at the door that his "client" just exited. Suddenly it comes to me the real reason why no one's reported seeing a beat-up stranger lurking in the halls.

His face goes blank, and I know my Danny has left the building. "Are you actually throwing *Roger* back in my face right now?"

"I wasn't talking about—"

"I killed Roger. Just go ahead and say it. I'm a murderer. Well, congratulations, now you're part of the club!"

"Ex*cuse* me?" I narrow my eyes at him, giving him a tread-lightly warning. But he's too far gone.

"How are we any different, Tuesday? By next week, *both* of us will have taken a life that that caused us pain. We *both* made the choice to do the wrong thing, to make our own lives better."

Tears sting my eyes. I never realized he was capable of wounding me this deeply. All this time, supporting me—is this what he really thinks of the choice I'm making? "I don't give a shit what you've been through in your life, Danny, you have no right to say that to me. You have *no idea* what this is like for me. It's always been about what's happened to *you*. Nothing is ever worse, no one's pain ever compares. You're going to waste your life feeling sorry for yourself and justifying your habits by blaming everyone else for your life. Grow up!"

He takes a step toward me, his fist raised, but before he gets too close he spins around and puts his fist through the drywall. My hands fly to my mouth, but I don't scream or make a sound. The moment of impact echoes between us loudly enough. Danny's breathing is heavy and panicked. So is mine. Blood drips from his hand. My reflex is to go to him, patch him up and hug him, and tell him it's all going to be okay. I want to take back the last ten minutes. I want to come in just a moment after the deal had been made, so I don't have to know about this. I don't want to lose another person. My last person. But I can't do the co-dependent thing again.

I pick up Danny's backpack, shove the pile of clothes he has strewn at the foot of "his" bed into it, and hand it to him. "Goodbye, Danny."

He doesn't say anything, just looks at me as he steps backward toward the door. The hurt in his bright blue eyes makes my throat close. Absurdly, I think of the amount of parking tickets he'll have on his car—it's been parked in the same spot for weeks—and I briefly consider offering him money. Then I remember there's no need. He's got a fistful of it in his pocket, and I felt more stashed away in the socks I just packed for him.

"Take care of yourself," I mumble, the lone nicety I allow myself to give.

He slams the door behind him. The vibration from the impact tingles painfully in my fingers and toes long after he leaves.

I move my poster of the Chrysler Building to cover up the hole he's punched in the wall, then sit on my bed and shake, the adrenaline coursing through me. I want so badly to pick up the phone and pour out everything that just happened to Murphy, the one person who knows both me and Danny better than anyone. But I can't do that anymore. My ties to Chatwick, and everyone I've ever thought to be important, are now severed.

# CHAPTER TWENTY

# RUBY

*Now*

It's the twenty-fourth of December. Christmas Eve, and Danny's birthday to boot. It's going to be a rough one.

I pull Blue through the open cast-iron gates and onto the gravel path, having abandoned the rental Sentra in favor of my trusty steed. I turn the radio down and slow to a respectful speed, listening to the sound of my tires rolling over gravel, pebbles pinging off the wheel well. My first car accident was in this cemetery. I was fourteen, and my mother dragged me along to clean up my grandmother's gravesite. I don't know if it was guilt from forcing me to participate in this morbid activity, or some bright shining impulse to seize the day as her own mother could no longer do, but Nancy offered to let me drive along this very path. If I was going to learn anywhere, it might as well be a cemetery, right? The people here are already dead—how much damage could I do? I was so nervous that when I turned a corner and headed down a hill, I overcorrected and smashed right into a tree. Granted, it was at about five miles per hour, but it still dented the bumper pretty good and scared me enough that I refused to continue driving lessons with Nancy. I worried the shared memory would be potent enough to serve as a permanent bad-luck charm.

I pull to the side of the path, exactly where I had parked for Danny's burial, and brace myself against the ten-degree air.

Without the sea of black suits and skirts and the smell of Aqua Net guiding me, I have to wander through a few rows before I find Danny's gravestone.

*Nice to see you can show up for a person once he's dead.*

There are tracks in the snow leading up to and away from the stone, and there is a bouquet of already-wilted red roses carefully balanced at the base, still in the plastic with the Martin's Grocery price sticker on them. I guess the etiquette of hiding how much you spend on gifts ends when the receiver can no longer read the tag. *Happy Birthday, Danny, have some flowers you're allergic to for $12.99. They'll rot into the ground, just like you.*

I wonder who left them. It wouldn't be Charlene. She would know Danny well enough not to bother with something he wouldn't appreciate. Or maybe not. Women tend to get all romantic about people after they're dead. Maybe it was some girl Danny had shot up with, or some tragic nineteen-year-old cashier who worshipped him silently when he came in to buy his Newports. Perhaps it was even a girlfriend, someone we had been completely unaware of sitting behind us at the funeral, as if our grief were all that counted. Someone who had been foolish enough to love him, and to think he would get better for her.

I stand with my hands in my coat pockets, looking down at the granite slab that marks the life of my friend. His name and the bookend dates of his existence are the only words etched into the stone. I'm grateful for the absence of any bullshit quip about the Lord and his infinite wisdom, or some quote Danny was known for. What would Danny choose if he had planned his death even more elaborately? "Beer is good, but heroin is quicker," perhaps. I catch a laugh trying to escape, and then I remember that Danny is actually decomposing under my feet and I choke on it.

*None of you bothered to try to help me when I was alive . . .*

My eyes are already puffy from last night's wine, and the sleeplessness that followed as memories of Danny and Murphy and Ally and Emmett flooded over me as I lay in the twin bed of my childhood. The tears that come now hurt as much physically as they do emotionally. They are persistent, and I wipe them away with my gloved hand to make room for more. I want to sit on the ground, to pull my knees up to my chest and talk to Danny, but it's covered in snow. Even if it wasn't, all I know to say is I'm sorry, so I whisper it to him now. I'm sorry for so many things I don't know where to start.

I feel a hand on my shoulder, and a scream escapes my throat as I spin around in defense mode, arms swinging.

"Hey-hey-hey, it's me. Jesus fuck!" Emmett cries, forearms raised to protect his face. "Careful, I'm forking out about a million dollars for a wedding photographer; I don't need a black eye to be captured on film for all eternity."

"Damnit, Emmett!" I cry, trying to catch my breath. "You scared me half to—" I stop before I say *death*. I look over his shoulder. "What are you doing, sneaking up on me like that? Where's your car?"

He crooks a thumb westward. "I live a block away. I walked."

It takes some effort to catch my breath and slow the hammering in my chest, the dehydration from the wine working against me. Emmett couldn't have known I was here, which means he came to visit Danny on his own.

"What are *you* doing here?" I ask, a bit more coolly than necessary.

He blinks at me. "It's Dan's birthday." He says it like it's the most obvious thing in the world, like I should be ashamed for not knowing. I guess it's sweet that he remembered, although I can't say I'm happy to see him. At the party last night, after my confession to Ally, he had cornered me about an article *The Times* had run about opiate use in Vermont. He had actually pulled the clipping from his pocket, prepared to discuss point-by-point where the article had gotten it wrong. At first I thought he was trying to pull me into one of our old debates, but then it became clear he thought I might have ghostwritten it, perhaps inspired by our friend's death. I had been too drained to do anything but laugh in his face. "Emmett," I had said, "if I had written an article for *The New York Times*, there's no way in hell I wouldn't take the byline, no matter who it pissed off here." He had then called me a "fame whore" before stomping off. Yes, that's me, in a nutshell. Ruby St. James: Account Manager. Anonymous city dweller. Non-practicing writer. Fame whore.

He must sense my leftover annoyance, because his normally perfect posture slumps slightly. "I'm sorry about, you know, the article thing."

"Whatever—it's fine," I say.

"I guess I'm a little on edge about the issue."

"Yeah, well, it's not easy to see the place we live portrayed negatively."

"You're doing it again."

"Doing what?" I spin on him.

"Being too nice. Too forgiving. It's not like you, at least not with me. You've been treating me like I'm dying ever since you found out about my heart."

I think about this for a moment. "Maybe. Or maybe I've just grown up." I can't resist adding, "Unlike some people."

He laughs. "That's a start."

We stare at the gravestone in silence for what feels like an eternity before I speak. "You know, I—of all people—was not naive about Danny. I knew . . . everything. And it doesn't take a giant stretch of my imagination to believe he turned to heroin. Especially considering the last time I saw him." I wince, trying to clear the image of his face, snarled with rage, and the raised fist that switched direction mid-swing to land in my dorm-room wall. "I just . . ." I don't know how to finish without sounding foolish, especially to Emmett. But there were other things that made Danny who he was. Other memories that I can't shake. How he always bought four of those hideous dyed carnations they sold at school fundraisers—one for me, Ally, and Tara, and one to bring home for Charlene—even though he was allergic. How he made up little raps at the lunch table to diffuse the tension of the latest debate between me and Emmett. How he wrote poems on napkins for Ally when one of her dogs died (this happened many times, as I was only one of the sick strays that her mother had a habit of adopting, particularly after Ally's father left).

After the last day I saw Danny, whenever I found myself worrying about him, I invented a life I felt he could realistically have led, had that moment in my dorm room woken him up. Sessions with a counselor, classes at a community college, maybe a nice girl to marry and have children with. It used to make me feel better about never finding my way back to being his protector. Now it just feels sad, like an alternate ending to a depressing movie's special features—it doesn't erase the pain of the real ending, where the hero dies.

Emmett appears to be waiting for me to finish my sentence until he realizes I have no intention of doing so. "You always saw the best in him," he says.

"Someone had to." I look at him sharply.

"Yeah. I mean, look how much good it did him."

He knocks the breath out of me with these words, like he bowled a strike right into my intestines. I turn my back to him and cover my tears with a little laugh. "Of course you would pick a fight with me *now*," I say. "Here."

"Hey, I'm sorry," he says. "I didn't mean . . ." He puts his hand on my shoulder, but quickly releases it. We are not an affectionate pair. In fact the first time we've ever hugged was at Danny's funeral. But like the rest of the group, Emmett and I are family. We're the brother and sister who swear they can't stand each other, but ultimately miss the challenge at any gathering where the other is not present.

"What are you even doing here?" I ask again, not ready to forgive him.

Emmett ducks his head and nods. Fair play. "Things changed between Danny and me, you know, towards the end," he says, reading between the lines. "We kinda...reached an understanding."

I stifle a giggle. "An understanding that he would sell you weed?"

He tucks his lips in defeat and rolls his eyes up to the sky, as if he's having a silent conversation with someone up there. He nods, as if he's decided something, and says, "Steph made that up."

"Oh yeah, right, Emmett! Look, it's really not that big a deal, I was just teasing."

"I'm serious, Ruby. She lied about my secret."

I'm stunned, momentarily unable to respond, save for the opening and closing of my mouth and the occasional pathetic squeak. "You mean, your heart . . . is fine?"

His eyes widen and he waves his hands. "No. No-no-no. That part is true. I do have HCM; I did have the operation. All that's true. Oh God, no, she would *never* make something like that up. I would never let her get away with it if she did. It just wasn't the secret Danny wrote down."

Again I am in the position where I desperately want to demand the dirt on my friend, but I can't without being a complete hypocrite. I can't share my secret with Emmett. Not until I talk to Murphy, anyway. Three months after Danny's big plan, none of us knows each other's real secrets except for his. So much for his "tell each other or else" threat.

But Emmett, to my surprise, reaches into his coat pocket and pulls out an envelope. *His* envelope. He opens it and slides out the little slip of paper with Danny's handwriting on it, looks at it a moment, nods again—another decision—and hands it to me. I take it without removing my eyes from his. I want to give him every chance to take it back before I read it. But he doesn't. So I read:

*"I am a drug dealer."*

And I burst out laughing.

His face falls.

"Emmett, what is this?"

"It's not funny. It's true."

"Yeah, okay. I'm supposed to believe that Nancy Reagan went from total abstinence to being some Chatwickian Kingpin?"

"Not a kingpin. Not even a dealer, really. I was a runner."

I scoff at him, searching his face for the joke. "Emmett. Come on."

"A few months after the operation, the bills started rolling in. The shitty insurance I have at the bank has a twenty percent coinsurance requirement, which came out to thousands of dollars we just didn't have. We bit off a little more than we could chew on the house; between the mortgage and Private Mortgage Insurance and property taxes and utilities, our paychecks were completely maxed out. But our salaries were just high enough that we didn't qualify for any financial assistance through the hospital. I was still recovering from the surgery and could barely make it through a full day at the bank, so Steph took a second job *stocking shelves* at Martin's at night." He shudders, and I get a flash of him in his red smock from his cashier's job in high school. "It still wasn't enough. We had credit agencies calling. It was a nightmare.

"So Steph was partially telling the truth. I *did* go to Danny one night to get pot because neither of us had been sleeping or eating particularly well. He, of course, was a total dick about it, and I ended up blowing up at him and telling him all about the surgery, the money problems, all of it."

I cross my arms, waiting for the giant leap from buying a little herb to transporting drugs.

"You know Danny always sold," he continues. "Once he got into the harder stuff, he sold it out of the back room of Borbeau's. That night he told me his runner had quit, and if I was willing to assume the risk and drive to and from Montreal once a week for a few months, it would pay. Big. Enough to get me and Steph out of debt."

"And you accepted, just like that?" Emmett, who found the answers to a final exam and turned them into the teacher without hesitation. Emmett, who graduated summa cum laude from VTU, without once indulging in the Adderall booster used by his classmates. Emmett, who premeditatedly hid the flashlight before slapping the mushrooms out of Danny's hand.

"No. I told him to fuck off. But when I went home, I found Steph crying at the kitchen table in her red smock, our mountain of bills in front of her. I couldn't let that happen again. It's my job to make her life better, but because of me . . . Anyway, the next day I went back and accepted."

"And Steph *let you*?" This is almost as hard to imagine, even knowing Steph for such a short time. I mean, she's a *librarian*, for Christ's sake.

"She didn't know about it right away, not until the envelopes full of cash started appearing in the mailbox. And she was *very* against it, but my mind was made up and there was nothing she could do to stop me. She wasn't about to turn me in. Then we'd really lose everything. That's why she leaked the HCM and the pot. She thought it would be enough to throw off suspicion."

I shake my head, still not convinced. "Did she actually think one of us would turn you in, if you told the truth? I mean, did she *hear* what Murphy and I kept secret for Danny?"

"Well, you two weren't the only ones in the room, remember?"

"Al?"

He nods. "I love her to death, Ruby, but that salon of hers is like the Chat's oxygen tank. Can you imagine the first time someone cried to her about their money problems? What she would whisper in their ear, convinced she was helping? She wouldn't be able to help herself."

Of course I understand. I didn't tell Ally the truth, either. I still haven't.

I look from him to Danny's headstone and back, as if one of them (at this point, I wouldn't even be that shocked if it were Danny) was going to break into a smile and yell, "Gotcha!" Finally I shove Emmett's arm, again and again, and the words find me. "Jesus, Emmett! Are you insane? You were a fucking drug mule!"

"I know."

"You could have gotten caught! That's a fucking felony! How could you be so stupid?"

"I was desperate," he says miserably.

"How did you even pull it off?"

"I honestly don't really know. Danny told me to dress like I was going to work, because it made me look more legit; he gave me a car that Borbeau's was working on—a different one each week—and the address of a mechanic shop up there. He told me he would give them my license-plate number and, when I got there, all I had to do was ask for an oil change. They hid it somewhere in the car, I crossed the border, I brought it back to Borbeau's, and I went home. A few days later an envelope of cash was in my mailbox—my cut, after they sold it all."

"To people who then repackaged it, cut it with who-knows-what, and then resold it to a bunch of addicts who need help, not something to shoot up their arm. A bunch of addicts like Danny."

"Oh, come off it, Ruby. You can't blame *me* for Danny's problem. I know you like to think so, but Danny was not some helpless victim. He made his own choices. He made the choice to let Roger die in front of him; and yeah, maybe given the circumstances, I can't blame him. But he made the *decision* not to come forward. He made the *decision* never to get help. He made the decision to numb it out with drugs. And he made the decision to die. To quit. That's not on *you*, and that's not on *me*."

I bite my lip, tears rolling down my face. "Danny didn't have the kind of life that you had, Emmett. He didn't have parents who brought him up to believe in himself. It's easy to sit in judgment when you don't have to walk in a person's shoes."

"But that's what you're doing to me!" he says, throwing up his hands. "Judging. When you have no idea what it's like, to be fighting not to lose what you've worked your whole life for. To have to send the woman you love off to earn more money to pay for *your* medical bills while you're sitting on the couch. You have no idea what that's like. Just like I don't know what it's like to grow up with a bipolar mother, or go through whatever your secret is."

He's right. I know he's right. Here I am, defending Danny's fucked-up choices and judging Emmett just because he made some of his own. And all that before we get to my own past. "I'm sorry," I say, "I guess I got defensive. You know, now that he's not here to defend himself."

"You *always* defended him. Even when Danny *was* here to defend himself. And most of the time he was smirking behind your back, like the little brother who just got away with something by telling Mommy that the other kids were mean to him."

There's a hurt in his voice, and in his eyes I see a frightened teenager realizing he was on hallucinogens against his will. I see a humiliated, gangly pre-teen sprawled out on the auditorium floor because Danny had stuck his foot out to trip him in front of the whole school. I see a little boy, gazing up at Murphy and Danny swinging from their knees in a moment of fearlessness he himself wasn't capable of. What that must have felt like, to a boy who was, at five, already set in his ways. Like the earth was shifting on its axis. Like he would never be good enough. Suddenly I see Danny grinning maliciously down at Emmett, raising his middle finger. Whether it happened or not, it certainly feels like it could have.

"Murphy didn't love Danny more than you, you know," I say, almost forgetting that I'm now speaking to Emmett the grown man, and not the little boy. "He loved you both the same."

A deep crimson spreads across his cheeks, already pink from the cold. I'm about to apologize for embarrassing him, when Emmett says, "Everyone has their favorites, though. Dan was everyone's favorite." He glances at me for just a second before tearing his gaze away again. I wonder for the first time if maybe Murphy's friendship wasn't the only thing he competed with

Danny over. Maybe it was mine as well. And Ally's, too. Danny needed us more than Emmett, and so he got us. And Emmett got left out. As much as he tried to make Danny feel like an outsider, he—Emmett—felt like one. I guess, for one reason or another, we all did.

I don't want to embarrass him any further, so I keep this thought to myself. Instead, I say the first thing that pops into my head. "I saw this movie a few years back, about this guy who could travel back in time and fix all the mistakes he had made. Any little thing he changed made all his loved ones' lives change completely."

"I remember it. No matter what he did, everything still ended up shitty, so in the end he did everything exactly the same."

"I read some interviews after I watched it. Originally it was supposed to end with the main character going back to the womb and strangling himself."

The words hang in the air for an uncomfortable moment, and I wish I hadn't said them.

Graciously Emmett clears his throat and changes the subject. "So you didn't write the article, but when are we going to see your name in print?"

I shake my head. "I don't think journalism is on the cards for me. I prefer fiction. It's . . . tidier." I remember something from the variety of conversations I had last night. "Ally thinks I should write about this," I say, waving my arm at the headstone, then at Emmett, and then sweeping it around to indicate Chatwick as a whole.

"Maybe you should. You'd have to be a *bit* of a journalist, though, to figure out the rest of the secrets. Of course you know mine and yours. And we know Ally's . . ."

"Well, Ally said hers wasn't true," I point out. My heart begins to pound. It feels only right to defend Ally when I know the truth, but we're getting too close to a topic I still can't discuss before talking to Murphy. Plus, Emmett is about as pro-choice as Glenn Beck, and I'm guessing his comment was meant to draw me out on a subject I don't have the energy to debate.

He nods in a way that tells me he thinks Ally is full of shit, then continues as if I hadn't spoken. "And I'm guessing you know Murphy's. Or that they're linked, somehow."

*All things done in the dark . . .*

"I don't know what Murphy's secret is," I say.

He gives me the same nod. *Yeah, right.*

"Really," I add. "And it's none of my business."

"You know he really loved you," he says out of nowhere. It's not a question, but a statement. Another statement that knocks the wind out of me. "Still does, I'd bet the house."

I force a laugh. "I think you're in enough trouble, without making ridiculous bets like that."

He smiles sadly. "Ruby."

I hear all his disappointment in those two syllables. We were having an honest moment, and I pulled away. It's going to take some time to break this habit. I swallow the lump in my throat and shake my head. "Murphy doesn't even know me. Not really. He hasn't for a long time."

"And whose fault is that?" He waits a moment for his point to resonate and then cuffs me on the shoulder. "See ya at the wedding." He turns to leave.

"Emmett!" I cry after he's walked a few paces toward the exit. Suddenly I feel desperate for him to stay. I'm not ready to say goodbye. To him. To Danny. To Chatwick. Emmett turns back. "Aren't you going to talk to Danny?" I ask. "That's what you came here for, right?"

He shakes his head. "I don't talk to him here," he says, but he walks back anyway, passes me, and snatches up the bouquet. "But thanks for reminding me. I wanted to make sure none of these things were left. Danny would have hated it." He starts to walk away again, but I grab his arm and pull him into a hug. Our second hug ever.

When we come apart, I turn to Danny's stone and say, "Happy Birthday, Danny." I try to keep a smile on my face when I say it. Just in case he's watching.

"Yeah, and Merry Christmas," Emmett says. We look at each other with sad, tucked-in smiles.

"Come on, I'll give you a ride home," I say.

He nods, slings his arm around my shoulder, and we walk back to my car. And for once we don't debate, or bicker, or dig at each other. We just let the silence settle over us. I look back at Danny's stone, left behind alone and in the cold. I try to convince myself that it's not him. That he's moved on to that hideously clichéd better place. That he's been forgiven for what he's done, and that maybe he's even forgiven himself. And us.

Halfway to the car it starts to snow. I've never been a big believer in the afterlife, but something tells me it's Danny's doing.

# CHAPTER TWENTY-ONE

# ALLY
## *Now*

I should have said no when Steph first asked me about red satin for the bridesmaid's dresses. She probably would have listened to me. But no, I kept my trap shut so Steph could have everything she wanted. Now I'm standing here six months pregnant, my belly looking like a giant tomato with a button at the center; I can only imagine how many times it will be pressed at the reception. Spanx engineered by NASA couldn't cover up this belly button in satin, the bitchiest of fabrics, if you ask me.

At least I'm not the only one who doesn't look her best. I finally wrestled Ruby into my chair to give her some highlights, insisting that the dress would clash with her hair and make her look sick, which it does. She wouldn't let me do more than a partial, always so cautious, ever since I made that one *tiny* mistake in high school. You couldn't even *see* the parts that turned black; I don't know why she had to be so dramatic about it. Anyway her hair is still too strawberry, and I did my best to give her a good up-do and makeup, but it doesn't look right together.

Emmett and Steph say their vows, the traditional churchy ones. Aaron is straight across from me, where the groomsmen stand. He catches my eye and winks. I swear when he does that, it gets to me just like it did when we were kids. And here we are, about to have a kid of our own. Someday *she* will get winked at and feel that skip in her heart that makes you stupid. What a scary thought.

Of course I don't know *for sure* it's a girl. My sister-in-law told me that not knowing the sex gave her that extra motivation to push, no matter how tired she was, and I thought that sounded sensible as anything, so we decided to be surprised, too. But I think it's a girl. I just have a feeling. Ruby said she had a dream it was a boy, but I think that's wishful thinking on her part. She's always been more comfortable around boys.

I try to pay attention to the service, but they're doing a full mass, and honestly it's enough to concentrate just on keeping upright. Finally they get to the part where the bridesmaids and groomsmen get to sit down, and I collapse into the front pew and fan myself with the program that was on my seat. It's hot as Halley's Comet in here. I'm guessing they crank up the heat for the old people. Ruby notices a trickle of sweat on my forehead and wipes it away. Every time she does something tender like that—something I picture her mother doing when Ruby was little—I worry about Ruby inheriting Nancy's dark side, too. I remember researching bipolar in the Chatwick High library, wanting to understand why Ruby's mom was the way she was, and read that it can be passed down to your kids, but sometimes it doesn't show up until your mid-twenties, which would be right about now for Ruby. Aaron tells me I'm a worrywart. Well, he better get used to it. As much as I love Ruby, can you imagine what I'll be like with my own kid?

I watch Emmett closely, looking for signs he's not taking it seriously, but he doesn't take his eyes off Steph for even one second. Good. I don't blame him; Steph *does* look beautiful, angelic almost. Her dress, well, I won't get into it because her family kept going on about how unique it is, but let's just say she could have saved herself the money by taking mine out of storage and tying a sash around the middle. It could have been her "something borrowed"! But besides the dress and the hair and the makeup—all beautiful on their own—she has that look to her. I've been to a lot of weddings over the years, and you can tell the brides who just want to get married from the brides who are truly in love with their husbands, and she is one of the second kind. She'll need it, being married to Emmett McDowell. I do not envy her. I love Emmett the same way Ruby does, in that we both want to kill him most of the time. He's become a little more thoughtful, though, a little softer, since his secret came out. Seems to me his heart condition is making him more aware he *has* a heart. Or maybe I'm just not taking everything he says as hard.

I hate to say it, but I'm glad we're at the finish line, that tomorrow this wedding business will be over. And it's fitting they're getting married on New Year's Eve. Today will be the last day of this insane year, and tomorrow we get to start fresh. The last few months have been exhausting, what with the wedding planning and the bridesmaid bickering and the pregnancy. And then there's the fact that this all started with Danny in a coffin, which I haven't really even had time to process, I've spent so much of my energy being mad at him.

People think I'm mad just because he lied about my secret, or because he's calling us out on our private business, but that's not true. Well, not entirely. I'm mad because he killed himself in the first place. I'm mad he became a heroin addict. I'm mad he never told me he was abused. You better believe *I* would have done something about it. I know people think of me as a bigmouth, but don't you think that might have been a *good thing* in this situation? Really, what good did keeping secrets do Danny in the end?

And maybe that's the point he was trying to make with his little suicide project. Maybe. I'm still too mad at him to think like that, and the hormones don't help. Plus, it's hard to forgive someone when you're looking over your shoulder all the time, waiting for whatever booby trap he's set up to reveal what you've *really* been hiding.

I know, I know. I'm a hypocrite. I'm the one who made us promise we would always be honest with each other. That stupid pact is what started all this in the first place. But hey, give me a break! When we made that pact, the worst thing we could think of to share—once I had told about my parents' divorce—was our middle names (mine is Dorothy, Emmett's is *Herbert*). Besides, obviously I'm not the only one who broke it. So back off!

"Josh, do you think you could move down a seat? I would like to sit next to Murphy. You know, my *date*," Krystal says to Emmett's brother, louder than seems necessary.

Honestly I don't see why Krystal goes to the trouble of embarrassing herself over Murphy. He certainly wouldn't do it for her. Most of the time she swears up and down they're not in a relationship and she's fine with that. She's still getting over what's-his-name that she dated since high school, and she's not ready for anything real, and blah-blah-blah. But then there's times like these when it's obvious she wants everyone to treat her like she's part of a legitimate couple. Weddings make people a little desperate, I think.

I'm glad I've never had to go to one of these things alone, with everyone else coupled off. Poor Ruby, the only one in the wedding party without a date. She's always been the independent one, though, trying to make it seem like it doesn't bother her that she's always single. Aaron thinks maybe it doesn't, but how could it not? I mean there's gotta be a reason she still keeps Jamie on her hook. Everyone gets lonely.

Ruby's parents are here, so is my mom and Murphy's parents, and Charlene, too, although I haven't seen her in a while. Ruby hugs Murphy's mom and Murphy hugs Ruby's in opposite corners of the reception hall, both mothers shouting about how the kids are so grown-up and how they turned out so well. I suddenly get a flash, like this is Ruby and Murphy's wedding and they're mingling with their own guests. I shudder. What a disaster that would be. Murphy's a Chatwick boy through and through, and if the last few years have been any indication, he would sooner jump off a bridge than settle down. And Ruby, well, now that I've seen her in New York, I can't help but notice how jittery and unsure of herself she is here, in the place where she grew up. Ruby's not comfortable in Chatwick, and Murphy's not comfortable a mile outside of it. They would have to be married over Skype.

Ruby sits next to me and Aaron at the head table, and I notice her refilling her champagne twice over dinner. Either she's loosened up over the years, realizing that just because her mother's an alcoholic doesn't mean she is, or else she is starting to show signs . . . When I make eyes at Aaron, he mouths, "Worrywart" at me.

Murphy gives his speech. His hands shake as he reads from his piece of lined paper, and his voice is a little wobbly at first, but he does good anyway. He makes a joke about Emmett making all the wedding plans because he's too particular to leave them up to Steph. He says how beautiful Steph is, and how lucky she and Emmett are to have found each other. It's one of those moments when it hits home that we're all grown-up. I'm sitting here pregnant, Emmett is getting married, and Murphy is giving a toast that doesn't have any burps or swear words in it. It's good and bad. Good because we're independent; we're choosing the lives we want to live. Bad because it's a slippery slope until we're old, and the first one of us has already died.

Elizabeth gives a beautiful toast, talking about how Steph was the first one to tell her she should go to college, and how Steph's support is what got her through some really hard times with her own family. Everyone cries. By comparison, Krystal's toast seems a little whiney; she manages to sneak in a reference to her surprise that she will be the last one married out of their little group. I think she thought it would be funny, but it was just kinda awkward.

The only fun thing about being at a Chatwick wedding and not drinking is watching how stupid everybody looks the more *they* drink. The dance floor is full of fools, and even though I'm dead tired and my feet ache more than they do after a full day at the salon, I dance, too. Your friends only get married once. Hopefully.

At one point Aaron and I are dancing in the middle of the floor, and Emmett and Steph are next to us. Ruby and Murphy see us and hip-bump their way through fourteen million of Steph's cousins to join us. It's like no one else is there, just our little crew, like always. I mean, it's Steph instead of Tara. And Danny's not here. But right now all that matters is the rest of us are together. My heart swells with the love I have for these people. My chosen family, who understand each other better than any outsider ever could, secrets or no.

And then Krystal is there. She swoops in from whatever corner she's been sulking in and she's got that look in her eye, like she's had about enough and is about to make a stand, ruining everyone else's time in the process. I shoot her a warning look and she relaxes a little bit, pretends she just came over to dance. She shakes her way in between Ruby and Murphy, who, in Krystal's defense, *are* a bit glued together.

Ruby arches an eyebrow at me, but she tries to pretend that getting boxed out doesn't bother her. She dances with me and Aaron instead, taking deep swigs from Aaron's beer. When Krystal leaves to request a song, there Ruby goes, back to Murphy, both of them throwing their heads back and laughing like they've never had a better time in their lives. If she's trying to butter him up before she tells him what she's hiding, I think it's working. The music changes to a slow song and I see a moment of hesitation before they clamp together, swaying back and forth.

I stop paying attention to them and look into my husband's eyes. It's not our song, but I remember dancing to it at our wedding, and even though my swollen tummy makes it hard to be near to each other, I know we're even closer now than we were the day we got married.

I hear a stomping of heels and suddenly Krystal is back. She puts her hand on Ruby's shoulder and gives her one firm push. "I'll take it from here, Ruby," she says.

Ruby takes one step backward from the force, but she doesn't say anything. She looks stunned.

"Uh-oh," Aaron says to me under his breath.

"Krys, I was dancing with Ruby," Murphy says.

"Oh, trust me, *I know* you were dancing with Ruby," Krystal slurs. "The little slut's been all over you all night. I'm just trying to take my date back."

"Excuse me?" Ruby says, whisper-yelling. I can tell she's at least *trying* to be respectful that we're at our friend's wedding, unlike Krystal, who seems to be itching to cause a scene.

"Uh-oh is right," I say to Aaron, leaving him so that I can guide the two girls off the dance floor. Krystal clings to Murphy's arms, like she's hoping he will start dancing with her and then the fight will be over, she wins. If you ask me, the prize isn't worth it. Obviously I love Murphy, but he has got to be the most selfish person I've ever met in my life. Murphy never does anything he doesn't want to do, and if he's doing you a favor, it's probably because he either owes you one or he's looking for you to owe him one. But these girls, it's like they think it's charming or something, his complete lack of thought for anyone else. Case in point, he doesn't defend either Krystal or Ruby, but just stands there and waits for me to clean up his mess. I'm a mother already, and I haven't even given birth yet.

I put one hand on Krystal's shoulders and one on Ruby's and lead them away from the crowd. They can't fight me off, I'm pregnant. Aaron, Emmett, Steph, and Murphy all follow us off the floor and into the lobby of the reception hall. I might not be able to put out this fire, but I can at least try to quarantine it before it spreads across the whole damn reception. No luck. It's already been lit. On the way out of the room I catch sight of Charlene, who is propping up the bar and cackling. Next to her is Nancy, who has a glass of clear liquid in front of her that I can only hope is water or seltzer.

"What is your PROBLEM?" Ruby explodes once we're through the doors of the hall and in the lobby. "We were just dancing! We've been friends since we were little kids. I can't dance with someone I've known my whole life at our friend's wedding?" Ruby is Fired Up. It's just like the halls of Chatwick High—Ruby fuming because one of Murphy's girlfriends was rude to her. Is it the alcohol that's aging her down ten years, or is she just under the influence of Murphy?

"I'm getting a little tired of this lifelong-friend bullshit," Krystal says, arms crossed. "I barely even heard of you, until Danny topped himself—"

"Watch it, Krystal," I cut in.

"Sure, Ally, stick up for your *best friend* Ruby, because I mentioned your *best friend* Danny. Did you know your *best friend* Ruby was *sleeping* with your *best friend* Murphy?"

I pause. How would Krystal know about that? I glance at my friends, who all look confused, except for Murphy and Ruby. Ruby shakes her head just enough so that I can see. But the cat's out of the bag now, so we might as well declaw it. "That was a long time ago, Krystal. What business is it of yours?"

Krystal holds one stubby finger about an inch away from my face and slurs, "One week after Danny's funeral—after I'd given Murphy the space *he said he needed*—I went to spend the night at his house. *Resuming our normal routine.*" She says this last sentence pointedly at Ruby, who is biting her cheek, her arms crossed now. "I smell perfume on my pillow that is *definitely* not mine. I ask Murphy about it, but he tells me I'm crazy. Then we go to New York, I hug Ruby when we get there, and for the rest of the day her *stench* is on my clothes, and I know. I know it was *her*." She points at Ruby, who is no longer shaking her head.

Oh.

When Ruby finally admitted Murphy was the father of her baby, I guess it wasn't a *total* shock. I mean, we all had our suspicions there was more than just friendship there. But it never occurred to me they *still* had something going on, after all this time. And what business does Ruby have *sleeping* with a man, when she hasn't even told him he knocked her up?

Aaron, good old peacemaking, tension-breaking Aaron, slugs

Murphy on the arm. "Jesus, Murph, change your sheets much?" I can't help it. I laugh.

Krystal narrows her eyes at me. "Oh, is that funny, Ally? It's so *funny* that your perfect little Ruby *screwed* Murphy, even knowing I was in the picture? Oh, but that's right! I remember, you don't place too high a value on fidelity, do you?"

I feel like I've been slapped. And I have a sinking feeling I know where she's going with this.

Aaron's face hardens. "All right, I've heard about enough of this. Let's go." He puts his arm around Krystal, gripping her shoulder, trying to guide her outside, even farther away from the reception. At this point, I hope he dumps her in a snow bank.

"Don't put so much effort into defending your wife, Aaron," she says, practically spitting as she talks now. "She probably wouldn't even *be* your wife, if you knew she had sex with Danny Deuso!"

He drops his grip.

"That's right," Krystal says, marching back to me, breathing her cheap-beer breath straight into my nose. "That's right, Ally, I read your *precious* secret. It was there in your purse on the bus ride home, and I read it while you were sleeping, and I didn't say anything until now because *I'm* a good friend. Loyal. But I'm not going to stand here and have you act like Miss Perfect, because you're not. You're not. You slept with Danny! You cheated on Aaron!"

And there it is. My secret is out. About a half second later, Ruby lunges for Krystal. Emmett catches her just one inch before her fist makes contact with Krystal's face. I can tell he didn't want to stop her, and I wish he had hesitated one second longer. As he drags Ruby away, she shouts so many swear words I haven't even heard some of them. She must have picked them up on the subway. Emmett puts his hand over her mouth.

"Ruby, shut up! Jesus, the whole hall can hear you!" he scolds her. She continues to struggle as Krystal stands there smugly, inching her way back over to Murphy, who keeps stepping farther away.

"Tell me this isn't true, Ally," Aaron pleads.

I say nothing. I can't. He looks at me, his eyes starting to glaze over with tears. His hands go to his head, his fists clench around clumps of the hair I took fifteen minutes to style.

"Was it his?" he asks hoarsely.

I blink. "Was what whose?"

"Was it Danny's baby?"

Oh my God, he still thinks I'm lying about the abortion, and now he thinks I hid it because it was *Danny's*! I shake my head. "No, Aaron, you've got it wrong—"

"Oh, SPARE me!" he yells, his arms flying up into the air.

"Aaron, let's just go outside and talk about this."

"I don't want to talk to you! Every time we talk, I get a different story. Speaking of which, real genius move, getting Ruby involved. What did you hold over her head to get her to go along with it?"

Suddenly I feel like a caged animal. My eyes search desperately until they land on Ruby. She is still struggling against Emmett's grip, his hand still clamped firmly over her mouth. She is shouting through it, and judging by Emmett's winces, trying to bite her way out.

Aaron turns to leave, and suddenly I know if he walks out that door without knowing the truth, I will lose him forever. But even if I tell the truth—if I throw my friend under the bus in front of everyone, in front of Murphy, who shouldn't have to find out like this—it won't make a difference. He won't believe me.

"Aaron, stop," says Murphy, stepping out from the corner to block my husband's exit. We all whip our heads toward him. What could he possibly contribute to this situation?

"I don't know about Ally and Danny, not for sure anyway—and if something did happen, it was a long time ago. But I do know this. Ally didn't have an abortion. Ruby did. Danny put Ruby's secret in Ally's envelope."

Our mouths hang open like we're trying to catch flies.

"How do you know that?" Aaron demands. "Did they tell you to say that?"

"No," Murphy says. "I know because I'm the one who got her pregnant. I knew about it and never said anything. That was my secret."

"It was when we weren't together!" I yell after Aaron, who is walking away from me. We are in the parking lot, and neither of us have coats on to protect us from the December—almost January—air. My teeth chatter, and in the back of my mind I'm worried about what a lowered body temperature will do to the baby. In the front of my mind, though, is desperation at the thought of my husband leaving me. Even after he seemed to believe what Murphy said, he still walked out. Because my real secret, that I slept with Danny, is upsetting enough, without bringing a secret pregnancy into it.

Aaron stops in his tracks. Turns. "So what, Al, you guys did it when you were like fourteen? You're telling me I wasn't your first? Where do the lies end?"

"No," I say, waving my hands. "No, it was that month when you first went away to college. *You* were the one who wanted to break up, remember? I was devastated! I loved you, and I wanted to make it work, but you thought it would be better for us to have some time apart, to figure out if it's what we really wanted. You can't be mad I slept with someone when we weren't together! *You* slept with Christie Bedard during that time, if you remember."

"Yeah, but I came clean about it, Ally! And as I remember, I had to work for *months* to regain your trust after that, and *still* you've held it over my head for a decade. Always bragging that I'm the only man you've ever slept with, like you're some saint. And all the while, you slept with one of our friends? Danny, no less?"

"I was hurt! I thought we would be together forever, and then you dumped me! I just needed . . . I needed someone to make me feel less hopeless. And there was Danny, telling me he always had a thing for me . . ."

I can hardly remember the night. The first night, anyway. It was late. I had drunk a good amount of wine, had a good cry over a chick flick, and then Danny called to tell me he had heard that Aaron and I had split. He wanted to see if I was okay. I was drunk, and alone. Tara had just left for college, and even though Ruby hadn't left yet, she was MIA most of the summer, so I didn't feel like I could call her. So I asked Danny to come over. He was there in minutes. He told me he was sorry, that Aaron was an idiot; that if he had me, he would never have let me go. And then he told me he had feelings for me—that he'd had a crush on me since we were kids. I basically mauled him, I was so hungry to feel wanted. And besides, I had always thought Danny was cute, in a below-the-tracks kind of way. I told myself it would just be the one time, but he kept showing up, never letting me feel down, never letting me be alone. After a week he told me he was in love with me, that he wanted to be with me. Instead, I got back together with Aaron.

"Always had a thing for you?" Aaron says. "Are you kidding me right now, Ally? We hung out with that kid every day. You're telling me he looked straight into my eyes, acting like we were all just such good friends, and the whole time he was trying to get you for himself?"

"No! I never knew anything about it until the night . . . it happened. I swear, Danny never said anything. He loved you, too, and he always respected our relationship. But then . . . we didn't have one and . . ."

"And he took advantage of you," Aaron says. It's more of a challenge than a question.

The countdown from inside the hall interrupts us. "Four . . . three . . . two . . . one . . . Happy New Year!" and Aaron and I just stand there, staring at each other, my heart in my hands. Aaron waits for reassurance I'm not sure I can give. Danny didn't take advantage of me, any more than I wanted to be taken advantage of. I may not have loved Danny the way he loved me, but I wanted him that night, and the night after that, and the week after that. The time he and I spent together was one of the most painful and beautiful times in my life, and when Aaron and I decided to get back together, part of me was sad to have to let Danny go. No relationship is perfect, and when things get rough with Aaron, I always have the memory of my time with Danny to get me through. But I can't say that to Aaron. My husband has to come before Danny's memory. So I just shrug, and decide it's okay to keep this one thing hidden inside my heart. No slip of paper is going to destroy my marriage.

# CHAPTER TWENTY-TWO

# STEPH

*Now*

Ally chases Aaron into the parking lot. Murphy drags Ruby off before she can storm away. Krystal, happy with the mess she's created, practically skips back into my reception, looking over her shoulder to make sure Ruby isn't behind her. I love Krys and all, and I get why she would be upset with Murphy, but I gotta say, after that little tantrum I wouldn't have minded seeing her get hit. And seeing Ruby so fired up like that was kind of thrilling. She's been so reserved since I've met her. Friendly, but like she was holding back. Can't take the Chatwick out of the girl, I guess.

It's just me and Emmett left in the lobby. "Welcome to the family, baby," Emmett says to me with a wink. He pulls me into a hug, kisses my forehead, and rests his chin on my skull. I love it when he does that. I hate to sound old-fashioned, but it's nice to feel tiny and protected. I should probably be upset, both by the fact that this drama is currently gobbling up all the attention and by the subject matter itself, but I can't seem to stop smiling. I'm married. I'm Emmett's wife. And the fact that his friends—my friends—have all humped each other doesn't seem like such an insurmountable crisis, considering the things we've been through this year.

Furthermore, it seems my strategy to reveal *just enough* about Emmett worked. Looks like everyone lied about their secrets, but we're the only ones who got away with it. I know he told Ruby about it, so hopefully that will satisfy Danny's requirement and we are taken care of, karmically speaking. I'm not too concerned about Ruby knowing. Out of all of them, *that* girl, apparently, can keep one hell of a secret. Thank God we paid off our debts and Emmett isn't doing that anymore. Every time he went up to Canada I thought *I* was going to end up needing a heart operation.

I hear the countdown and kiss Emmett at the stroke of midnight. I can only hope this is the first of decades of New Year's kisses we will share. I sigh and bury my head into my new husband's chest, breathing him in. I don't ever want to leave his side, don't want to be away from him for even one minute tonight, but I pull back.

"I should go check on Ally," I tell him. "Make sure she's okay." He nods, smiles. I get the sense I've passed some kind of test by not throwing a fit about the disruption. I feel more like I've been hazed. I grab Ally's coat and, as an afterthought, put on mine. If Aaron ran off, she could be outside alone and need to talk, and Lord knows how long that's going to take. As acclimated to the cold as any native Vermonter, I'm still in a strapless wedding dress, for Pete's sake.

I push open the door of the reception hall and peer out into the darkness. "Al?" I call. No response. The parking lot is empty of people and silent, except for . . . what is that creaking? I scan the rows of cars and find Aaron's truck rocking back and forth, the windows all fogged up. I giggle to myself. Those two. I hope Emmett and I have as active a sex life as them, when we've been married for five years and/or I'm pregnant with our first kid. The latter of which should happen any day now, if all goes well. I know Emmett's going to be okay. I know it. But I'm not taking any chances.

I turn and walk back into the hall, ready to return to the festivities. I decide to go to the bathroom first, and on the way I hear voices in the stairwell. I know I shouldn't listen, but it could be Krystal and Ruby about to resume where they left off, and bloodshed is not exactly how I want this night to end.

"—this *whole* time?" It's Ruby.

"I'm sorry, Ruby, I—"

"*How* did you know?"

"Danny."

"But *he* didn't even know until *after* you guys fought. I thought you never spoke after that?"

"We spoke once. He called me after he took you to your first appointment at Planned Parenthood, to tell me what was happening. Danny convinced you to put the abortion off for a few days, to give me time to get down there."

"He *said* that?"

"He said he didn't care whether I stopped you or not, he just thought I should know and that I should be there."

"But you didn't agree? What? Too busy with your *perfect, pure* little girlfriend?"

"That's not fair."

"Don't talk to me about what's fair, Murphy Leblanc. Jesus, did you ever love me at all?"

Whoa! Now I *really* shouldn't be listening.

"Of course I—"

"Because I don't see how you could say you love somebody—how you could even claim to be my best friend—when you knew I was going through that and you didn't even . . . you didn't even . . ." Her voice breaks, and I can tell she's crying. Or struggling not to cry.

"You weren't exactly innocent, Ruby. You made Danny swear *not* to tell the father of your child that you were even pregnant. Your *best friend.* I've been waiting for you to tell me yourself for ten goddamn years! How do you think it made me feel, to be cut out of a decision like that? How do you think it made me feel, that you wanted so little to do with me you would do *that* to a life we made together, without even talking to me about it?"

"If you were so *hurt* by it, why did you sleep with me the day after the funeral? Why did you maul me at Ally's Christmas party? You didn't seem too hurt then."

That little sneak! Right under Krystal's nose? Even if they aren't an official couple, Murphy couldn't at least be a little more discreet? Krys was *at* that party.

"You didn't let me finish. I *was* hurt. But in the end, I knew you were making the only decision you could, given our . . . circumstances. I stayed away because I respected your decision to keep me out of it. I left you alone so that you could do what you wanted and move on."

"Yeah, that sounds like you, Murph. So *selfless.* I'm sure it had nothing to do with the fact that you got off scot-free and didn't have to give up your little backup girlfriend," Ruby spits back. "I lost everything, Murphy. And what I didn't lose, I gave away. Not just for me. It was so that *you* could be free to do what *you* wanted. I didn't want you to be forced to stay with me if I decided to keep it, and I didn't want you to have to go through the pain if . . ."

" . . . you decided to abort."

"Right. Only those weren't the only two options, Murphy."

They're both quiet for a beat. Oh God, I think I know what's coming, and I only wish I could see Murphy's face. "What are you saying to me?" he asks.

"I didn't get the abortion. I had the baby, and I gave it up for adoption."

Just as I think I'm about to pass out at the thought of Murphy Leblanc being a father, the lobby door swings open and Charlene tells me to get my ass in gear because it's the last dance. My feet are heavy as lead as I walk away from the stairwell, where a bomb the size of Canada has been dropped on Emmett's best man. I let Charlene lead me to my husband, whose tie is now wrapped around his head, and join him to enjoy the last few minutes of our wedding.

# CHAPTER TWENTY-THREE

# RUBY
## *Back then*

"That's it, honey, you can do it. Push! Push!" The nurse props me up, her small frame almost completely wedged between me and the inclined bed. A vague worry that I will crush this nice woman floats around somewhere in a distant part of my brain that can still think about things other than my own pain. She was assigned to me when I came in without the standard-issue clueless male to hold my hand and curse at for doing this to me in the first place. She wipes the hair off my forehead, slick with sweat from eight hard hours of labor. The epidural wore off around hour four.

I don't know the nurse's name. I'm sure she told me, but I blocked it out, along with the million other details of this day. Less to try to erase from my memory later. I allow her to wipe my brow, rub my shoulders, feed me ice chips. I allow her to take care of me like I haven't been taken care of in a long time. Every time she touches me, I stifle a cry until the pain comes again, so that I have an excuse to let it out. It's not just the baby ripping through my body, it's my heart.

When at last the baby is born, the doctor, whose name I also pointedly ignore, asks me if I'm sure I don't want to know the sex; if I'm sure I don't want to hold the baby. I shake my head, tears rolling down my cheeks like the rain that streaks the windowpane that I have now rolled over to face. I squeeze my eyes shut so I won't see anything. The baby cries, and a pain like I've never felt before rips through my body. I want nothing *more* than to know the sex of the life I've carried inside me for the better part of a year. I want nothing *more* than to hold that life in my arms. "Get it out of here," I whisper instead. They move quickly and exit the room, but I continue to whimper, "Get it out of here."

The nurse stays behind. I want her to leave so I can cry the way I need to. Loudly, ferociously. But I don't want her to leave me, either. I can't be alone so suddenly after having a little partner attached to me for nine months. She stays and "cleans me up," as she says. No matter what she does, I still feel inhuman. I can't believe millions of women go through this voluntarily, and more than once, in some cases.

"You must think I'm a monster," I say to the ceiling, afraid to meet her kind eyes. "I just couldn't—"

"Oh, honey, no." She walks up next to the bed and lays a reassuring hand on my arm. "Some people want to hold them, for closure's sake. Some people think it will just make it harder. Nobody's judging you, because either way, what you've done says more about the kind of person you are than anything that comes after."

I try to smile, to show her that what she says has helped me. But it hasn't, and I can't.

"Are you sure there isn't anyone I can call for you?" she asks. "The adoptive parents . . ."

"They're already here," she says. "Do you want to see them?"

I shake my head. I chose them from a binder full of desperate barren couples, all smiling at me, their blurbs all trying to convince me they would be the perfect family for my child. Lucy and Michelle run a bookstore in Delaware. They found each other later in life and opted to adopt rather than shoot themselves up with hormones and sperm. I liked the idea of my child hiding in book stacks and living in a small state. I made sure the adoption agency told them about the history of mental illness in my family. They were okay with it, so I was okay with them. But I was very specific when we set up the terms for the adoption. I allowed them to pay my medical expenses so I wouldn't have to go through my parents' insurance. I allowed them to come to some of the doctor's appointments. But once I had the baby, I didn't want any contact. They said they would still tell the kid, when it was time, that he or she was adopted (once the kid learns his birds and bees, he would naturally have some questions), but they would keep my identity a secret. When he turns eighteen, if he wants to find me, he'll have to go through the agency, and the agency will have to contact me. I'm already dreading the day, eighteen years from today, when I will have to make that decision. Or worse, if I don't have to make it, because he doesn't want to know me. But at the same time, I can't imagine waiting eighteen years.

"Anyone else I can call for you? Your family?"

I shake my head. There's no one. No one even knows I'm here, except for Lucy and Michelle. Well, and my Resident Adviser. After I threw Danny out, I confided in my RA so she would appeal to the university to keep the other half of the room unoccupied, due to my "special circumstances." I figured she was a safe bet, since she's bound by confidentiality and could be an emergency contact, should anything bad happen. But tonight when I woke up in a puddle of embryotic fluid, rather than wake her up, I slipped a note under her door. I was perfectly capable of taking a cab myself, and I didn't know her well enough to obligate her to share this experience with me. About every five minutes during labor, I thought about calling Ally. Even after all this time with no contact, she would drive here like a bat out of hell if I picked up the phone.

My parents were easier to keep in the dark than I thought. I saw them once, at parents' weekend, when I was still not far enough along to show. After that I made stuff up—I was skiing with my roommate in Aspen for Christmas; partying in Cancun for Spring Break. All the things I should have been doing in my freshman year of college. After my second trimester (when I could no longer throw on an oversized sweater and claim the Freshman Fifteen), I begged out of every dinner request by my father, citing homework or a date. I lived in fear he would get frustrated at my excuses and show up at my dorm one day, but my worry was for nothing. He isn't that kind of dad. I'm sure the people in my dorm and my classes have figured it out, but I've made it a point to keep them strangers. They don't say anything about it; they just wait until I pass to whisper. In that way, college isn't much different from Chatwick.

"The father?" the nurse asks. "You left that blank on the birth certificate."

I tell her the same lie I told the adoption agency. "I don't know who he is." I had to say this; otherwise I would have had to have Murphy sign off on the adoption. I was too scared, either that he wouldn't sign or that he would, without a fight. I seesaw about which would be worse.

"Are you sure you don't want to see him?"

A current of panic shoots through me. Does she mean the baby or the father? Is my baby—Lucy and Michelle's baby—a boy? I can't know that. I can't. So I don't ask her to clarify. I just nod. Either way, I'm sure.

The nurse turns to leave, but I stop her.

"How long until the pain goes away?" I ask.

"Well, you'll be sore for a few—"

"—that's not what I mean."

I knew, when I made this decision, it would be hard. Even before my fight with Danny, the one where he basically called me a murderer, I had already been waffling. The judgment of my drug-dealing, stepfather-killing friend was not what put me over the edge. I still went to my appointment, but after I had been prepped and was lying there with my shaking legs in the stirrups, I sat up and shouted at them to stop, that I couldn't go through with it. I knew I couldn't keep the baby, but I also knew that, without me and Murphy for parents, it might have a chance of a good life. A chance to make two other people's lives whole.

The nurse looks at me, pity filling her eyes. Normally I would find it condescending, but right now I can accept it.

She sits on my bed. "I've never given a baby up for adoption, but my first child was born early, much too early. Stillborn." Her eyes moisten. "I would imagine that, even though your baby is alive and well, it feels something like that."

I nod. Perhaps.

"I can't say you'll ever be completely free of it, honey. The first few weeks will be the hardest, because your body will be telling you it's time to feed the baby and your hormones will be all out of whack. It will get easier after that. Every day will get a little easier, and then one day you'll wake up and you'll feel almost normal. And soon after that, you'll be grateful."

"Grateful?"

"I know it sounds crazy, but one day you will heal, and you'll be grateful you got through it. And you will be grateful for the choice you made, because it means a better life for four people. You, the new parents, *and* the baby."

*Five people*, I think. *Murphy*.

I worry that she is about to call Jesus into the conversation, belittling the women who did keep their feet in those stirrups and make the choice that was right for them. I don't have the strength to defend them, but I don't think they're any less brave than I am. They'll never be the same, either. But she doesn't launch into a pro-life sermon.

"I know I've only known you for a day, Ruby, but it's the hardest day you will probably ever have. And if it means anything to you, I think you're the bravest young woman I've ever met."

"I don't feel brave," I murmur. How can I? Right now I feel like marching down that hallway and yanking my baby out of Lucy and Michelle's proud and loving arms. Right now I feel like everything I've done to protect this secret was completely insane. It was crazy to think I could pull this off and walk away unscathed. I thought it would be the best thing for everyone. For Nancy, whose mother once let it slip that her bipolar worsened after the stress and hormone changes that came with having children. For Murphy, who was in no way prepared to handle this. For the baby, who deserved a chance at a family who wanted it. And for me, who just wants to have the big life I always dreamed of. But right now, my life seems very small. Seven pounds, nine ounces small.

I cry into the nurse's arms until she administers a sedative and I drift off to sleep.

The next morning I wake up, check out of the hospital, and try to pretend it was all a dream.

# CHAPTER TWENTY-FOUR

# RUBY

## *Now*

I tug on the brass handle of Charlene's—her deli, not her house—pleased to find the door is no easier to open than it was ten years ago. Muscle memory kicks in, and I perform a combination of deftly aimed kicks and yanks before the door swings violently open. The patrons inside do not so much as glance up from their newspapers or tear their eyes from the chalkboard menu above the deli counter. They study it as if they don't have it memorized, as if they won't be ordering the same thing they did yesterday and the day before that. On the first day of this new year, already they are breaking their resolutions to eat more healthily, to try new things. I'm sticking with mine: to be honest. With others, but most of all with myself.

A man in line is wearing a blue jumpsuit with the word "Borbeau's" in block letters on the chest pocket. I don't recognize the man, but part of me feels like I should approach him, tell him I knew Danny, tell him I'm sorry he lost his coworker. But upon closer inspection, I see it's not a man at all. It's a boy. About the age Danny was when he *started* working at Borbeau's. This boy is Danny's replacement. Working on New Year's Day even though the shop is closed, either because he needs the money or because he's picked up where Danny's side business left off and there are lots of people just itching to break their resolutions.

He even has sandy hair like Danny's, but his eyes aren't nearly as blue. And his presence isn't half as magnetic.

Murphy sits in one of the red-pleather upholstered booths that Charlene removed an aisle of liquor to make room for, back when she became the owner. (Chatwick near-rioted over the change.) He's in the booth farthest from the door, as if we're likely to have any privacy anywhere in this town. But he suggested we finish the conversation from last night here, rather than at his apartment, exactly *because* it's public. Even considering how we're both feeling right now, at his place it would be too easy to get off the topic.

*They're both really good at ignoring problems.*

I'm a bundle of nerves as I slide into the seat opposite him. We make small talk about the weather for a few minutes: how unusual it is for the temperature to be above thirty-five degrees at the beginning of January, how a Nor'easter is due later in the week but should hold off long enough that my flight home won't be affected. I've never felt more awkward making small talk in my life, because I'm sitting with Murphy Leblanc and we're supposed to be past all this. An observer might think we're on our first date, rather than our last.

A waitress comes over who can't be more than sixteen. Plump white rolls of skin spill over the sides of her low-rise jeans, a lacy hot-pink bra strap peeking out from a black camisole. I want to ask her how she's not freezing, and that makes me feel old. I ask if Charlene is here, but the girl tells us with a smirk that she is home, "recovering." I'm not surprised; as I climbed into Murphy's truck after the reception, I saw my parents piling her into their car to give her a ride home. Charlene's car remained in the lot for the hours that he and I stayed there talking.

Once our order is in, we twirl straws and rearrange cutlery.

Murphy is the one who called this morning to invite me to lunch. Let him speak first.

"Quite the drama last night, huh?" he starts.

He hopes I will take over from here, but I just smile and nod, take a sip of my drink. I'm too afraid to say anything. He has every right to be furious with me, and yet he seems . . . normal. I'm waiting for the other shoe to drop.

He continues, "Mom says it's not a wedding without drama." I wonder if he's already told Cecile what we talked about last night, but I decide he couldn't have. If Cecile suddenly became aware there was a grandchild who had been kept from her, I would have heard from her already. It's part of the reason I did not tell Murphy I was pregnant. I was afraid I wouldn't be strong enough to stand up to her, and the decision would be out of my hands.

"It was nice to see Cecile," I say.

"She misses you. You know she still has our prom picture on her mantel, still in the little cardboard-thingy it came in?"

A breathy laugh escapes my nose. "Really?"

"Kept it up the entire time me and Taylor were together, too. Used to drive her crazy."

The victorious little thrill that goes through me at this is embarrassing, but hearing Taylor's name reminds me of last night's conversation. I had demanded to know who Murphy had told about the pregnancy, and he had replied, "Only Taylor." I should have been happy, I guess, that he protected the information. But the thought of Taylor being the person who helped him through such a heavy period, despite knowing the circumstances that created the child, made me feel ill. I picked a great girl to set Murphy up with, and then I tried to steal him away, and when that didn't work I slept with him anyway. And in the end, Taylor was his best friend and I was the enemy.

"Listen, about—" Murphy starts.

I hold up a hand to stop him. "Do we have to go through it all again?" I ask. Last night, I told him everything: when I found out I was pregnant; all the thoughts that went through my head; what happened when Danny showed up and what happened after; how I kept it a secret from everyone. Murphy told me how he found out—Danny had called him after the first Planned Parenthood appointment; it was why Danny wanted me to wait a week, to give Murphy the chance to be there for me, to be part of the decision. He defended his choice to stay out of it—he was hurt, he was scared, he didn't feel he had a right to interfere. I justified why I didn't tell Murphy myself—I was hurt, I was scared, and I didn't want him to interfere. We didn't accomplish much, beyond draining his gas tank from the blasting heat while we talked circles around each other.

He looks at me now, swallows. "I think you know there's more to be said. I think you know that's why we're here." I realize he's nervous too, his eyes unable to focus on mine for too long, before darting around. "I just stared at my ceiling all night, thinking of questions I should have asked, things I should have said different."

I don't tell him that after we parted, I had the best night's sleep I've had in ten years. But not before sitting at the kitchen table with Nancy, who was waiting up for me when I got home. We shared a kettle of hot cocoa and a plate of blueberry pancakes she had whipped up after the wedding and placed in the oven to keep warm. After having several days to digest the news that I had hid an entire pregnancy from her, she told me only how sorry she was that I had gone through that alone. She thinks I made "the most beautiful decision" she could think of, and that she's never been prouder of me. I was still nurturing the anger from learning that Murphy abandoned me, knowing full well what I was going through. "You have to remember, baby girl," Nancy said, "not everyone is as strong as you. In fact, not many people are."

"Okay," I concede. We both received new information last night, but when we weigh our secrets pound for pound, even I have to admit his new burden is more significant. "Where do you want to start?"

"I was so mad last night, but when I got home all I could think about is how you went through all that alone. I'm sorry."

I stay silent. My instinct is to tell him it wasn't his fault because he didn't know, but now I know that's not entirely true.

"What was it like? Did you have anyone there with you?"

I blink at him, realizing he could only be talking about one thing. "I don't want to talk about the birth," I say.

"But—"

"Murphy. It's off-limits. I'm sorry if that's not fair, but no." I can't go there. I will never stop crying if I do. The memory is mine, and no matter how descriptive I am, there's no way he can share it.

As the waitress delivers our sandwiches in red plastic baskets, Murphy grinds the ice in his cup with his straw, his jaw set. "Can you at least tell me if it was a girl or a boy?" he asks when she leaves. Neither of us touches our food.

I swallow. If only we could have started with a softball. *Why didn't I see any stretch marks, the day after Danny's funeral?* perhaps. (Answer: You weren't looking for them.) "I don't know," I say. "I asked them to take the baby away right after."

His face falls again. I feel like I have to give him something. So I say what I've never said out loud. "I feel like it was a boy."

He gets a little sparkle in his eye. I know he's picturing tossing a baseball around with a hyperactive little boy with a mop of black hair in his eyes. The sparkle vanishes as the daydream does, the anger from the impossibility settling in.

"Doesn't it *bother* you that a piece of you—a piece of *us*—is walking around in the world not knowing us? And we don't know if he's happy, or safe, or feeling abandoned?"

"Of course it does. It bothers me every day. Every single day I worry about that. And I'm really sorry to say it, but now you will, too." As I say it, I wonder if it's true. All these years I've envied Murphy for not knowing. I even resented him for it, even though it was my doing. But now, knowing that he knew I was pregnant, I wonder. Will it be the same for him? Will it stay with him, crashing into him at random times with varying degrees of strength? Or will he be able to shrug it off, like getting hit by a pitch? Take his base and forget about it by the time he gets his next turn at bat.

The silence after this stretches on and on until finally Murphy asks, "He would be, what, ten years old?"

An alarm sounds in my head, and I stiffen. "Nine," I say.

"Do you know where he lives?"

"Murphy, the adoption is closed."

"I know that. You told me that."

"I understand this is all brand-new, and maybe your gut is telling you to find him and try to be a part of his life, maybe even to try to get him back—"

"I didn't say I was going to—"

"I'm begging you not to do that. I'm begging you to leave him alone. He has the parents he has, they're all he knows, and I don't want his life to be turned upside down. No matter how either of us might feel, we have to think about what's best for him."

He raises his hands in surrender as I talk, dropping them with an awed smile when I finish. "Wow," he says.

"What?"

"Look at you. You're a mother."

When a tear slides down my cheek, he puts one of his hands over mine. With the other, he pulls a napkin from the dispenser and gives it to me.

When I recover myself, I tell him, "If he ever tries to find me—us—I promise I will include you in the decision to meet him or not."

He looks at me skeptically, then does the goofy face as he tries to raise one eyebrow. I laugh, wipe my hand on the napkin, and reach across the table to do it for him.

"I promise," I repeat as my finger makes contact. "My turn to ask questions now," I say, pulling my hand back and swatting away the remaining tears. What I want to know is unimportant, but it will change the subject. "This might seem stupid, after all this," I say. "But I have to know why you and Danny fought before he came to see me in New York."

"Ah," he says, "I can finally tell you. It was Ally."

"*Ally?*"

"I figured out that something happened between the two of them. Or at least, I suspected. It was right after Ally and Aaron got back together, and we were all at Danny's for poker night. The two of them kept exchanging this *look*, like they had a secret together. So when Ally and Aaron stepped outside for a smoke, I just lost it on him."

"Why? What did you care?"

"Aaron wasn't just some guy Ally was dating, he was our friend. I didn't like the way Danny slid in and took over, the minute his back was turned."

I knit my brow. After all the three of us had been through together, it doesn't quite compute.

"It seemed like he was doing a lot of that, that summer," Murphy adds.

Ah. "You thought there was something going on with me and Dan?"

He nods. "After what happened with us, you shut everyone out except for him."

I have to smile. How wonderfully *high school*, with all the seriousness of what we've been through, that Danny Deuso and Murphy Leblanc fought over a couple of girls. "Nothing happened, Murph. Danny and I were never more than friends."

He shakes his head. "That night he called me, to tell me you were pregnant and that you were going to . . . that was the last time we ever spoke, and I didn't even say anything. He just told me what was going on, and where I could find you, and then hung up. I think he and I probably could have gotten over the fight, eventually, if I had shown up for you. But I didn't, and when I tried to reach out when he got back into town, Danny didn't want anything to do with me. I don't blame him."

I reach across the table to hold both his hands in mine. There's nothing I can say that will make him feel better about this. If there's one thing I've known since I was a little kid, it's that sometimes things suck and you can't do anything about it. It will never be okay that Danny and Murphy wasted that time, that any of us wasted that time with him. It will never be okay that Danny is gone. It will never be okay, truly okay, that I gave away my baby, and it will never be okay that I didn't tell Murphy about it.

"I love you, Ruby. You know that, right?" He says it without looking into my eyes, just like the night he first said it.

I sniff back the fresh wave of tears and nod. "I love you, too. But where does that leave us?"

He shakes his head, and in that gesture he is saying what we both know. There is not enough love to compensate for what we've done to each other, and there was never quite enough to compensate for our differences. Even if I moved back to Vermont, I could never live in Chatwick again. And unless it's Chatwick, for Murphy it might as well be the moon. I can't ask him to meet me halfway, or even a third of the way. He belongs here every bit as much as I don't.

"I could never say never. Not to you. But right now . . ."

"It's just so unfair," I say. The words escape me, and I know they are from the most childish part of me, which used to believe in the fairy tales I would read by flashlight, before the days when Danny threw rocks at my window. I have long since known that love doesn't conquer all. "It's just—" I hasten to cover.

"I know," he says, "we never got to be together."

I nod. My heart soars. Finally knowing that this is something he regrets, too, is a gift. A painful one, but a gift all the same.

The waitress comes back and Murphy hands her a credit card without looking at the bill. "Maybe things can change a little now," he says after she leaves. "I mean, I miss talking to you. Maybe we can start there."

Damnit, Murphy. Here we are, an inch from finally closing this thing up, and he's got to crack that door open a millimeter. I nod, say of course, we'll keep in touch this time. But we won't. It's too hard. And as much as eighteen-year-old Ruby would have clung to that crack in the doorway, I can't.

"You know I think he had the right idea," he says. "Dan, I mean." The doubt must show on my face, because he explains further. "Maybe he wasn't just trying to get back at us for the way his life turned out. Maybe he really wanted to bring us all back together."

I have to laugh. "And Emmett thinks *I* saw the best in him."

"Really, though, don't you feel better now that the truth is out on the table?"

I think back to my peaceful night's sleep, to the lightness of my shoulders, to the pictures on my phone of all my friends. Maybe that *was* Danny's intention. Or maybe he was just stirring the pot. Either way, I can't regret coming home. I can't regret reconnecting with people who were once my family. And I can't deny that the burden on my shoulders feels a little lighter.

Speaking of which . . . "You can tell them, if you want," I say. He knows I mean tell our friends about the baby.

"No," he says. "It's your secret to tell or not tell."

I shake my head back. "It's not just mine anymore. That's how this works."

He thinks for a moment. "Okay. Then it should just be ours."

He grins wickedly as he shrugs his Carhartt jacket on. It seems that he and I will always have secrets that no one else knows. No matter what Dan may have wanted.

We stand to leave, and Murphy pulls me into a hug. "I think you did the right thing, giving the baby up," he says into my hair. "And I'm really proud of you—the woman you've become—despite everything." I hold him tighter, refusing to let go until I can blink the tears back into my eyelids. "Just . . . get back to writing now, okay?" he adds.

I pull back, laugh. Nod. I think I have some good material. As we make for the exit, a familiar face passes through the door.

"Hey there, Miss Ruby," Shawna says, as if it were hours since my last shift at The Exchange, instead of years. I do not keep as cool. Seeing Shawna after such a nerve-racking and awkward conversation is like a glass of water after a marathon, and I thrust myself into her ample bosom for a hug. Murphy stands awkwardly to the side, and I wave him off.

*You can go*, I think.

Our eyes connect as he hesitates. *Are you sure?*

He still looks hesitant, and I know he's thinking the same thing as me: will this be the last time we see each other? Probably not. The last time I thought we'd never see each other again, I wound up pregnant, tied to him forever.

*Go*, I think, pointing at the door with my chin. *You can go now. I'm okay.*

He turns, opens the door, and walks through it. The air outside is so cold the latch is frozen, and the door refuses to close all the way, even when the waitress tugs and tugs on it. Finally she gives up and leaves it open just a crack.

"What are you doing in town?" Shawna asks. While she collects the takeout order she will bring home to her family, I tell her I was a bridesmaid at Emmett McDowell's wedding, which makes her laugh. She remembers Emmett as the pain-in-the-ass kid who would come in and point out the racks that weren't perfectly straight, never offering to rectify the situation. We grab an empty booth—cooling food be damned—and catch up. She tells me she has her own bookkeeping business, a dream she was too afraid to pursue until The Exchange closed and she had no choice. Her daughter, Ashley, who in my mind is seven, is getting ready to graduate from high school. She will go to prom this year, and Shawna's business is doing so well they were able to purchase her a car when she got her license last spring.

She asks me how I am and what became of me, and I can tell she is yet another person who is hurt that I lost touch. I tell her I live in New York, that I think I'm finally ready to start writing.

"Donna always did say you weren't going to set the world on fire," she says with a sad smile.

I let my lips reverberate. "Most of the time I don't even have the energy to search for the matches."

"I hear that, sister," she says. "Speaking of fire . . ." She points her chin at the door, where moments ago Murphy made his anticlimactic exit from my life. "What's going on there?"

I shrug. "Nothing."

She cocks her head, surveying me, looking for clues. I fear it's beating on my sleeve—my heart, as broken as it was when I was eighteen, but without the same concentration of grief and hormones rushing through it. "Old flames take the longest to burn out," she says.

"Maybe," I say, "but I think we've damn near stomped it out. Now—"

"—it's all over but the crying," we say in unison, quoting from one of the songs we used to sing while closing up the shop at night.

When our laughter dies down, Shawna shakes her head. "I have a feeling about you two. Maybe now isn't your time, but I'll be doing your makeup for your wedding someday. I just know it."

I don't argue; there's no point with Shawna. I simply smile and shake my head. "Maybe a little less glitter than for prom, yeah?"

# DANNY

*Now*

I watch them gather one by one. Emmett is first, perpetually punctual, and he hoists several camp chairs from his trunk, staging them and restaging them around the fire pit. Next to his own chair he places the full twelve-pack cooler on a pile of grass clippings left behind by some stoned teenage employee of the Chatwick Parks & Rec Department. Earlier today, Emmett exchanged the key to the park's gate for $50, palming the money and sliding it into the kid's outstretched hand like he's seen in movies.

Before long the others start to arrive, these people I watch over. The same people I was charged with watching my entire life, even though I didn't know it at the time. It was a while after my death before I stopped being angry with them. I thought they should have saved me, but once I got here, I realized that wasn't their job. The living have this Hollywood notion that friends are meant to save each other, but really we're all just there to exist alongside each other, occasionally holding someone else's pain in our own hearts to grant them a moment of respite.

Ally comes next, the only one accompanied by a guest. She bounces constantly now, in part to comfort the baby swaddled tightly into a kangaroo-pouch contraption, in part to comfort herself. This is the first time she's left the house in weeks, and she feels a sliver of the insecurity that Ruby wrestles with when she's in Chatwick—unsure of her place, now that she has a new role. Isabelle is less than a month old, and it shows in the bags under Ally's eyes, the hair free of its usual careful coloring and styling, the pooch that remains from her stretched belly. She is still every bit as beautiful as the girl I quietly lusted after for most of my adolescent years. More, perhaps. She loves Isabelle fiercely, but motherhood has been surprisingly hard for her to adjust to. Breastfeeding didn't work out, no matter what she tried, which has made her feel like a failure, and while her heart is fully charged, she is exhausted and overwhelmed by the demanding little life she holds.

Aaron pretty quickly forgave her for her tryst with me, under the condition that she never again invoke the name Christie Bedard. She hasn't since, but she will. And he will throw my name back in her face. That's marriage, from what I've seen. Regardless, she asked her husband to stay at home for this gathering. She wanted to say goodbye to me without Aaron looking for some sign of residual feelings. Fearing a hormonal surge, he didn't argue. Besides, I'm already dead; I'm not exactly a threat to him anymore. Not that I ever really was.

Murphy comes next, his nerves dampening the ferocity of his usually confident swagger. He hasn't seen or spoken to Ruby since their lunch on New Year's Day. He's picked up the phone to call, especially when he wakes from one of his nightmares, but he always hangs up before pressing Call.

Not long after the wedding, he told Krystal it was over. He was never going to commit to that girl, and he didn't want to waste her time. He did her a favor, but she doesn't exactly see it that way.

He's been a suspiciously good "uncle" to Isabelle, constantly dropping by with new toys she's too young to play with, picking her up and making a fuss over her. Ally is confused by it, but grateful for the few minutes she can duck out of the room to take a shower.

Ruby is the last to arrive, her anxiety surrounding her in a fog that no one but I can see. She hasn't been home since the wedding, but she's talked to Emmett several times, and she and Ally talk every Thursday evening. When Izzy was born, they Skyped, giggling as Ally held the baby up to the webcam as if she were Simba from *The Lion King*. Because of all the time she's already taken away from work, and her rigid new self-imposed writing schedule, Ruby wasn't able to come home for Ally's baby shower *and* this gathering. Ally chose this. She had plenty of women at her baby shower, but no other woman in the world could understand *this*.

The crew greet each other warmly. Ruby and Murphy are the last two to embrace. Neither of them knows what Steph overheard in the stairwell. She's never told anyone, including her husband, further proving that she is too good for our Emmett.

They speak, one by one, about me and about the slip of paper they each hold in their hands. A secret of theirs that I scribbled angrily before ending my life. A game I *thought* I was creating just to mess with them, to shake them out of their monotonous existences. It served a much higher purpose in the end. If I hadn't outed them, they would have drifted back apart the minute I was in the ground. And worse, their secrets would have remained as buried as my body, never to be dealt with. Even now, Ally and I, of all people, are the only ones who have told the whole truth. *Ally* and I.

I can't really blame the others. Like most of us, they don't want to shine a light on the darkest parts of their souls, the weakest parts. They were sure, like all of us are sure, that no one could possibly love us, if they knew who we truly are. What they don't understand—what I didn't understand myself, until now—is that those dark, weak parts are not ugly. They are not unlovable. They are what make us beautiful. Resilient. Strong. They turn us into who we were meant to be. The way to be sure that happens, and to be sure we won't be crushed by the burden, is to redistribute the weight a little so that someone else can come along, wedge their shoulder under it, and help us carry it.

Emmett starts off the ceremony, reading the same fake secret Steph did months before. He is happy to report his condition remains stable, and he is adjusting to "life at a lower intensity." (After this, he will pitch this phrase to Ruby for her next writing project, to which she will reply, "Write your own damn book.") He apologizes to the crew for hiding his illness from them, but they wave him away. Who are they, not to forgive him? When he's done talking, he tosses the slip of paper into the fire, and everyone cheers. Ruby shows no sign that she knows his real secret. Murphy doesn't, either, although he was in on the scam. The garage Emmett went to? In Montreal? I had no connection to it. When Murphy's brother came for his weekly weed purchase, I made sure to tell him all about the big joke, including the dates of Emmett's "drug runs." Just as I suspected, the little puppet ran straight to Murphy, who took over from there, leaving envelopes of cash in Emmett's mailbox in the middle of the night. He never said a word to anyone, and I wish I had thanked him. And now that Emmett is out of the woods, I *really* wish I could tell him what we did, just to see the look on his face. God help me, I still get a chuckle out of it.

Ally goes next. She talks about our time together, and how—as much as she loves Aaron—she misses the way I used to let her be the worst version of herself, the weakest and the meanest, because with everyone else she felt like she had to be perfect. She's learning to let go of the mean, but share the weak. When she's done talking, she tosses her slip of paper into the fire, and everyone cheers. The sick thing? I preferred her at her worst because I knew she needed me. In the end, I was made of some of the same stuff as Roger. Ruby knows that.

Murphy relays my phone call telling him that Ruby was going to have an abortion. He says how much he regrets letting her go through it alone. He tells them he's been trying to change, to grow up, to get ready for a family. Emmett doesn't notice the look he shoots at Ruby when he says it, but Ally does. When Murphy's done talking, he tosses his slip of paper into the fire, and everyone cheers.

Ruby apologizes for hiding her pregnancy from Murphy, careful not to use the word "abortion." A lot of questions came after their secrets were revealed, and piece by piece the truth about what happened between them, the year leading up to the pregnancy, came out. Depending on who you ask, it is either a love story that has yet to find its true end (Ally), or a simple tale of a horny teenage boy who got in over his head, as he would do *anything* to lose his virginity (Emmett). Only I know the truth.

Ruby talks about how my death has made her deal with things she hadn't gotten over, flicking her eyes to Murphy. She says at last she's truly moving on, and perhaps she finally is. Jamie, her old boyfriend, is coming to New York this summer to spend time with her, even scope out some "flats," if all goes as well as it has been going on the phone. They've even talked about weekend getaways to some snowy, rustic cabin in Vermont—somewhere outside of Chatwick, but close enough to visit "the family." A change of pace from the city, where they can pour prose into their notebooks by a roaring fire. When Ruby's done talking, she tosses the slip of paper into the fire, and everyone cheers. Murphy, perhaps, a little less enthusiastically than the others. He knows they can't be together, and yet he can't imagine her belonging to anyone else.

Ruby pulls out another slip of paper—mine—which she saved because it was one of the last things I ever wrote. During this visit home, she will visit my mother and collect the notebooks I filled up with poems and heroin-induced rants. She doesn't know it yet, but she will use them in her second novel, which will be about me. About all of us.

She hands the slip of paper to Murphy, her partner in my crime, and Murphy reads it to the crew. He and Ruby remember aloud the night Roger died, and all the nights leading up to it. The stones against Ruby's window. The first of their late-night phone calls. The bruises and cuts. Everybody cries, but when Isabelle joins them, they laugh. Then Murphy tosses my secret into the fire, and everyone cheers.

They have forgiven me my sins, and now I can move on, but I stay to watch for a while longer. I watch them as they hold hands—a little too "Kum bay ya" for my taste, but okay. I watch the fire take their slips of paper, five pages of grief and love and shame igniting, pieces of them breaking away, little orange embers escaping into the black, cloudless sky.

They sniffle and watch, hypnotized, until the sound of a police siren jars them. They scramble to collect their chairs, the remainders of their bottles of beer. They run away, laughing, huddled together like a pack of wolves. They separate only when it comes time to jump into their cars and peel away from trouble, only to end up back together at Margie's Pub.

Look at them.

# ACKNOWLEDGEMENTS

First of all, I have to thank my agent Stephanie Kip Rostan and my editors Shana Dreys and Sara O'Keeffe, for championing this little piece of my heart. Your knowledge, guidance, and cheerleading have been much appreciated by this newbie.

Next, to my friends and family, thank you for the years and years and YEARS you listened to me bitch about how hard it is to get published, without once outright saying that I should give up on the dream.

So many thanks to the wonderful people who read this book in its early phases: Randy Coble, Shayla Ruland, Cathy Wille, Meredith Tate Servello, Kathryn Saris, Loren Bowley Dow and my mom, Deborah Plant, (who, reverting to her schoolteacher days, put a checkmark at the top of every page that didn't contain a spelling or grammatical error), and to Louise Walters, my mentor through the WoMentoring Project. Without question, your honest feedback and relentless encouragement is what made this manuscript worth publishing in the first place.

I would be remiss if I didn't mention the beta readers for my first novel: Rebecca Nichol, Brian Holmes, Jaci Mills, and Veronica Grenier. Even though that book was not published, you gave your time and patience as you slogged through my early drafts and offered constructive criticism and ideas. Perhaps almost as important, you helped me get used to receiving feedback without inhaling a Costco-sized chocolate cake in the process.

To Meredith Tate Servello and Kristin Fields, thank you for all the advice and support you've offered me in the process of trying to get published. Thank goodness for Twitter, or I would never have met you! And to Amy Burrell Cormier, my writer friend, for understanding the trials and tribulations of being a writer. May we one day (tomorrow?) be sitting with a pitcher of margaritas, laughing about our naiveté.

The most meaningful compliment I received, and will ever receive, about this novel came from my sister, Stina Booth, who said she teared up at the end, sad that the story was over. If you knew her, you would know this is the highest praise conceivable.

And finally, I must acknowledge the most patient man in the world: my husband, Randy Coble, for dutifully playing video games or watching ESPN (anything I'm not interested in), so I can zone in on my writing, for cooking dinner on the nights I need more time to write, for making me take a break when he knows I'm burned out, and for holding my hand when I doubted the ability to make this dream come true. Abubus.